Shortlisted for the
2010 *Orange Prize*

ENGLAND, 31 AUGUST 1939: THE WORLD IS on the brink of war. As Hitler prepares to invade Poland, thousands of children are evacuated from London to escape the impending Blitz. Torn from her mother, eight-year-old Anna Sands is relocated with other children to a large Yorkshire estate, which has been opened up to evacuees by Thomas and Elizabeth Ashton, an enigmatic, childless couple. Soon Anna gets drawn into their unraveling relationship, seeing things that are not meant for her eyes and finding herself part witness and part accomplice to a love affair with unforeseen consequences. A story of longing, loss and complicated loyalties, combining a sweeping narrative with subtle psychological observation, *The Very Thought of You* is not just a love story but a story about love.

THE
VERY THOUGHT
of YOU

A NOVEL

ROSIE ALISON

WASHINGTON SQUARE PRESS

New York   London   Toronto   Sydney

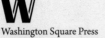

Washington Square Press
A Division of Simon & Schuster, Inc.
1230 Avenue of the Americas
New York, NY 10020

Epigraph: "Late Fragment," from *A New Path to the Waterfall*, © 1989 by the Estate of Raymond Carver. Used by permission of Grove/Atlantic, Inc.
"Oh, Lady Be Good," words and music by George Gershwin and Ira Gershwin copyright 1924 (Renewed) WB Music Corp. (ASCAP).
"The Very Thought of You," written by Ray Noble, used by permission of Range Road Music, Inc.
"The Way You Look Tonight," words by Dorothy Fields, music by Jerome Kern © 1936 T.B. Harms & Company Incorporated, USA. Universal Music Publishing Limited (50%). Used by Permission of Music Sales Limited and Shapiro, Bernstein & Co., Inc. o/b/o Aldi Music. All Rights Reserved. International Copyright Secured.
"somewhere i have never travelled,gladly beyond." Copyright 1931, © 1959, 1991 by the Trustees for the E. E. Cummings Trust. Copyright © 1979 by George James Firmage, from COMPLETE POEMS: 1904–1962 by E. E. Cummings, edited by George J. Firmage. Used by permission of Liveright Publishing Corporation.

First Washington Square Press trade paperback edition July 2011

For information about special discounts for bulk purchases, please contact Simon & Schuster Special Sales at 1-866-506-1949 or business@simonandschuster.com.

The Simon & Schuster Speakers Bureau can bring authors to your live event. For more information or to book an event, contact the Simon & Schuster Speakers Bureau at 1-866-248-3049 or visit our website at www.simonspeakers.com.

Designed by Kyoko Watanabe

Manufactured in the United States of America

10 9 8 7 6 5 4 3 2 1

Library of Congress Cataloging-in-Publication Data

Alison, Rosie.
   The very thought of you : a novel / Rosie Alison.—1st Washington Square Press trade paperback ed.
      p. cm.

1. World War, 1939–1945—Evacuation of civilians—England—Fiction. 2. World War, 1939–1945—Children—Fiction. 3. Families—England—Fiction. 4. Yorkshire (England)—Fiction. 5. London (England)—Fiction. I. Title.

   PR6101.L4515V47 2011
   823'.92—dc22   2010048262

ISBN 978-1-4516-1397-1
ISBN 978-1-4516-1398-8 (ebook)

For my daughters Lucy and Daisy

And did you get what
you wanted from this life, even so?
I did.
And what did you want?
To call myself beloved, to feel myself
beloved on the earth.

RAYMOND CARVER,
"LATE FRAGMENT"

Contents

Prologue

+ I +

Evacuation

1939

+ II +

Affinities

1939–1945

+ 45 +

Back to the Old House

1946–2006

+ 261 +

Acknowledgments

+ 311 +

Prologue

May 1964

My dearest,

Of all the many people we meet in a lifetime, it is strange that so many of us find ourselves in thrall to one particular person. Once that face is seen, an involuntary heartache sets in for which there is no cure. All the wonder of this world finds shape in that one person, and thereafter there is no reprieve, because this kind of love does not end, or not until death—

From Baxter's
Guide to the Historic Houses of England (2007)

Any visitor travelling north from York will pass through a flat vale of farmland before rising steeply onto the wide upland plateau of the North Yorkshire Moors. Here is some of the wildest and loveliest land in England, where high rolling moorland appears to reach the horizon on every side, before subsiding into voluptuous wooded valleys.

These moors are remote and empty, randomly scattered with silent sheep and half-covered tracks. It is unfenced land of many moods. In February the place is barren and lunar, prompting inward reflection. But late in August this wilderness surges into bloom, igniting a purple haze of heather which sweeps across the moors as if released to the air. This vivid wash of color mingles with the oaks and ashes of the valleys below, where the soft limestone land flows with numerous streams and secret springs.

It is hallowed territory, graced with many medieval monasteries, all now picturesque ruins open to the sky. Rievaulx, Byland, Jervaulx, Whitby, Fountains—these are some of the better-known abbeys in these parts, and their presence testifies to the fertile promise of the land. The early monastic settlers cleared these valleys for farming, and left behind a patchwork of fields marked by many miles of drystone walls.

Nearly two centuries later, long after the monasteries had been dissolved, the Georgian gentry built several fine estates in the valleys bordering these moors. Hovingham Hall, Duncombe Park, Castle Howard and others. Trees were cleared for new vistas, grass terraces levelled and streams diverted into ornamental lakes—all to clarify and enhance the natural patterns of the land, as was the eighteenth-century custom.

One of the finest of these houses, if not necessarily the largest, is Ashton Park. This remote house stands on the edge of the moors, perched high above the steep Rye Valley and theatrically isolated in its wide park. For some years now, the house and its gardens have been open to the public. At one corner of an isolated village stand the ornate iron gates, and the park lodge where visitors buy their tickets. Beyond, a long white drive leads through a rising sweep of parkland, dotted with sheep and the occasional tree. It is a tranquil park, silent and still, with a wide reach of sky.

Turning to the left, the visitor sees at last the great house itself, a Palladian mansion of honeyed stone, balanced on either side with curved wings. Topping the forecourt gates are two stone figures rearing up on hind legs, a lion and a unicorn, each gazing fiercely at the other as if sworn to secrecy.

The house appears a touch doleful in its solitary grandeur, an impression which only intensifies when one enters the imposing but empty Marble Hall, with its scattering of statues on plinths. Red rope cordons mark the start of a house tour through reception rooms dressed like stage sets, leading this visitor to wonder how the house could have dwindled into quite such a counterfeit version of its past.

The guide brochure explains that when the last Ashton died, in 1979, there remained only a distant cousin in South Africa. Mrs Sandra De Groot, wife of a prominent manufacturer, appears to have been so daunted by her inheritance that she agreed to hand Ashton Park over to the National Trust in lieu of drastic death duties. But not before the estate was stripped of its remaining farmland and other valuable assets. Two Rubens paintings were sold, alongside a Claude Lorrain, a Salvator Rosa and a pair of Constables. Soon after, her lawyers organized a sweeping sale of the house contents—a multitude of Ashton treasures accumulated over three hundred years, all recorded without sentiment in a stapled white inventory.

One pair of carved George IV giltwood armchairs, marked; one Regency rosewood and brass-inlaid breakfast table; one nineteenth-century ormolu centerpiece . . .

Antique dealers from far and wide still reminisce about the Ashton auction of 1980, the final rite of a house in decline. It is said that a queue of removal vans clogged the drive for days afterwards.

Mrs De Groot was apparently not without family feeling, because she donated a number of display cabinets to the National Trust, together with the house library and many family portraits and papers. In a curious detail, the brochure mentions that "the exquisite lacquered cigarette cases of the late Elizabeth Ashton were sent to the Victoria and Albert Museum".

According to the notes, Ashton Park had fallen into disrepair before its reclamation. But the curators retrieved plenty of family relics and mementoes, and the walls are now hung with photographs of the Ashton sons at Eton, at Oxford, in cricket teams, in uniform. A look of permanence lingers in their faces. Downstairs are photographs of the servants, the butler and his staff all standing on the front steps, their gaze captured in that strange measure of slow time so characteristic of early cameras.

Beyond the Morning Room and past the Billiard Room, a small study displays an archive of wartime evacuees. It appears that an evacuees' boarding school was established at Ashton Park in 1939, and a touching photograph album reveals children of all sizes smiling in shorts and gray tunics; handwritten letters, sent in later years, describe the pleasures and sorrows of their time there.

In the last corridor there is only one photograph, an elegant wedding picture of the final Ashton heir, dated 1929. Thomas Ashton is one of those inscrutably handsome prewar men with swept-back hair, and his wife Elizabeth is a raven-haired period beauty not unlike Vivien Leigh. Their expressions carry no hint of future losses, no sense that their house will one day become a museum.

On high days and holidays, Ashton Park attracts plenty of day-trippers. An estate shop sells marmalade and trinkets, while the gardens offer picnic spots, woodland trails and dubious medieval pageants on the south lawn. And yet visitors may drive away from Ashton Park feeling faintly dejected, because the spirit of this place has somehow departed.

This melancholy cannot be traced to any dilapidation. The roof is intact, the lawns freshly mown, and the ornamental lake looks almost unnaturally limpid. But the dark windows stare out blankly—a haunted gaze. Beyond the display areas are closed corridors and unreclaimed rooms stacked with pots of paint and rusting stepladders. The small family chapel remains but is rarely visited: it is too far out of the way to qualify for the house tour.

Perhaps it is the family's absence which gives Ashton its pathos. It appears that there were three sons and a daughter at the start of the last century, and yet none of them produced heirs. By what cumulative misfortune did this once prosperous family reach its end? The brochure notes do not detail how or why the Ashton line died out, yet a curious visitor cannot help but wonder.

But for all this, one can still stand on the sunken lawn and almost apprehend the house in its heyday, even amidst the signposts and litter bins. One can imagine how others—in earlier times, in the right weather—might have found in this place a peerless vision of English parkland.

There is one tree which particularly draws the eye, a glorious ruddy copper beech which stands alone on a small lawn by the rose garden. It was on a bench under this tree that the duty staff recently found an elderly woman sitting alone after closing hours, apparently enjoying the view. On closer inspection she was found to be serenely dead, her fingers locked around a faded love letter.

Evacuation

1939

1

London, 31 August 1939

THERE WAS A hint of afternoon sunshine as Anna Sands and her mother, Roberta, stepped off their bus into Kensington High Street. To Anna, the broad street flickered with color as shoppers flowed past her, clutching their bags. Beyond the crowds, she could see the parade of shops tricked out with displays of every kind: tins of toffee, new-minted bowls and cups, rolls of ribbon, hats, coats and gloves from every corner of the empire.

Mother and daughter set off down the wide pavement, Anna swinging her arms, always a little ahead. But she kept crisscrossing in front of her mother, as if uncertain whether to turn and hold her hand. For tomorrow, early, she and thousands of other children were to be evacuated from London—"In case of German air raids," her mother had told her airily, as if this was a standard routine for all families.

"Once this crisis is over, you can come straight home again," she had explained. Anna was looking forward to country life— or seemed to be, when asked. There were things to buy for the journey, but Anna's impending departure hovered between them and lit every moment with unusual intimacy.

Roberta's nerves and Anna's excitement meshed into mutual high spirits as they strolled through the penny arcades, just for the fun of it, before reaching Pontings, the famous drapers, with its fluted pillars and white-iron galleries.

This was Anna's favorite shop, an Aladdin's cave of colored cloths and trimmings, laden with rolls of silk and swathes of damask. On the ground floor, beyond the hanging boas, she chose herself a white handkerchief starred with violets.

"*Thank* you," she said, kissing her mother.

While Roberta queued to pay, Anna glanced upwards to the bright atrium above, where sunshine streamed through the stained-glass flowers in rays of colored light. Anna's eyes swam around the shop, with its reams of ribbons and baskets of glinting buttons, brass, silver, mother-of-pearl. The sounds of the shop receded as the dream light washed through her until, for a moment, she vanished from herself.

"You can carry your package, my darling," said her mother, breaking her reverie. Anna sprang to attention, and was the first out of the shop, planning the next purchase. At Woolworth's they bought a small cardboard case and luggage labels for Anna's journey, then they crossed the road to look for shoes.

Shiny brown lace-ups they bought, at Barkers. They smelt new and luxuriant. They reminded Anna of her father in his uniform, with his big black boots. She and her mother had seen him off a month ago, just after her eighth birthday; he had swung her right round when she hugged him good-bye. Sometimes he sent her letters with funny drawings, describing his army drills. She wasn't really worried about him, because it was common knowledge that most of Hitler's tanks were made of cardboard.

"Britain has the greatest empire in the world, so the war won't last long," she announced to the bespectacled lady who fitted her shoes.

Then mother and daughter were out on the street again. It was time for Anna's promised treat: a knickerbocker glory. She had seen American films in which children sat at counters, with ice creams in tall glasses. That was her dream.

Roberta led the way through the art deco splendor of Derry and Tom's department store, along lavish blue carpets, whisper-quiet, until they reached a wall of lifts and stepped into a cool chamber of copper and nickel.

"Fifth floor, ladies and gentlemen, world-famous roof gardens," chanted the liveried lift boy. The gardens had opened with much fanfare a year ago, but they had never visited: it was too dear.

But today was special, and they emerged to glittering sunlight amidst the rooftops of Kensington. Before them, a profusion of flowers stretched away on every side, outstripping all their hopes. There was a Spanish garden, with a terra-cotta Moorish tower, and tumbling bougainvillea. Beyond, through a winding courtyard, they found themselves in a water garden of lily pads with a hint of gleaming carp. Another turn took them through dainty Elizabethan arches with climbing roses.

They found their way to the café, with tables set out beneath striped umbrellas, and a fountain tinkling nearby. From the tall menu Anna picked her ice cream with care: vanilla and chocolate, topped with cream and cherries and nuts. To her mother's relief, she did not seem disappointed when the towering confection arrived.

A small palm-court band played familiar melodies, muting any sound from the streets below. The unreality of the place and the peculiar occasion of their visit only increased their light-headed pleasure in each other.

"Before today, have you ever sat in a garden in the sky?" asked Anna.

"Never," laughed her mother, "nor would I want to, without you here too."

"When I get home again, can we come back here?"

"Of course, sweetheart."

"With Daddy too?"

"*For sure*," said Roberta, and clasped her daughter's hand.

Later, when the ice cream was finished, and the teacups empty, and the garden's secrets all explored, they set off together, subdued, for home.

It was not until they reached the store's entrance lobby that

Anna admitted the one shadow lurking over her day: she had no bathing costume.

Anna had seen the newsreels about evacuation, and they all showed children traveling westwards, to the seaside, to Devon and Cornwall. She longed to join them, but feared that with all they had spent that day a bathing costume would be one item too many to ask for.

"But how will I swim?" she blurted out.

Roberta paused to hear her child's fumbled request, and knew at once that she must keep this afternoon intact, not scupper her daughter's hopes. Back to the lifts they went, and up to the sporting department. With abandon, Roberta spent two shillings on a blue striped bathing costume, and saw her daughter's face shine with pleasure. It was more than she meant to pay, but it perfected the afternoon. Then they set off for the underground station, united in satisfaction.

As Anna skipped ahead, Roberta rejoiced in her daughter, knowing that she was bright and resourceful, with an uncluttered face easily lit by smiles. That tiny gap between her front teeth gave her a frank charm.

They clattered down the station steps, Anna always in front. A train rolled in and opened its doors, and passengers stepped past them. Suddenly, on the half-filled platform, Roberta found herself brimming over with love for her straw-haired child.

"Anna—" she said, and Anna turned, her eyes bright and clear. In that instant, Roberta sensed the spontaneous rise of her daughter's soul, which had flickered to life in her eight years before. She reached out for her daughter and held her fast in her arms. For a moment, they could feel each other's heartbeats.

"I love you, my darling," said Roberta, stroking her daughter's hair.

Anna looked up at her mother with unblinking eyes.

In the years to come, she would remember that fragile day, its touchless light, their quiet elations.

2

Warsaw, 1 September 1939

INSIDE THE WARSAW embassy, Sir Clifford Norton had been up most of the night; now he watched a pale-blue dawn that was serenely oblivious to their troubles. Vaguely, he realized that the last summer of the decade was over.

All night his staff had been working in shifts, everyone engaged in these final frantic negotiations to stave off war. Typists had been rattling away, telephones ringing, messengers coming and going, even his wife had been there with her small portable typewriter, encoding and deciphering telegrams.

Danzig, Danzig, Danzig was the word on every letter and report. The Polish port had rapidly grown from a place to a principle, Norton reflected, as Hitler demanded its release into the Reich. Now they were facing a diplomatic deadlock, and the embassy was on emergency alert. But at this early hour, some of the staff were still napping on camp beds, and Norton was alone in his office waiting for the next round of telegrams from London.

Suddenly craving the new day, he pushed his curtains right back until he could feel the arrival of daylight, subtle, spreading, now obscuring his desk light. The brightness cheered him; there was still a time for spurious delight.

The eerie disquiet of these last summer weeks had been contagious. Warsaw was gripped by a strange *Totentanz,* the restaurants overflowing with odd gaiety and the hotels thronged with journalists firing off telegrams and spreading rumors. The shops had run out of sugar and candles, and the Poles had been burying their silver and crystal in gardens and parks.

The telephone on his desk rang, startling him. Five forty-five A.M. It was the consul in Katowice.

The Germans are in. Tanks over the border at 5 A.M.

The news struck Norton distantly, as if it was a piece of history which might roll past him if he stepped aside. This was the moment they had all been waiting for, yet it had never seemed inevitable.

Norton had not yet put on his shoes. The floor beneath his feet seemed to push upwards, hard. He felt as if he were living in the third person. He put down the telephone and spurred himself into mechanical action, cabling the news to London, rallying his staff.

In the embassy, people came and went as if in a dream. Only a few hours ago they were still negotiating the price of peace, they thought, but Hitler had outmaneuvered them all.

At six A.M. Norton heard an air engine and went out onto the embassy balcony. Straight ahead in the clear sky, he watched a German fighter plane swooping over the Vistula. Sirens wailed, and there was a boom of antiaircraft guns. That was a shock; the first air raid in Warsaw so soon. War had reached them already.

3

London, 1 September 1939

Anna lay on her back, suspended in the stillness of sleep. Roberta sat on the bed and smoothed back her daughter's hair until she opened her eyes.

They both smiled, then Anna reached out her hand.

There had been so many things to prepare for the evacuation. They had already picked up the new gas mask, in a box you could carry over your shoulder. The previous evening, Roberta had carefully packed Anna's case with three changes of clothes and her wash things. And her bathing costume, of course. Her mother also produced a surprise book as a special treat. Into this she had slipped a loving letter and a family photograph.

Roberta had stowed the food in an extra bag, because she didn't want Anna to open her case and have everything else fall out. There was a tin of evaporated milk, some corned beef, two apples and a bar of chocolate. There was also a luggage label with Anna's name and school on it, and her age.

"A label, round my neck?" asked Anna, surprised. It felt strange, the itchy string against her skin.

Anna had already decided not to take her teddy with her, in case anyone laughed at him. So she propped Edward on her pillow and kissed him good-bye.

"I won't be long," she promised him.

Roberta was so anxious as she fed her daughter that she had no chance to feel sentimental. But she was careful to be loving, not impatient, as they put on their coats and left their Fulham house. There was little time for Anna to look back at the green front door and be sad.

But as they walked together towards the school, both of them began to feel the ache of parting. The coming separation made Roberta breathless—it would be several days before she could know where Anna had been sent. She thought with dread of some dismal, dirty house.

"You *must* keep your hands clean," she said.

Walking along in the cloudy sunshine, war seemed remote and unimaginable. Roberta wondered how she could be doing this to her beloved daughter. Perhaps war would not touch them. Perhaps it would not happen. Would any German planes really fly as far as London?

After her husband joined up, her first thought had been to leave the city with Anna. But they had no family outside London, nor the means to move. So, like other reluctant mothers, she had signed up for the evacuation scheme: all the parents at Anna's school had been urged to take part. At first she had thought she could go with Anna, but was later informed that only nursing mothers would be able to stay with their children. *It'll only be temporary,* Roberta told herself.

Anna, meanwhile, had no such trepidation. She assumed that all the evacuees would be going to the seaside, like a holiday. She had only ever been on a beach once before, at Margate, and she was longing to run through wet sand again. And now she had her own bathing costume, packed and ready.

She was expecting adventure; she had read so many fairy tales that she longed to set out into the world alone. Like Dick Whittington. The long road, the child with a small case, it seemed only natural.

Her shoes were polished, her socks were clean. She carried her kit with pride. She did not fear parting; her mother's face felt closer than her pulse. She could not yet imagine any rift.

Beneath the red-brick gaze of the old Victorian school they

joined an uneasy crowd of mothers, fathers, children, all there to say farewell. Children were crying, some of them howling. Mothers also were weeping. A sudden sadness washed over Roberta, though she and Anna were too resolutely independent to make any public display of sentiment. But still Roberta's resolve wavered. She sought out a head teacher to ask where the children would be going.

"Buses will take them to St. Pancras station."

"Can we go with them there?"

"No, I'm sorry," he said defensively, "you must say good-bye here."

There was a long wait in the school yard, and children sat on the ground, yawning. Roberta and Anna stood together, not saying much, just holding hands. Soon they were organized into class lines, with teachers ticking names on clipboards. Roberta was proud that Anna looked so pretty, so bright and fresh.

She could always take her back home again.

Suddenly the buses arrived, coming on from another school in World's End. Before Roberta had the chance to change her mind and retrieve her child, the crowd's momentum had swept Anna's class forwards. Without a backwards glance, Anna hurried to find a seat. She put down her bags and realized that, after so much waiting, she had hardly said good-bye to her mother. She pressed her face to the window.

There she was below, looking up at her—gleaming brown hair, and a smile meant for her alone, wishing her every joy and all good things.

"Good-bye, Mummy!" called Anna, through the glass. Suddenly, she began crumpling inside as she fixed her gaze on her mother. She could feel the pull of her mother's eyes right through her—until she was going, gone, and Anna was away on her journey.

She sank down in her seat. The bus had a sour smell of stale cigarettes which made her nauseous. She yawned in the heat;

there wasn't much air. She felt odd—excited and suspended in a strange new world, where anything might happen. She did not miss her mother yet, because she was still so firmly rooted inside her—her face, her voice, her touch.

But for Roberta the separation was immediate. She walked back home from the school feeling limp, like a wilting plant. The trees she passed looked parched and weary, and the pavement was cracked beneath her feet. The dryness of late summer was all around her, and the streets seemed unnaturally deserted.

Had she made the right choice?

4

A NNA'S SCHOOL BUS arrived first at Paddington station and sat there dead-engined for an hour. An inconstant sun came and went, making the children fidgety. Some of them disembarked there, but not Anna.

Her bus pushed on to St. Pancras—magical, colorful St. Pancras, a riot of exotic brickwork. Anna had never seen this station before. Climbing from the bus, she glanced upwards at red Gothic spires rising to the sky—they looked like the towers of a fairy-tale castle, the first step in a great adventure.

Inside, the vast vaulted space thrilled her. Steam was rising from the trains; their smokestacks were trailing wisps of white up to colossal arched girders. Beyond the platforms, the sky was framed like a stained-glass cathedral window—an infinite window of bright blue.

But she was being pushed forwards, and there was little time to stop and look. The station was seething with crosscurrents of children and parents; it was hard not to get caught in the wrong queue. Station announcements and men with loudspeakers only aggravated the chaos. Many children seemed to have brothers or sisters, some of them very young and wanting to go to the lavatory. Anna felt strong in herself, and sorry for those who were looking miserable. She clutched her belongings carefully—the case, the food bag, the gas-mask box.

She longed for the seaside.

A great clock hung over the sea of bewildered children, ticking away the morning. Gradually, Anna's excitement began to dwindle, and the magic of the steel cathedral faded as they queued along the platform, waiting for something to happen. They stood, they sat on the ground. The platform was grimy, and there was an acrid smell which burned her nose.

"Where are we going? Where?" The whisper of unanswered questions swept up and down the lines of children, dozens of young faces screwed into supplicant expressions.

At last her group was led towards a train. Mrs. Martin, her class teacher, ticked her off a list as she clambered on board with her cases.

She had nobody to say good-bye to, but as the train drew away she joined the throng at the window, and waved at all those mothers and fathers whose faces were fixed on the departing children.

The train rolled slowly through North London, past dingy backs of houses, small tended gardens, smoking factories. Anna felt as though she were in a film. The train speeded up, more places flashed by, and fields began to roll past her window.

She remembered her mother's gift book and unwrapped it: to her joy, she found *The Yellow Book of Fairy Tales,* with scary drawings of sea serpents and gnarled witches. Her mother's photograph and letter made her a little tearful, but she was fixed on being as brave as a fairy-tale orphan, setting out to prove her mettle.

Only she did wish for a brother or sister.

The train stopped and started. Every now and again, somebody with a clipboard came to check that all was well. The toilet was blocked, and this was causing problems. Anna dreaded smelly lavatories, so she was careful not to drink or eat much.

At last the train pulled in at a station. Nothing happened for a while, then doors started slamming, and voices shouted down the corridor, "Everybody out!"

When they reached the platform, Anna saw they were at Leicester. She didn't know where that was. Some of the children were being led towards the exit; others were directed onto a new train. As the crowds flowed round her, Anna felt suddenly dizzy—should she climb onto the train, or find her new home here? She stalled where she stood and felt sick and faint, facing this invisible crossroads to her future.

"Is Leicester at the sea?" she asked a woman with a list of names.

"No, dear, nowhere near the sea."

That settled it. Anna did not want to stop here. She joined the queue for the new train, even though nobody seemed to know where they were going.

She made for a window seat.

"When do we get to the sea?" she asked a patrolling teacher. His eyes were quizzical.

"You mustn't be too disappointed if you don't end up at the seaside," he said. "Anyway, it's too cold for bathing at this time of year." Anna asked no more, but sensed with a sickening heart that she was on the wrong train.

She began to worry. She watched and watched out of the window, hoping for a glimpse of the sea on every horizon. They seemed to roll through empty countryside for too long. Clutching her food bag and book, she fell asleep. Her legs did not touch the floor but swung from side to side with the train's motion.

In the late afternoon, the train slowed and she woke up. They were pulling into a station on a great bend. Anna saw the sign: York.

"Everybody off!" called the supervisors, hurrying down the corridors. Anna was jolted to her feet and scrambled together her belongings. She stepped off the train and followed the line of children. They marched up many steps and over a long bridge, stretching across the station's majestic curve. Birds were flocking in the great glass roof. Somebody blew a whistle, and they flapped away into the open air, startling the children.

Were they seagulls? Anna watched them, wishing she knew more about birds.

Billeting officers were waiting for them, ticking off their names. Only a few children remained from Anna's school.

She looked about her at a crowd of unknown faces.

"Where are we going?" she asked a man with a beard. He stopped and looked down at her small, anxious face. "We're just taking you all to the billeting hall now. There'll be tea for you there." He spoke gently, with an unfamiliar accent. She didn't dare to ask, this time, if the seaside was close by.

The children were quickly marched off into hot and dusty buses. Anna looked out at the towering station hotel with its neat banks of flowers. *So this is York,* she thought.

Fortunately, it was only a short drive from the city before they reached a school hall. There were a couple of hundred children there, and kindly women greeted them with drinks.

"Where are we?" asked Anna.

"You're in Yorkshire!" replied a stout woman with spidery red veins on her cheeks. Anna didn't know anything about Yorkshire, except that it was for poor people, factory people. That scared her a little.

She was placed in a row of chairs and checked for head lice. Once cleared, she was given a bun and a cup of milk. Some of the adults were hurried and a bit snappy, but others looked her in the eye and took the time to smile.

She ate her bun on one of the benches by the big windows, trying to make sense of the scene before her. She could see that adults were wandering around the hall, watching all the children. They were talking to a man sitting at a big desk, and pointing at different boys and girls. Were they being picked, like vegetables at a market stall? She sat down next to Becky Palmer, one of the few girls from her school who had come this far with her. Becky was soothing her little brother, who had wet himself. Women walked past, looking them up and down.

Her heart was fluttering: a bit of her wanted to be chosen, but she also dreaded the people she saw. It all seemed so differ-

ent to the seaside holiday she had dreamt of. She didn't want
to be in Yorkshire with unknown people—she had a picture,
suddenly, of factories and smoky faces.

Anna began to notice that all the women with nice faces
were choosing girls—and she was sitting beside a weeping boy
who had wet himself. Well, she wasn't going to leave Becky just
because of that. Just then, a purple-faced woman with bristles
on her chin walked by and Anna felt relieved that young Ben
was still crying.

Suddenly the doors opened and a dark-haired woman in a
smart coat strode into the hall. A younger woman hovered at
her shoulder, as if attending her. The elegant woman seemed
to swing forwards in her high heels, and her light coat swayed
as she walked. She made straight for the chief billeting officer,
who rose and spoke to her with deference. Anna watched from
her bench as this new lady turned and surveyed the hall, leaning back on one leg and subtly rocking her other heel, like a
dancer.

The chief officer stood on a chair and clapped his hands to
ask for silence.

"Mrs. Ashton here has thirty places left at Ashton Park, for
those aged between seven and thirteen—boys or girls. Any
children fitting that description, come over here now please."
Children began to shuffle over, but Anna rose quickly and went
to the front of the line.

She was captivated by this mysterious, beautiful woman—
Mrs. *Ashton*. Her hair was glossy and dark, and her clear level
eyes traveled around the hall with a glint of amusement.

My mother would admire this woman because she's a lady,
Anna thought.

She looked down the line behind her: a straggle of boys and
girls, all bewildered by their long day. The billeting officers
were hurriedly taking down their names, and issuing them with
postcards to send home. Anna watched closely as Mrs. Ashton

waited there with effortless poise, talking a little to her assistant, and asking a small girl about her journey.

A billeting officer gave a signal that everything was in order.

"All set? Come along then," said Mrs. Ashton, striding away on her heels. Anna hurried to keep up, and clambered onto yet another bus, already half-filled with children.

The bus rolled out of the city through miles of flat wheat fields, until gradually the ground rose higher and the road began to twist and turn more. At last light, they climbed up a steep bank, where the bus engine struggled round sharp corners.

Then daylight was extinguished, and they traveled in darkness. There were no streetlamps, just the empty road. The bus rumbled on and the children fell asleep in the dark, heads falling on shoulders and laps, cases and gas masks scattered all about the floor.

At last they reached a humpbacked bridge and entered a village.

"Here we are"—Anna heard Mrs. Ashton's voice. She strained her eyes and glimpsed some iron gates. The bus rattled over a cattle grid, then slid silently up a long driveway. There was a sudden turn to the left and Anna found herself looking out at a great dark building, with lit windows. They passed through more gates into an oval forecourt. The bus slowed to a halt, and the children were roused.

"Don't forget to bring *all* your cases," said another voice.

They followed each other off the bus like a flock of startled sheep. Anna was one of the first out. Clasping her things close, she followed Mrs. Ashton up the stone steps to a pair of tall doors: through them, they emerged into a magnificent marble hall, with a blue-domed ceiling which seemed to reach up to the sky.

Anna felt her eyes on stalks. What would her mother say about such a place? All around stood silent Greek statues: a naked man hurling a plate, a great dog baring its teeth, a sleeping lion. The children huddled together on the checkered floor, their small voices echoing in the vast hall.

Mrs. Ashton clapped her hands.

"Welcome, all of you, and I hope you will be happy with us here at Ashton Park. I am Mrs. Ashton. This is a special house, and we hope that you will enjoy it and care for it as we do. There are teachers and staff here who will look after you, like your schools at home. And this is Miss Harrison, who will be your matron."

A hefty, iron-haired woman stepped forwards, wearing the blue uniform of a nurse, with a watch pinned to her tunic. She looked a little fierce, and her twitchy, bespectacled eyes seemed to lack eyelashes; Anna preferred Mrs. Ashton.

But it was Miss Harrison who divided them into groups— boys, girls, younger, older—and led them up a great stone staircase.

They came to a long corridor with a red runner carpet. The matron showed them into a large room of washbasins and partitioned lavatories, before leading them, through yet more corridors, to various dormitories lined with rows of beds.

Anna was placed in a dormitory named "Wisteria," on the second floor. She had a plain iron bedstead, and stiff new sheets. She took out her nightdress, and stowed her other things neatly away under the bed.

Curiosity took her to the window: she peered through the curtains—but all she could see was dark distance. Perhaps the seaside was out there after all.

There was one more queue for the basins and the lavatories, before Anna collapsed into bed, thinking of her mother as she fell asleep.

Downstairs, Thomas Ashton waited for his wife to join him for a late dinner. Their large dining room had been transformed by three new refectory tables, ready for the evacuees' breakfast.

Elizabeth arrived at last, her eyes glittering. Over these last few weeks, she had worked tirelessly to prepare for the evacuation, extending the sleeping quarters, buying the provisions, recruiting her helpers. Only this morning, she had walked through the top corridors with her new matrons, admiring the clean airy dormitories.

"They're all settled upstairs now," she reported.

"And the beds are full?"

"Oh yes. The billeting halls were still busy when we left."

"Let's hope there aren't too many tears tonight."

Elizabeth looked over at him, and tilted her head as she spoke.

"We can give them something good here, Thomas."

He smiled and touched his wife's hand. He was moved to see her so engaged.

"I'm looking forward to meeting them all tomorrow," he reassured her.

Thomas had been surprised and delighted by Elizabeth's willingness to open up their lives like this. And not a day too soon: Hitler's dawn invasion of Poland had been reported all day long on the wireless.

"I've been thinking about the Nortons," he added, picturing their friends in Europe's most incendiary spot.

"They'll get out of Warsaw."

"I hope you're right."

But none of them, Thomas reflected, would really escape the coming war. The front line would stretch all the way into the home front this time, with airplanes reaching far into enemy cities. He was glad if Ashton could at least act as a refuge for a few evacuees.

Since Easter, the house had become a shell of its former self, with many of the male staff called up to local regiments. There was an expectant silence in the empty corridors, waiting to be broken by the sound of these children. Other people's children.

They retired to their bedroom, and Thomas brushed Elizabeth's long hair as she sat at her dressing table. A recent ritual which soothed them both.

Later, lying in bed, Thomas sensed a subtle shift in the atmosphere of the house. Ashton had been childless for so many years, yet now the very echo of the Marble Hall seemed muffled by the children sleeping upstairs.

The change in the air sent him effortlessly to sleep.

5

THE NEXT MORNING, eighty-six children woke up in a strange new house.

Anna lay in her bed for a few minutes, wondering if she was allowed to get up yet. But light was streaming through a gap in the curtains, and she could not resist looking out at the view. There was a window seat—so she clambered onto it and peered out.

Here was her new world. Wide, unfenced parkland sloped gently up to the sky, ringed at the horizon by dark woods. Sheep grazed undisturbed on the grass plain, which was dotted with a few solitary trees and a single white track. It was a sight of great calm and quiet.

Another girl joined Anna.

"Lots of grass," she said. "I'm Beth," she added.

"Those tree guards means there's deer. I've seen them in Richmond Park," said another girl. Katy Todd, she was called. She seemed to know a lot of facts.

The door opened abruptly.

"Time to dress!"

It was the matron in her blue tunic, sending them all off to wash.

Ten minutes later a great gong rang out, and all the evacuees assembled in a long line on the first floor. Anna glanced round at the hushed faces waiting there. Two or three girls she knew from school; she would talk to them when she could. Then they were off, following the person in front, a long crocodile of children moving rapidly down to breakfast.

Anna was flustered, but felt the pleasure of her new shoes. The girl in front of her was older, with long legs. She had to hurry to keep up, as the line of children rattled down a great stone staircase. Anna was moving fast, her knees pumping up and down as she fixed her eyes on the girl in front.

A stab of pain suddenly juddered through her body as her right knee rammed into a sharp decorative leaf sticking out from the banister. She pulled away her knee, disengaging the iron from her flesh—leaving a deep gash there.

She felt sick at once, but kept running. Breathless, she limped after the girl in front, into a great crimson dining hall where huge portraits loomed down from every wall. Children were standing in rows by long tables.

Anna's shin felt sticky and wet. She looked down and thick warm blood was sliding down it, seeping into her sock. She pulled out her handkerchief, white, embroidered with violets, her mother's gift from Pontings.

Her knee hurt as she dabbed at it. She could see the glistening red of raw flesh in the open wound, and her handkerchief was sodden.

There was silence, as they waited for grace. An ooze of sweat ran down Anna's temple and her upper lip was wet. She felt sick. She tried to keep standing but dizziness was spinning her head.

"For what we are about to receive may the Lord make us truly grateful." Anna saw the grain of the wooden floor rising to meet her—like water draining fast down a plughole, the light rushed out from her.

She struck her head on the floor as she fainted, and the girl beside her called out for help. Elizabeth Ashton appeared and knelt down. She called for a napkin and, wincing, covered the wound. Crouching on the floor, she raised Anna in her arms. The other children were sitting down now, eating and watching.

Anna emerged from deep, sweet oblivion to a strange room. She saw a high white ceiling edged with intricate patterns, like cake icing. Her body felt limp and damp. She looked up into the face of a stranger—a stranger with an anxious face and dark glossy hair.

Elizabeth looked down at the pale girl in her arms. She was so slight, yet her eyes, relit, shone with life. This was a clean child, a pleasure to hold.

"What's your name?" she asked softly.

"Anna Sands." She wanted her mother, and stifled a sob.

"We're going to take you upstairs, Anna. How did you cut your knee?"

"I banged into the railings," said Anna. She felt obscurely guilty about the mess of blood. "Sorry," she said, "I'm so sorry."

"Don't worry about anything. Just breathe calmly for a few moments until you're ready to move."

The matron, Miss Harrison, appeared with a damp cloth, and Mrs. Ashton vanished with a smile. When the matron examined the wound, she realized that it would require stitches, and the village doctor was called for.

Anna was left waiting in her dormitory. She lay on her bed, pressing the cloth against her knee, worrying about her bloodied socks because she only had three pairs. Nobody came, and she missed home. She wished she had brought her teddy with her, after all. She gazed up at the crack lines on the ceiling and felt cut off from everyone.

At last the doctor appeared with the matron, and checked her over.

"We'll need to sew you up, my dear," he muttered. He looked like a severe doctor from the card game Happy Families, all whiskers. But his eyes were crinkly-kind as he undid his black bag and made his preparations.

Anna looked away when he produced the needle, and winced with pain as the matron held her leg; she had never known such shocking sharpness. Tears seeped through her screwed-up eyes.

After the wound was dressed, the doctor smiled, showing his gummy teeth.

"Have a rest, and then you can run out and play with the others. But be careful not to bump yourself."

Anna counted to a hundred many times, then went downstairs, warily, this time. Breakfast was long over and she joined the other children in a great paneled room called "the saloon." Someone blew a whistle and Mrs. Ashton appeared.

"We're going to divide you into classes now, so please come up, one by one."

Anna was put into a class with Miss Weir, who had come with a group of children from Pimlico. She was young and pale, with sandy hair. And a gentle face. There were fourteen children in her class, boys and girls. Anna had an eye for Katy from her dormitory, who seemed to know things.

Another whistle was blown, and they all followed their new teachers. Miss Weir led them to their classroom, but it wasn't like a normal schoolroom. It was tall with carved ceilings and there were marks on the yellow wallpaper where furniture was missing. Some simple wooden tables and chairs had been laid out in rows, and a blackboard rested on a stand. On one wall hung a darkly varnished portrait of a man with his dog; in the distance behind him was a great house, and Anna wondered if that was Ashton House.

"The summer is over, but you can look forward to a new term now," said their teacher as cheerily as possible, before outlining their lessons. Anna listened, but looked out of the window too, watching the sheep move slowly across the parkland. She had never seen so much grass.

"Write a few sentences about you and your family," said Miss Weir, handing them books and pencils.

My name is Anna Sands. I am an only child. We live in
Fulham and I play in Bishop's Park, usually. My father

mends antiques and my mother helps him. He has gone
away to the army. My mother can play the piano.

A gong rang for lunch, once, twice. Everything now would be
marked out by gongs and whistles, and handbells. Anna did not
complain; she was longing to eat, after missing breakfast.

In the afternoon, all the children were assembled in the
Marble Hall to meet Mr. Ashton for the first time.

When she saw him from behind, Anna assumed he must be
old, because he could not walk. He was sitting in a wheelchair.
But when she faced him properly, she saw that he had a young
face. He was handsome, even, and very polite, though his legs
were oddly thin.

Mrs. Ashton wheeled him round to shake hands with all the
evacuees. He had a lovely smile, bright and friendly, Anna noticed. Perhaps he was not really much older than her own father?

When they reached Anna, Mrs. Ashton paused.

"And this is the girl who had stitches in her knee—"

"Ah!" he said. "So you're the young lady who lured the doctor from his village rounds?"

"Yes, sir—sorry, sir," mumbled Anna.

"Well, I very much hope you're feeling better now?" he
asked with gentle eyes.

"Yes, sir," she said, and smiled. He was kind, not frightening—she could see that at once. More, she trembled with secret
pleasure at being singled out by such a gentleman.

The wheels of his chair squeaked a bit on the polished stone
floor as he moved on, and quite suddenly Anna felt sorry for
him and his wife. She worried that Mrs. Ashton might not be
happy being married to a cripple—they couldn't go dancing together, and she could imagine Mrs. Ashton dancing. That must
make him sad, too, she thought.

How could such a beautiful woman be married to a man
who couldn't walk?

~

That afternoon, the evacuees were allowed to play outside. Limping a little with her bandaged knee, Anna followed the others into the gardens on the south side of the house. There were lawns and yew walks, and woods to explore. Small, hedged gardens, and steep banks to roll down.

On every side stretched the parkland, as far as Anna could see.

Bands of children ran across the vast sunken lawn beyond the saloon, chasing each other up and down its banks. There was a subtle bloom to the air, and to the weather. Coming from a city, Anna had never seen such a wide sky; it stretched out above them all like something freshly opened.

She couldn't really fathom why she was here, or what sort of place it was. She hopped down a bank with her arms raised to the wind and her head thrown back, yelling as she went, like the others.

From his study window Thomas Ashton watched the children playing tag on the lawn below. Their freewheeling grace touched him—all that spontaneity.

A shiver of unknown emotion rippled through him. He wanted to strike the right note with these children: to encourage them, and enjoy their high spirits, as was proper for someone with an open heart. But he must not let them unsettle his hard-won balance, either.

He wheeled himself away from the window and turned on the wireless to hear the latest news.

The children, meanwhile, wandered through the grounds until supper time. They knew nothing of Hitler's invasion of Poland. Nor did they ask any questions as they went upstairs to their dormitories.

The slow, silent power of the house was beginning to reach them already.

6

———•———

ON THE MORNING of 2 September, Roberta Sands woke early, dressed herself and made some tea. She overfilled the pot, brewing for her absent husband, out of habit, then sat for a long time in the kitchen.

She knew that all the other evacuees' parents would also be suffering a weekend of eerie quiet—waiting to hear about their children, wondering when war would be declared—today, tomorrow?

All around her were the final shreds of summer. A vase of fading roses from the garden, dusty geraniums in a pot, a spattered back window which she had not cleaned since the spring.

It was a Saturday, so there was no need to hurry off to work. She wandered through the empty rooms, putting things in order. Until she found herself sitting on the stairs, gazing down at the patterned tiles on the hall floor, unable to move.

Anna had been born upstairs. It was a small Edwardian house in a grid of near-identical terraces in Fulham. The front rooms were dark, facing north onto a street narrowed by two rows of pollarded limes.

Anna had the brightest room, with a back view. They had their own small lawn, but the grass was always sparse, because it lacked sunshine. Only at the turning point of the day did the sun rise high enough to cast an unblinkered eye onto their modest enclosure. But from Anna's window they could gaze onto other, larger gardens with cherry trees and magnolias, where the sunshine gleamed off luxuriant grass late into the afternoon.

Roberta made her way to Anna's room and glanced at some

colorful petunias on a distant lawn. Their very exuberance gave her an ache of separation.

Where was Anna's new home?

She had never valued their family routines enough, and now they were over—yet she found the transitions to this new time oddly untraceable. Outside, the ugly corrugated roofs of the air-raid shelters looked as if they had always been there.

She went downstairs again. Her old upright piano was lying open, its ivories throwing out a pale gleam in the dark front room. She banished the silence by playing an Al Bowlly song, but it felt too feckless, so she drifted into a lullaby.

Photographs of her husband Lewis and Anna were propped on a side table. She felt watched, and strangely guilty to be at home without them, just waiting for news. So she decided to go out for a walk, perhaps along the river at Bishop's Park.

She stepped out into a subdued city, tightening her coat belt as she went.

Later that day, Lewis sat in his bell tent near Salisbury Plain. It was raining—had been raining all day. Every item of his uniform felt damp. Rain was sliding down the tarpaulin sides of his tent, and his heavy boots were caked with wet mud. Their company commander was waiting for the weather to ease off before the next drill—unlikely before supper, thank God.

He sat cross-legged with a book on his knee, writing to his wife. He closed his eyes and imagined Roberta on one of her habitual walks: a sensuous blue-eyed brunette strolling through the park. She always carried herself with a graceful swing which could make her appear slightly available.

And yet he would hate her to change anything. He sometimes let her walk a little ahead, just to admire her. If she turned to wait for him, then her eyes would flash backwards in an expectant glance; he loved that look, always would. Somehow, the rapid flicker of her moods shone right through her face—she carried her own personal weather, as subtly shifting as a sea sky.

Lewis returned to his letter. He was good at gallant endearments from a distance, but he did worry about being too dour in person. He was a diligent furniture restorer with a small family business, but no more than that. Would Roberta wake up one day and realize he was not enough for her?

I'm still getting used to the strange ways of army life, he wrote, but felt reluctant to describe their banal routines: polishing buckles, erecting tents. They were busy much of the time, but there were also frequent between-times, when they all seemed to be waiting and waiting for the war to begin. Everything hanging on the news from Poland. He felt mapless in this new world, with his wife unattended, and their child in an unknown house.

Where is Anna's new home, he wrote, *have you heard yet?*

"I am speaking to you from the Cabinet Room of 10 Downing Street."

On the morning of Sunday 3 September, Anna was sitting with a silent crowd of children in the Ashton saloon, listening to Mr. Chamberlain on the wireless. All the evacuees had been assembled to hear the prime minister's broadcast just after eleven o'clock, when his solemn, hangdog voice announced that they were now at war with Germany.

"You can imagine what a bitter blow it is to me that all my long struggle to win peace has failed . . . I know that you will all play your parts with calmness and courage."

Anna felt keenly for her father, picturing him in his uniform. And would there be bombs, now, over London, with her mother sheltering in the cellar?

Mr. Ashton switched off the wireless.

"It is unlikely that very much will happen to begin with, so please don't worry yourselves about anything," he said with a steady face. "And now I suggest you all write to your parents—to tell them you have arrived at a safe new home."

The children were guided into the dining room, where each place was set with a sheet of lined paper and a pencil. Anna sat down and tried out her new curly handwriting, keeping her letters close to the lines.

Dear Mummy, my train went to Ashton Park in Yorkshire. It is huge. We play in the gardens a lot.

Roberta opened the letter as soon as she saw it on her return home from work. It didn't say much. She looked at the postmark—three days old. She read it over and over, to see if she had missed some nuance. Eight-year-olds could chatter away, but wrote as little as possible.

Tomorrow, she would go to the library and look up Ashton Park on the map. She had thought Anna would be in a family house, with foster parents, but this sounded like a school. Perhaps that was better. She had given Anna a signal to let her know if things were too dire—she was to write, *Can you send me some extra socks?* Yet what if Anna had forgotten?

In the front room, the absence of her husband and child was palpable in the unlit silence. She rolled down her makeshift blackout curtains, then turned on a lamp and wrote to Lewis at his training camp:

I don't know much about her new home yet, but her first letter was cheerful.

7

IN WARSAW THE mood was mysteriously euphoric on 3 September. Britain's declaration of war was greeted by rejoicing crowds spilling through the streets, and Poland's Colonel Beck arrived at the British embassy with a bottle of champagne. He waved to well-wishers from the embassy balcony, but Norton had never felt less like celebrating. It was an unnatural jubilation, he thought, an odd gallows glee, and a desperate hope that if Britain was on their side now, and France too, there must surely be hope yet for Poland.

But any elation faded rapidly as Allied planes failed to appear and the Nazi tanks rolled on undeterred. Not for the first time, Norton felt acutely ashamed of Britain's vacillating support for the Poles. The news from the front was desperate, with reports of the Polish cavalry being mown down by German tanks. And it was rumored that almost the entire Polish air force had been destroyed on the ground, in a single Luftwaffe raid.

By 4 September, waves of German bombers were attacking Warsaw. Norton and his wife stood on the embassy roof, and watched the city burn. Within hours, heavy air raids forced them and their staff to abandon the embassy and head eastwards. There was little room for a chauffeur, so his wife insisted on driving their Plymouth herself.

"You've barely slept for days, and I've spent all summer getting to know the roads," she said.

Norton's wife had always been unflappable. Sometimes people asked him why she was called "Peter," but as he watched her mobilizing the embassy evacuation, he thought how apt her nickname was: she was irrepressible, like Barrie's pantomime boy. With her short hair and angular face, she had never been pretty, but Norton loved his wife for her energy and bracing candor.

She drove him through the night, in pitch darkness. Their car was right down on its springs, and she navigated by moonlight.

At one point she lurched abruptly into a copse, and the jolt of her braking woke him.

"Stukas," she said, "we'll wait here." He heard the engines rumbling overhead.

"You should have woken me earlier—I might have died in my sleep," he muttered. She glanced at him sideways in the dark.

"You would've probably woken up just *as* you were dying."

She kept on driving for several days, until they reached the eastern town of Krzemieniec, where the diplomatic corps were regrouping.

"It looks like the backdrop for a ballet," said Norton, admiring the pretty hillside town as they unloaded the car. But the next morning, six German planes appeared from the west and dive-bombed the marketplace, packed with peasants and their loaded carts.

It was all so sudden. Houses collapsed, and screaming people scattered in every direction. A shrieking horse bolted through the market, his twisted cart clattering over cobblestones. Other dead horses littered the streets. Norton found a woman streaming with blood in a crater, and he pulled her out, while his wife ran to help an old man trapped by a wall.

The rest of that day was spent digging out bodies from the debris. Twenty or more houses were destroyed, and over fifty people died outright, but many more were injured. Norton tried to cable London with reports of this civilian slaughter, but the wires were down.

The diplomats huddled together in that broken town until

the thirteenth day of the Nazi invasion, when news came through of a sudden pincer invasion by the Soviets from the east, sealing Poland's ruin. Then they all knew it was time to leave.

The Nortons drove to Kuty, a small town separated from Romania by a river. There, Norton got out his visa stamp, and signed as many British visas as he could for refugees trying to escape Poland. Then he and his wife joined the interminable queue across the border bridge to safety, and began their long journey back to England.

When they at last found their way home to London, the parks were empty and the streets swollen with inert piles of sandbags. The city had a strange, corpse-like air.

It was a few days before Norton realized what was missing. It was the sound of children, walking home from school, running to the corner shop, waiting with their mothers at bus stops. As if the Pied Piper had passed through London and lured them all away.

Affinities

1939–1945

8

6 October 1939

Dear Mummy,
There are lots of trees and conkers here. Yesterday we made
a big pile of leaves and hid inside it.

ANNA HAD NEVER noticed autumn before. Back home, the sheer cliffs of terraced streets blocked the light and hid the seasons. There was summertime when you ran about outside, but after that she could only remember darker days, and the long wait for Christmas. Wet leaves on the pavement and bare branches against a white sky.

But here, now, in remote Yorkshire parkland, Anna saw the glory of autumn for the first time. Great avenues of trees towered with color. Wide lawns glinted with ripe conkers, and gusts of wind swept down leaves in fiery drifts. The weather reached right through her fingertips and deep inside her, until she felt different and new.

Today, a sparse drizzle had driven the other evacuees indoors, but Anna lingered outside for a while, strained by playing with children she barely knew. In the empty garden the roses were oddly still, as if arrested in time. The quiet was such that only a sigh of rain could be heard, close or far.

At that moment, under a sullen sky, Anna realized she was disappointed. Only weeks ago, she had thought they were being sent to the seaside, all of them. She had pictured herself running on soft sand, in an endless afternoon of sunshine with no school. Now she wondered how soon she could get back home to her mother.

Beside her stood a cluster of flaking roses, yellow but edged with brown, and torn by rain. They had no scent. The box hedges were stiff with raindrops which quivered on small points. Anna flicked a hedge with a stick, and water sprayed over her bare shins.

I have a uniform now. Does that mean I'm staying here longer? I'm fine but I miss you. Please write soon. Lots of love, Anna.

The day they all lined up for their uniforms had felt like a turning point. Gray tunics for the girls, gray shorts for the boys, white shirts for both. There were a few standard sizes, and many of the evacuees drifted around in clothes too big for them, cuffs rolled up. But the next morning, when they filed in for assembly, Anna noticed how they all looked more or less the same now.

She counted six teachers at the school—or seven, including Mr. Ashton. They were led by Mr. Stewart, a Scotsman who had been a headmaster in Pimlico. His back was army straight, and he hid behind a mustache flecked with gray, like Mr. Chamberlain. Anna often saw him set off for solitary walks, picking his way through the fallen leaves with a stick.

Some of the children were always homesick, sniveling with tears which seemed to blend into their colds and runny noses. But Anna didn't cry. As the weeks unrolled she began to pride herself on being one of the braver evacuees, who could adapt to anything. She still missed her home, but a part of her now wanted to see this adventure through to its end.

She had never known a place with so many secrets to explore. There was a watchful statue of Father Time on the lawn, and an abandoned palm house in the woodland—and beyond, a pet cemetery marked with strange names. Inside the house, the corridors were hung with ghostly portraits of forgotten people, and hidden attic steps climbed up to dusty storerooms crammed with old furniture and papers.

One of the older children discovered a disused nursery. A painted room, once cornflower-blue, now faded somewhat and piled with old toys. It became a secret den for some of the bolder girls, including Anna. There was a doll's house, still peopled by pretty porcelain dolls with faces of startled happiness. An old rocking horse stood patiently to one side, with a scraggy mane and frayed stirrups. Dusty wooden puzzles were stacked on shelves. Tin soldiers, too, and a windup drummer whose drumbeat still worked if you turned the key. Dolls with unruly hair, and teddies missing their glass eyes.

Did the Ashtons have a daughter, Anna wondered, locked away in another part of the house?

"Whose was the doll's house in the old nursery?" she asked casually one day, as Mrs. Robson, a housemaid, was folding laundry.

"That'd be Miss Claudia's," she said, "Mr. Ashton's little sister—died of the flu as a girl."

Anna breathed in sharply. A dead child, a dead sister, at Ashton Park. Perhaps there was a family curse.

"And Mr. Ashton, was he always . . . lame?"

"Oh no," came the emphatic reply, "he was the finest young man in Yorkshire. Running, riding, dancing, everything."

Brisk Mrs. Robson seemed unfussed by this revelation, but Anna felt herself flinching. To change so drastically—that was terrible!

What happened to him? Anna wondered. Perhaps war wounds had crippled him. Perhaps he had won medals for bravery in the Great War, leading his men. Or perhaps it was a car crash . . .

"That's *awful*," was all she could muster, hoping Mrs. Robson would be more forthcoming.

"He copes. There's many to help him."

Mrs. Robson was busy counting pillow slips, but she glanced over at the child, who was suddenly damp-eyed at Mr. Ashton's misfortune, and became stern, irritated even.

"There's worse things than being an Ashton, even if you're crippled. Save your pity for those as go down the mines every day—if you break your body there, you're finished, like a broken tool. Mr. Ashton has plenty to enjoy, plenty to be glad about. He's all right."

There was a firm note of reproach in the older woman's chiding, but all Anna's sympathy was welling up for the kind, gentle man who tried so hard when he taught them. She had not realized how much he had lost.

By the time Mr. Ashton arrived at her next lesson, she felt a shiver of secret embarrassment—because she had been thinking about him. He had triggered her pity, and there was no ridding that from her heart now, as she watched him wheel himself to the front of the class.

Thomas Ashton swiveled his chair by the teacher's desk, then looked across to see fourteen young faces gazing up at him, expectant, respectful, perhaps a little nervous too.

How very strange it all was. To find himself teaching this group of unknown children, all under ten. Their first Latin lesson.

"Let us begin at the beginning," he said, clearing his throat. "*Amo, amas, amat, amamus, amatis, amant—that* is what all children learn first in Latin, the verb *to love.* Learn *amo,* and you will open a door onto one of the great lost languages of the world."

He smiled as he said this, hoping the children would relax.

"It is all quite simple after this," he went on, wheeling himself over to write the words on the board.

"Just repeat after me. *Amo*—I love. *Amas*—you love. *Amat*—he or she loves . . ."

He began to chant the words and the children followed him.

"*Amo—amas—amat—amamus—amatis—amant.*"

"Again."

The children recited it over and over, understanding nothing, really, of their stiff chorus. *I love, you love, we all love.*

"That's very good," said Thomas, halting their chant with a raised hand. "Now you can speak Latin. Remember these words, and they will never leave you."

He smiled, and saw three rows of open young faces gaze back at him, guileless and obedient.

Was teaching really so very easy, he wondered, remembering his own boarding school, the hectoring masters, the routine canings, the nameless daily fears. He felt no wish to do anything other than help these motherless children.

"Even today, you will find that Latin turns up in odd places," Thomas said, and he passed around a coin on which they saw *Georgius Rex* written underneath the picture of the king.

"Have you always been a Latin teacher, sir?" asked a girl, Katy, with pigtails.

The question came abruptly, and pricked Thomas. He saw himself suddenly as they must see him: a man in a wheelchair, apparently infirm, drilling them in a dead language. He should not feel the need to explain himself to a group of children, surely?

"No, I have not always been a teacher," he said with a slight shrug, looking across at the curious faces before him. "Things are not always quite as they seem. I was once a diplomat," he added.

"What's a *dip*lomat, sir?"

"Somebody who works to keep the peace between different countries."

"Can they stop wars?"

"They try to."

"Can they stop this war, sir?"

"If only," he said wryly, "but there have been many blunders."

Silence. He looked round the room, suddenly stricken by these trusting faces looking up to him, waiting for their teacher to reassure them that all would be well. He smiled as convincingly as he could.

"But I have no doubt that we will see Herr Hitler off: it will only be a matter of time. And then you'll all go home again."

A pang of unease tugged at him as the children showed such willing relief, all of them, wanting to sense victory right around the corner, just because he had said so.

"But in the meantime, *you will learn your Latin words*," he tutted at them with mock fierceness. Several faces broke into smiles, but then the gong rang, and the next lesson was upon them.

Thomas wheeled himself away; Anna Sands from the back row got up to open the door for him.

"Thank you, Anna," he said brightly, but she averted her eyes, shy of him. Watchful eyes, he noticed, as he left the room.

Anna returned to her seat. Did the Ashtons have any children of their own, she wondered? She hoped so. He must be a kind father.

9

THOMAS MADE HIS way back to the estate office, which had been transformed into a staff room. Opening the door, he found himself suddenly face-to-face with Ruth Weir, the sandy-haired young teacher from Pimlico.

"I'm so sorry," she said, for no clear reason.

"What about? This is meant to be your place too." She was clutching a stack of books and looked flustered, with startled eyes. He hoped it wasn't because of his abrupt entrance.

"Have you found anywhere to stow your things yet?"

"I was just trying to find a corner—"

"Here," said Thomas decisively, wheeling himself over to a set of wall cupboards. "I've been meaning to clear these, and now I have the rest of the morning to do so." He looked up and gave her a reassuring smile. "By the time you return here at lunchtime, this cupboard will be yours."

She smiled her thanks and disappeared to her lesson with an armful of books and pencils. The room without her felt suddenly still and empty.

A whistle shrieked in the distance. Thomas glanced out of the window, and saw Jock Stewart supervising some boys' races on the front lawn.

Turning back to the overflowing cupboard, he allowed himself a mental sigh. For days he had put off clearing out all these pointless old accounts books. He locked his chair brakes and settled his feet on the ground, and began to make a rubbish pile.

When Thomas reached the second cupboard, a leather-bound christening album fell at his feet. *Thomas Arthur Ashton,*

March 1900 said the gold lettering on the spine. He picked it up, unclasped the brass lock and abruptly opened a door onto his past.

There was his family, staring up at him. The photographs showed a formal group assembled outside the chapel, but even within the stillness of a photograph Thomas could sense their hidden lives. At the center stood his father, Robert, bracing his shoulders and staring into the camera defiantly, as if proud to be marking this new century with a third son. Beside him, his mother, Miriam, looked so poised, her luminous pale face enhanced by an oyster silk dress. Cradled in his mother's arms, the infant Thomas had an attentive gaze and a thin, rather adult face, he thought. At their side hovered William and Edward, his older brothers, clearly fidgeting for a chance to run wild in the early spring weather.

Thomas could remember his mother telling him all about the elaborate pomp of his christening party, the crowded reception spilling out into the gardens, where his father had planted his christening tree—a copper beech sapling—to much applause from family and friends. Afterwards, in the crimson dining room, the guests had sat down to a banquet entirely sourced from the estate: meat, fish, tender vegetables, fresh bread, even the cheese, with a steady flow of vintage wines from the cellars.

The sound of cheering roused Thomas, and his eyes flicked back outside to the boys running their races on the south lawn. He watched them for a moment, enjoying their reckless speed. One boy tumbled on the grass, then picked himself up as if nothing had happened. Thomas could still remember those easy boyhood falls—and rolling down the grassy banks of the rose garden with his sister, Claudia.

Turning back to the album, he noticed with regret that there were no pictures of his sister there: she was born two years later. Yet all his earliest memories were shared with her. Playing in the blue nursery, with its looming rocking horse and scattering of tin soldiers. Or hiding behind the leafy palms in the saloon, listening to their mother playing Schubert on the piano.

Every morning they would visit their mother in her dressing room. She had a view to the lawns, and a small writing table crowded with letters and exotic bijouterie. Sometimes they watched her brushing her long chestnut hair, and then there was the familiar clink of rings and bracelets as she took the jewels from her ring dish and put them on. She never wore her wedding ring at night, "because it makes my finger go stiff," she told them.

"When I grow up, can I have your rings?" Claudia asked one day.

"Of course you can, my darling," their mother replied, "and Thomas can have this bracelet for his wife," she added, to be fair.

Thomas had felt instantly possessive about her white-gold bracelet—so elegant, so delicate, already part of his future. He watched his mother slip it on her wrist and snap shut the clasp.

Those were the Edwardian years of plenty, Thomas now recognized, when the rooms overflowed with rich trailing draperies and potted palms, and his mother's exquisitely colored figurines were scattered on tables covered with ornate cloths.

There had been many reassuring family traditions, which he still liked to retrace in his mind. He could picture the long light of summer evenings, when the Ashtons and their guests would sit out on the garden steps, under the colonnade, with drinks and stories. Sometimes, he would accompany the butler on his clock-winding rounds. There were grandfather clocks, carriage clocks, hanging clocks—some that chimed, some with swinging pendulums, all requiring regular winding with their own key. Stillwell, the butler, held all the clock keys together on one ring, and he occasionally let Thomas do the winding.

"Gently does it—gently, gently," he would mutter, stooping

his back awkwardly to check on the boy. "Be careful not to force the mechanism."

Thomas never looked up to notice Stillwell's face, though now he fancied he could imagine the butler's anxious expression, as if reliving the scene outside himself.

Every spring, a man would climb up on a high ladder to polish the great crystal chandelier suspended in the Marble Hall. When he was finished, the crystal drops glistened like the purest water. Or if Thomas stood below it and looked upwards, the chandelier shone like the sun against the painted azure sky of the high-domed ceiling, where a half-naked man played his lyre amongst the clouds.

"That's Apollo," his father explained to him one day, "Greek god of the sun, and music too. Decent of him to join us here in Yorkshire—very decent."

Thomas's parents were frequently away at their Regent's Park house in London, but whenever they returned to Ashton, a mood of relaxed gaiety would flow once more through the house as their trunks and suitcases were carried upstairs. Twice a year, they held dances in the gilded-oak saloon—a long, many-windowed room which glowed in the late afternoon sun. Sometimes, Thomas was allowed to stay up for the occasion. Guests would assemble in the Marble Hall, and he would shake their hands without ever quite recognizing their faces. He retained an impression of the men throwing back their shoulders to carry their bellies, while the women seemed always to be tilting their heads to one side, as if to balance precious objects on their noses.

At the center of any room stood his parents. He would never forget his mother in blue-shadowed silk, sweeping into the dining room on his father's arm, truly beautiful.

"You're an Ashton," his father would fondly tell him, to the mild annoyance of the others. For Thomas had inherited his father's arresting blue gaze, which Robert, in his vainer mo-

THE VERY THOUGHT OF YOU 57

ments, believed was the gift and guiding spirit of the Ashton family. When Robert looked into his youngest son's face, he saw a pleasing mirror of his own soul.

History, too, pervaded Thomas's childhood. Family portraits looked down at him from the walls, and he ran his fingers across the calf-backed books accumulated over generations in the library.

In one corner of the library was a secret door, subtly encased in dummy books, which revealed the gallery steps at the flick of a catch. Thomas knew that this device had been installed by his grandfather, and he felt a rush of complicity with him whenever he clicked open the door. He would spend hours walking along the brass rail of the library's gallery, touching all the old books, histories, Greek poetry, atlases, editions of old dramatists.

All over the house, Thomas sensed the presence of earlier Ashtons—in the air, in the smoke rising from the great carved fireplaces, always watching. He could walk through every room secure in the continuity of generations, with ancestors whose names were known and remembered.

But minor intimations of an imperfect world had still intruded upon his early years. When he was eight, his aunt Mary came to visit, and walked with him to the statue of Father Time on the south lawn.

"I used to swing round him as a child," she said fondly, scraping away a little moss from his pedestal. "He looks so much smaller than I remember."

As she turned to face the house, Thomas was startled to recognize that Aunt Mary used to live here, and that he, too, would one day be a stranger at Ashton like her. His elder brother William would inherit the house, and install his wife and children. He would be only partly welcome, no more than an uncle to the new heirs. For some weeks, he wandered round the house staring at favorite pictures and clocks with a puzzled sense of incipient loss.

There was, too, the eerie warning of the local monasteries, which they visited every summer. Laden with baskets of food and drink, cars would carry them to the picturesque ruins of Rievaulx and Byland, perfect spots for a picnic. He and his brothers would race about on the broken walls, jumping over the stumps of old pillars. Until a stray breeze would make Thomas stop, and look round at the mighty walls reduced to piles of tumbled rock. Here was Rievaulx, once one of the greatest abbeys in the land, where now the grass grew right up to the altar. Where soaring broken arches framed sheep grazing on the far hill.

Thomas could recall sitting quietly with Claudia on an open staircase, and rubbing his hand over the sheer stone steps. The tricks of time were all about them, stones worn smooth by wind and rain, but this was the oblivion of somebody else's past.

"This stream runs into the river in our park," his whiskered father once explained to him, as they walked along the small beck at Rievaulx. "They named the abbey after the river here— Rievaulx, valley of the Rye. It's a broader river through our land, but it's the same source."

Thomas had looked into the rocky shallows of the water, and blithely speculated that all the life and spirit of this ruined abbey had simply drifted downstream a few miles and settled with them instead, in the seemingly imperishable splendor of Ashton Park.

Outside, the cry of children grew suddenly more insistent. Thomas wheeled himself to the window, and realized that it was the break before lunch.

Girls and boys were thronging the lawn in scattered groups, and queuing for the swing. For a while, he watched the random formations of children, just checking that none of them looked excluded.

His wife wandered onto the lawn. He felt faintly guilty about spying on her unobserved, but kept watching. Jock Stewart followed just behind her, and began to swing the lunch bell high and low, drawing the children towards the dining room.

He watched his wife standing on the crest of the lawn steps, as dozens of children raced past her. Until a girl stopped there, Anna Sands, and reached up her hand to Elizabeth. Thomas felt his heart lurch.

But his wife would not accept the gesture. She patted the girl on the shoulder a little awkwardly, and sent her on her way.

Thomas winced, and pushed himself off to lunch. Her pain was his pain. What were they, he asked himself, but a childless couple in a vast house, surrounded by other people's children?

10

EVERY MORNING, A housemaid brought a tray of tea to the Ashtons' bedroom. Sometimes the maid would open the door to find Elizabeth in triptych, reflected in all three of her dressing table mirrors as she brushed her long hair. And if Elizabeth turned to thank the maid, her reflection would glance round three times too.

Elizabeth persisted in keeping her hair long at a time when most women cut theirs. She had long dark hair tinged with copper, which she groomed with a set of silver hairbrushes. Thomas would watch her at her dressing table, with her hair falling down her back, brushing and brushing. When white strands began to appear, she first plucked them out, then discreetly dyed her hair until she could no longer remember its true color. A woman in her thirties should not have any white hairs, she was clear about that.

Once she had completed her dressing-room rituals, Elizabeth would emerge into the school. Crisply dressed, with her distinctive clipped walk echoing through the Marble Hall.

Anna could recognize her footsteps at once. From a distance, half-afraid and half-intrigued, she would often watch Mrs. Ashton in her silken blouse, with her skirt barely shifting as she walked. Her shoulders and long neck appeared still and poised, even though she moved briskly. Her face, too, was unflinching. She did not smile much, and always seemed to be setting off somewhere else. Probably because she didn't teach any lessons like her husband. She was usually busy organizing everyone else—the matrons, the kitchen staff, the housemaids.

Ashton Park was more like a proper school now, with rotas and rules, and Anna always did what she could to stay out of trouble. At first she had been afraid of dormitory life, where nothing could be secret and she had to undress in front of other children. Yet she had got used to that, as well as the thin blankets at night, and the cold days when they all took turns to sit on the old tepid radiators. But she was often hungry.

"Don't you know there's a war on?" muttered the cook, if she saw the children's disappointed faces.

Yet despite these austerities, Anna now often relaxed into happiness. There were group games of hide-and-seek right round the house, and her heart raced with the elation of playing with so many children. Sometimes, when she hid in a cupboard waiting to be found, she had to bite her knuckles just to stop herself from whooping out loud.

But although Anna appeared cheerful, even to herself, she was troubled by bad dreams at night. Sometimes her mother would grow old very suddenly, all gray and withered, or her face would begin to bubble with warts, with her small, straight nose turning bulbous and ugly. Anna would run to save her, but the scene would dissolve into a chase, with a faceless, implacable man following them everywhere, through cupboards, down streets, into every dark corner.

She cherished any remembered glimpses of her mother, but too often her face was unclear—a shape, a glance, her head turning, no more. Sometimes, Anna simply could not remember what she looked like. Yet she dreaded her mother's hair turning white in her absence.

She began to wet her bed, unleashing a cycle of fear and shame. She would wake suddenly in cold, sodden sheets, and know with a shiver of panic that the matron would be furious with her.

Miss Harrison was fiercely impatient with any bed wetters. She would publicly scold the offending children at breakfast, making them stand up one by one, before ordering them up-stairs, shamefaced, to change their sheets.

Every night, Anna prayed solemnly for a dry bed. She avoided drinking any water, and went to the lavatory as many times as she could. Yet in the dead of night she would still wake up to a slippery damp mattress, the sheets icy-wet against her legs, her heart chilled with fear.

Every third Wednesday, the children had to troop down to the laundry room in a long line, dumping their sheets in wicker baskets. One morning, Anna was the first down, and she saw the junior matron slip out the key from a crockery cabinet to unlock the door.

Two nights later, she woke up alert and afraid in a wet bed. But she remembered the key to the laundry room. Quietly, she stripped the offending sheet from her bed and used it to sop up the wet mattress. Then she rolled her sheet up into a ball and started to creep downstairs.

First down the top stairs, where every step seemed to creak. Then she decided to walk down the forbidden mahogany staircase, to avoid the long corridor past the matron's room. Down she went, clinging to the banister so as not to slip on the polished wooden steps.

She worked her way through the dark, cold hall, which glowed with lunar light off the marble floor. Now she had to pass Mr. and Mrs. Ashton's rooms, and get down the steps to the basement. She heard an owl hooting outside, and her own feet scuffing the stone floor as she reached up, at last, for the laundry-room key.

She opened the door and felt her way round the dark room, not daring to turn on a light. She found the drawers where the sheets were held, and pulled one out. She couldn't see in the dark if it was exactly right—it seemed to be a thicker sheet. So she felt for another. That was the one she would take.

She folded up her wet sheet as neatly as she could, and

stuffed it into the back of the nearest drawer. Then, with her heart drumming, she relocked the door and crept upstairs the way she had come.

The Marble Hall was already showing the first glimmer of light as she hurried back to her dormitory. Another child stirred as she tiptoed towards her bed, but nobody woke up. She folded her blue, rough towel, and placed it over the wet patch on the mattress. Then she laid the new sheet over the top, with the bedclothes too, and fell into bed, exhausted, though not forgetting to remove her wet nightdress.

The next morning she dressed quickly and straightened out her bed. At breakfast, there was no fierce summons from Miss Harrison.

Twice more, she awoke suddenly in the night with icy wet sheets against her skin. Twice more, she ventured down to the locked laundry room successfully. But on her third trip she encountered something which she would never forget.

She was safely down the mahogany stairs, and through the Marble Hall, and was about to head down the final flight of stairs to the laundry room. Her journey took her past the great paneled door which opened onto the Ashtons' suite of rooms. Occasionally, the children saw the door open in the daytime: they could glimpse a crimson sitting room, and a door beyond leading to the Ashtons' bedroom.

As she left the Marble Hall behind her, she was shocked to see that the Ashtons' door was open and their light was still on. She heard voices, and dashed to hide behind a Chinese lacquered dresser in the corridor's corner. Cowering there, she waited with dread to hear the clack-clack of Mrs. Ashton's heels walking towards her. Blood pounded in her ears as she crouched there, still clutching the damp sheet.

No footsteps came near her, but there were sounds, and Anna strained to listen. She could hear an agitated voice— Mrs. Ashton, she thought—from the next room. It must be the middle of the night. Didn't they know their door was open?

After a few minutes Anna crept out from her position, and moved quietly, slowly, towards the stairs. But as she did so, her eye was drawn through the open door to a large oval mirror hanging on the crimson wall. She saw something move and looked again.

It was Mrs. Ashton, naked.

Sheer shock branded the sight on her mind. She caught only glimpses, as Mrs. Ashton moved in and out of vision through the bedroom reflected in the mirror. But it was a searing vision of a woman's body. Anna had never seen her mother naked, and the sight of Mrs. Ashton's mature breasts and dark bush of hair was astonishing to her. She was repelled and entranced. Is that what would happen to her own skimpy body one day? She stayed rooted to the spot, her eyes fixed to the mirror, listening.

Though she could only catch snatches of what was being said, she recognized a desperation which frightened her. Mrs. Ashton was swearing and choking on foul words at her husband. Violent language she had never heard before. Guttural sounds which chilled her.

She crept away as silently as she could.

Elizabeth Ashton was drunk. She was walking up and down naked in her bedroom, swearing, sobbing, showing Thomas the menstrual blood smeared down her legs.

"I'm bleeding again," she cried. "I'm bleeding."

She swore at Thomas, gagging on a string of ugly expletives. It was a strangled voice, hysterical, before she doubled over with weeping, her breasts pressing against bare legs.

Another month and still no pregnancy. Thomas sat by silently on their bed, longing to soothe and pacify her, but knowing he could not reach her yet. Sometimes, when Elizabeth menstruated, her raving grief could not be contained. Drink unleashed this frenzy in her. She drained the room of any space for his emotions; he just had to wait for her to collapse onto the bed in a drunken sleep as he knew she eventually would.

Both of them were exhausted by her misery. There were times when Thomas longed to be left alone, but he felt responsible for his wife's unhappiness. They were both damaged people now, both locked into their drama together. Some self-destructive urge made Elizabeth stay with him. She would neither leave him, nor would she adopt a child.

At last she sank onto the bed and her sobs ebbed into sleep. He covered her and switched off the bedside light. The door remained open till morning, when the kitchen maid spotted it on her way to the dining room. She shut it before the children came down to breakfast.

In the morning Anna saw Mrs. Ashton stride through the Marble Hall, trim and elegant as ever, her face a mask of distant composure. Anna stole a glance at her breasts, so discreetly tidied away now behind the silky blouse. Then she felt ashamed and anxious.

Did all adults cry out in such pain behind their bedroom doors?

It was only once more that Anna wet her bed, and she allowed herself to be rebuked by the matron rather than go on her dark journey to the laundry room.

But whenever she saw Mrs. Ashton now, she felt a strange bond with her. Because Anna knew she was unhappy, even if she did not know why. Mrs. Ashton's sadness was her secret now, too.

She found herself puzzling over an unfamiliar pang inside. Mr. Ashton's words came back to her, from his lesson. "Things are not always quite as they seem." She thought of his smiling face, and his wheelchair, never mentioned. She thought of Mrs. Ashton and her secret sorrow. She found herself troubled by a new twinge inside—an ache she could not quite fathom.

It was as if her heart had been suddenly tuned into a strange new wireless station for other people's sorrows. And their vibrations would not quite let her go, even if they had nothing to do with her.

11

· —— ·

SOON AFTER THE evacuees' arrival, Thomas began to dream that he could dance again. Whether the children had awakened something in him, he couldn't say, but suddenly his dreams transported him into wide, bright rooms of flowing waltzes and swift, intricate foxtrots on sprung floors. Dreams in which he could feel himself dancing, yet watched himself too, both dancer and audience. So vivid were his sensations that he would awake with a pleasant ache in his legs, surprised to discover that he had only been dreaming.

The dreams took him by surprise, but did not sadden him: they were rejuvenating. As if the past was still inside him, within reach. Sometimes he whirled around a ballroom with Elizabeth, or he gazed into the eyes of other, earlier lovers, from the days when he was a young diplomat stepping out in Berlin.

There was one tender night in Berlin which Thomas would not forget. A ball at the French embassy, when he held Elizabeth's waist and led her deftly round the dance floor, as if nobody else was there. When their marriage was only weeks old.

Her eyes were fixed on his, and she began to laugh, exulting in their moment together. *I am dancing with my wife,* he thought. *This is us—you and me, together.*

"Happy?" he asked her.

"So happy," she said, "so very happy."

He could not contain his own joy as he spun her round the floor, the music flowing through them and the tenor crooning his love song.

Oh sweet and lovely lady be good,
Oh lady be good to me . . .

Even now, ten years on, he could still remember her eyes reaching into his own. Later events could never quite cancel out what once had been. There was still that time, whatever came afterwards.

As he sat at his study desk preparing for the day's lessons, his thoughts wandered back further, to the summer of 1914—and the day when his mother had taken him out from school to watch a polo match in London. He could remember standing with his sister, Claudia, amidst the Hurlingham Club's ornamental gardens, waiting to see their brother William, whose cavalry regiment had just returned from India. It was a day of great excitement for them all; they had not seen William in over two years.

He appeared with a familiar wave, taller, darker haired, more dashing than Thomas ever remembered. He had grown a lustrous mustache, and his powerful legs filled his riding boots.

"Our team is being drilled for a summer of tournament wins," he explained casually.

That was a great afternoon for the Twelfth Lancers. They played with grace and speed and intuition. For a moment, when William fell and their mother Miriam rose with a cry, it looked as though the afternoon might be blighted. But William was unhurt, and his team played on to win the Subaltern's Cup with ease.

Afterwards, a sea of colored hats flooded the lawns as the spectators congregated for tea and sandwiches. Claudia danced about, euphoric to see her eldest brother, and entranced by the braid and brass buttons of the cavalry uniforms. Here was the full pageantry of the empire, with its glinting array of young men. Claudia pulled Thomas along to watch the military band down by the lake. As the crowds died away, the bandsmen paraded with a final slow march, their spurs glimmering in the late-afternoon sunshine. Thomas noted the strange slow double-step performed with solemn grace even by the stoutest bandsmen.

Everyone knew that war was in the air, and the proud vale-dictory note of the brass band caught at the hearts of many mothers. Archduke Franz Ferdinand's assassination was every-where discussed.

"If war happens, it will be over by Christmas," was the line which Thomas heard passed around Hurlingham that day.

> *Be thou my guardian and my guide,*
> *And hear me when I call;*
> *Let not my slippery footsteps slide,*
> *And hold me lest I fall . . .*

Even after war was declared, school went on as usual for Thomas. Beneath the soaring fan vaulting of Eton College Cha-pel, he continued to sing rousing Anglican hymns. Glancing upwards, the chapel's carved medieval stone made any present troubles seem somehow insignificant.

> *We blossom and flourish as leaves on a tree—*
> *And wither, and perish, but naught changeth thee . . .*

Daily they prayed for those who had died at the front. Roll calls of boys' names were read out, boys who had so recently walked down the school streets. But Thomas was still hedged in by his lessons, competing for the History Prize, and running for his house team. Never thinking much about the war, even when his brother's cavalry regiment crossed the channel to France. Until his housemaster called him into his study after lunch one day.

"It was a dawn raid. He was leading his men with the courage you would expect. I'm afraid they were unable to retrieve his body."

William, his indomitable brother, whose thick legs had strained the top lace of his riding boots.

Thomas was excused from afternoon school, and sent off to running practice. He ran and ran, and the breath of life streamed through his lungs, and the ground pushed up against his feet as he pounded along the track. But he could not stop himself imagining the alien landscape, and the random moment of his brother's death in the trick light of dawn. He had vaguely assumed until then that any British deaths were those of incompetent soldiers, without his brother's verve or timing. Now, with William caught out, he glimpsed the roulette of survival on the front.

He took tea in the High Street with his brother Edward, already in the uniform of the school's cadet corps. They ate muffins, and all their thoughts were for their mother and sister: they could touch on their own grief only through sympathy for the women in their family.

A few weeks later William's memorial service was held at Ashton Park, despite the absent corpse. Only his bullet-scarred helmet had been retrieved. Miriam Ashton was distraught and held on to Claudia, stroking her hair. It was no comfort to her that William had been heroic, because the soaring death toll had already devalued the worth of any one sacrifice. Nor could she lose the imagined moment of her son's pain in death: the phantom shrapnel kept tearing through her own guts.

Thomas's father was silent, but inside he wept at the memory of his son, whom he saw as a better version of himself. He was privately mortified that he could not have died in his place. But he was also pricked with guilty sorrow by the three young laborers from the village who had also died that month, yet would not be treated to the ceremony of William's memorials. He ensured that flowers were sent to their mothers.

William's leather trunk was returned by his regiment, all his chattels neatly packed by his batman, his shaving kit, his ivory hairbrushes, his silver flask and cigarette cases, his letters. It gave an oddly ordered impression of war, Thomas thought. His mother would not allow the trunk to be unpacked: it was locked up and stowed away, upstairs, somewhere safe.

Her anguish was only deepened when her next son, Edward, finished his schooling and arrived home for a visit in his uniform. In 1915, he trained for a month at Aldershot before his regiment was sent to the front.

When fifteen-year-old Thomas returned home to Ashton Park in the holidays, he found an altered place. All the young men from the estate had left to join the local yeoman rifles. For the first time, he and his sister saw the great shell of their house empty of parties. The fires were unlit, and the deserted corridors echoed to their footsteps. Memories of William's commanding presence crowded in on them, in every unused room.

Their mother had removed herself to London, to help run a soldiers' canteen at Waterloo. Their father struggled to keep his estates going in the absence of so many laborers, then succumbed to his wife's wish to turn Ashton Park into a hospital. At least the house was full again, thought Thomas. For the next few holidays, he carried supplies up and down the mahogany stairs to nurses in starched uniforms. He and his sister watched with appalled fascination as limbless young men were wheeled around in bath chairs on the front lawn. Claudia longed for Edward to come home on leave; Thomas dreaded his mutilation.

School was little better for Thomas, because every day brought fresh news of casualties from their teams, their school plays, their choirs.

Edward wrote home from Flanders, letters which at first— but only at first—commended the bravery and spirit of his company.

Dear Thomas,

I imagine with pleasure your daily routine at school.
Enjoy it for me and do not hurry to join us. Here, death is so
familiar that it weakens our will to live. What does it matter
if the sun shines? Why should I shave?

Our bravery is bovine. We expect to die, and prepare
for it daily. But just when you think you are resigned and
emptied of fear, and free to fight, then a chance thought
makes all the old hopes flood back in again and, with them,
all the fear fueled by hope.

Yesterday my fellow patrolling officer was picked out by
a shell. It blew off his head. It could have been me.

But I have William for company, in his way. I feel his
presence with me here, cheering me on, bringing me luck.

Stay away as long as you can—

> *Your loving brother,*
> *Edward*

The letter felt oddly rhetorical to Thomas. The writing was neat, the paper unsmirched. Was it really so bad? Thomas forgot the fights he had known through his childhood with Edward, and felt sucked into the abysmal world of the trenches. He could sense the stinking mud which was so often described, the infernal soup of earth through which the soldiers waded, while he, Thomas, ate buttered muffins over a stoked fire at Eton.

Edward survived as the men in his company fell. Through the long nights, he often recalled the sunlit lawns of his Yorkshire childhood. For too long now, he had left behind all that comfort and delight—first for the chilly dormitories of boarding school, and now, barracked with his men in trenches, with the stink of gangrene rising amongst them. The natural flickers of fellow feeling, of seeing how the limbs of working men were as good as his own, had made him doubt his inheritance. He would go back to his home a changed man—a better man, he told himself.

But in 1917 he slipped into the infamous Flanders quagmire of Passchendaele. Running along slippery duckboards on a wet night, he was blown into a flooded dugout by a shell which shattered his right side.

At last a blighty, he thought, *I'll be home at Ashton for Christmas.* But he had not reckoned on his weakness, nor the depth of the mud, nor the distance to the duckboards. He hung on to a wooden rafter in the darkness and called for help, but the sky was loud with the clamor of shells. He tried to move forwards, but there was no firm ground beneath his feet. He thought of Bunyan's Christian, in his Slough of Despond, and prayed for help. But there was no true faith in his prayers, only panic. The mire was too thick to swim through. With his good arm he clung to the wooden beam, but the mud was heavy, pulling on his boots, drawing him down.

The sky was fitfully lit with the blazing flares of war. His shattered shoulder was throbbing with pain, and his too rapid breathing only sunk him further. The meteoric splendors of the battle sky echoed the involuntary flashes of light inside his own dimming mind.

Images flickered through him, of his pale-faced sister, of the yellow wallpaper in his room at Ashton, of bare white legs on the rugby pitch at Eton. The aroma of his mother's scent seeped through his breathing, and he felt the touch of her white embroidered handkerchief. He wished he had spent more time with women. If he could just keep afloat till dawn, somebody would surely find him and fish him out. Christmas at Ashton Park, breakfast with new-laid eggs and toast.

After an hour, as freezing weariness and pain loosened his grip, he slipped downwards to darkness. He tasted the mud for a moment, thick, suffocating, before it flooded his lungs and he drowned.

Nobody in his company knew where he was, but they were sure he had not deserted. He was missing, presumed dead. Too many had vanished into muddy oblivion, and would surface only later, as picked bones, when the summer skies dried up the unnatural quagmire.

Ashton Park now lacked a second body to bury at home, and Miriam's heart was broken. She clutched at consolations in the air around her, and began to speak to her dead sons through mediums.

My dear Thomas,

How close we are to the spirit world, if we only learn how to listen and open our eyes! Last evening, with the help of Mrs. Ostleton, I had a sighting of Edward. He was smiling. He looked as he did before going off to the war. He told us that William and he are together now, and happy, too. We need not despair. We are all together, now and forever. Take courage, dear Thomas. I will tell you all about the vision properly when I see you soon. We must help your poor father, and Claudia, through this terrible time.

Your loving mama

Thomas was at first shocked by his mother's retreat into the spirit world of her Anglo-Irish youth. But he, too, sometimes felt the presence of his brothers' spirits, in his head, and in the promptings of his conscience.

His mother was desperate not to let her beloved last son go to the front. But like all his friends, Thomas went to war as soon as he had completed his schooling.

"It is not a question of *choice*, Mama," he told her.

He found himself at Aldershot, where long lines of faceless barracks were interspersed with barren parade grounds. A monotonous landscape, manufactured and unreal. Thomas was drilled in the art of marching and the skills of open combat, which by all accounts were worthless on the front.

> My dear Claudia,
>   I think of you at Ashton, with all the convalescents. I can imagine how much you must cheer them up.
>   Strange to think that Edward trained here, at Aldershot. The barracks are worn and shabby—did he ever say which building he was in?
>   Memories are to be cherished. I think of William and Edward daily, and the thought of them bolsters me. Other times, I am still shaken by their loss.
>   Take care of Mama. I know how she will suffer if I go too, and so I will do all I can to return to you.
>
>   Your loving brother,
>   Thomas

Thomas was an eighteen-year-old marching on a parade ground when the Armistice was declared, releasing him back to civilian life. With a mixture of relief and regret, he left behind his dreary barracks and returned to the Ashtons' London home, Sussex Place, a wedding cake of a house in Regent's Park, all pillars and porticoes.

His father and mother were waiting for him there, to rejoice in their living son, who carried now the weight of his brothers' unused lives. Claudia joined them for a champagne toast in the drawing room, but privately felt that any celebration was inappropriate.

After two glasses, Miriam Ashton became lachrymose and reached out to her only son.

"You're lucky, Thomas," she said.

"I know that," replied Thomas, a little abashed.

"No, I mean something else, I believe you have *luck with you*—"

"Please don't say that," chipped in Robert, unusual though it was for him to contradict his wife.

"You can be sure that Thomas and I will take good care of ourselves for both of you," said Claudia, eager to pacify.

Miriam smiled and laughed, but Thomas was subtly shaken by his mother's longing for his good fortune—what if lightning struck, or he fell from a horse; how could he fulfill all the hopes she had for her remaining children?

It was not long afterwards that an epidemic of Spanish influenza swept haphazardly through Europe. At Ashton Park, the cook's daughter was the first to fall ill. Rachel Barry shivered and sweated, and her mother stayed with her through the night, giving her water, sponging her face and body. Rachel recovered, but the fever spread rapidly through the rows of recuperating soldiers in their hospital beds. Within days, three men and a young nurse had died.

Sixteen-year-old Claudia, helping with the nursing work, was taken ill on the third day of the outbreak. She lay in her old familiar bed, overlooking the broad sweep of parkland. Her head burned hot and she began to slip in and out of delirium, like the other victims.

Robert and Miriam Ashton were telephoned in Sussex Place. They caught the first train to York, and forbade Thomas from joining them. For two days they sat by Claudia's bedside in desperate agitation. They sponged her, they talked to her, they tried to rouse her. They walked up and down the room, and rocked in their chairs, and gripped at their own fretful fingers until they were sore. But they could not reach their daughter—her soul was drifting free. Sometimes, in her delirium, she seemed to be talking to her brothers, as if they were standing at the end of her bed.

Her decline was too swift. Miriam was watching her daughter's white face when she stopped breathing. Suddenly Claudia's eyes were empty and still. She had vanished into the light of the sky, and nothing could bring her back.

Miriam howled out loud, in animal sounds. Half-delirious with exhaustion, she held her daughter and breathed into her mouth, hoping for a shudder of life. But the girl was dead as stone.

Robert stumbled into the room, and found his wife holding their dead daughter in her arms. He held them both, and tears seeped down his face for Claudia, for Miriam, for all of them.

Thomas, waiting for news in London, was stunned by this capricious aftermath to the war. There was nothing to steady his heart but to walk, and he walked all day and late into the evening through the streets of London, through the darkening park, until exhaustion overcame him. Soon after dawn, he caught the first train to York, sleeping fitfully on the way. But when he arrived at Ashton Park, his mother sent him away, back down to the village, for fear that he, too, might get infected. It was another ten days before they would allow him to come into the house.

By then the epidemic had passed, but not before they had suffered five deaths at Ashton Park. The house hospital was wound up and rooms which had been stripped for wards were left empty and forlorn, still smelling of disinfectant.

There seemed to be an excess of iron buckets lying around the house.

Thomas felt he had been cut off at the roots. In the months that followed, he grew oddly estranged from himself. A profound detachment separated him from hope, and his heart was numbed, leaving him distanced from the quick of his feelings.

As soon as he could, he escaped from the silent dining room of his grieving parents, first to Oxford, later into the Foreign Office. He wondered if perhaps his marriage, too, hadn't been an escape from that time of loss. He felt a familiar twinge of regret that he had too readily yoked Elizabeth to his burden of sadness.

Certainly, Ashton Park had receded from his life after his

siblings' deaths. For some years he had avoided his childhood home. But now, two decades later, it was both strange
and rewarding to find the house filled with voices once more,
with children running around the place. They felt right here,
Thomas reassured himself, despite the sorry cause of their
arrival.

12

———•———

A NNA'S FAVORITE TIME at Ashton was after supper. Most of their day was regimented, with lessons and chapel services and meals in the dining room. But there was always that empty time before the bell for bed, when they could race around the house—when friendships were formed and new games devised, and unexpected things happened.

Anna loved to roam the dark corridors and unused rooms scattered about the house. There was a luggage room upstairs, stacked with musty cases and old paraphernalia of tennis rackets and cricket bats: she made a den there, behind an open trunk. But once she showed it to Beth Rothery, other children used it as their hiding place too, and the place lost its mystery.

Some evenings she would run down to the parlor by the kitchens, where there was an old stand-up piano. Her mother had taught her to play "Danny Boy": it was the only piece she knew, but she could play it with two hands, like a proper pianist. Still, she liked it best when there was a mob of children there, strumming chopsticks and pinging the piano strings, everyone singing and dancing about.

Over time, their games turned to dares, led by Billy Carter, who climbed out of his dormitory window onto the stone ledge beyond and crawled his way round to the girls' dormitory. But they dared him to go back to bed along the corridor, where Miss Harrison caught him, and made him stand against the wall for two hours.

Another time, Anna pulled a short straw: her dare was to

knock on a teacher's bedroom door during the night, then run away.

"Mr. Stewart! Mr. Stewart!" suggested Katy Todd, enjoying somebody else's risk.

"His room is too far," argued Beth.

"Miss Harrison, to see if she wears a wig—"

"Miss Weir, I'll only do Miss Weir's room," said Anna, already scared by what she had to do, but glad at least when they agreed with her choice: she hoped that kind, unhurried Miss Weir would not get too angry.

The girls in her dormitory stayed awake until Miss Harrison had finished patrolling their floor. Then Anna crept out of bed and onto the long red runner carpet which snaked down the corridor, and round to Miss Weir's room.

She glanced back. Katy Todd was peering after her, checking she was doing her dare properly.

She edged round the corner. There was a night-light at one end of the landing, for the younger children's dormitory. Softly, slowly, she stepped towards Miss Weir's closed door. Her breathing was rapid, her eyes alert. She raised her hand—and knocked, as quietly as she could.

Then turned and ran. But slipped and stumbled for a moment. Panicking, she picked herself up and raced for the corridor corner.

She heard the door behind her open, heard a voice.

"Hello?"

She glanced round, saw Miss Weir standing at her door in her nightdress, looking after her. Just for a moment their eyes locked, before Anna turned round the corner, raced back to her dormitory and dived under the covers.

"Did you do it?" whispered the others.

"Yes. But she saw me."

"Is she coming?"

"I don't know—"

Anna's heart was still racing, and she thought Miss Weir would appear at any moment to haul her out of bed. But the minutes passed and nothing happened. Anna's breathing calmed; the others fell asleep.

But Anna kept replaying that puzzled look on Miss Weir's pale, lamp-lit face as she ran away from her. She felt troubled, somehow, as she slipped away into sleep.

The next day, she tried to avoid Miss Weir, hoping that she had not recognized her in the dim light of the corridor. But after assembly she met her in the Marble Hall.

"Anna . . ."

She shuffled over awkwardly, crabwise, unable to meet her teacher's face.

"Is everything all right, Anna?"

"Yes, miss."

"But last night you knocked—"

"I'm sorry, miss, I shouldn't have bothered you."

"I'm not chiding you, Anna. Is anything wrong?"

"Nothing, miss."

"Why did you knock then?"

Anna looked up anxiously, then blurted it out.

"It was only a dare—"

"I see." Miss Weir tilted her head.

"I didn't really *want* to do it."

A look came over Miss Weir's face: Anna did not know whether it was cross or curious.

"When are we going home?" she asked with orphan eyes, then felt immediately guilty about playing for pity. But Miss Weir's face softened at once.

"We don't know that yet, I'm afraid."

Anna dipped her head, looking crestfallen, but worried she might laugh.

"I hope it won't be too long before you go home," said Miss Weir gently.

"Yes, miss," said Anna, fighting back a smirk, trying to look solemn.

"Do knock on my door if you ever need help, but stay to talk next time."

"Yes, miss."

"Off you go then . . ."

Round the corner, back in her classroom, the other girls gathered round her.

"What did she say?" they asked. Beaming, but still shaking in relief, Anna told them how she had pretended to be homesick and got away with it—not a punishment, not even a rebuke, nothing. She basked in her completed dare, knowing she had won some glory with the others.

But as the day went on, she found herself feeling a touch uncomfortable—guilty that she had played a homesick child, and made fun of Miss Weir's kindness. She felt shabby.

Never again, Anna decided. In future, she wouldn't cheat on anyone.

That morning, as Ruth Weir spoke to Anna in the hall, Elizabeth Ashton noticed the teacher and child talking together.

Something about the pair of them struck Elizabeth, with a pang. By the time she had checked the new rotas in the staff room, she realized that her pang had been a moment's jealousy. It was their casual complicity which had pricked her.

This whole school enterprise had been her initiative, and she, surely, should be the one who could connect with these evacuees. But she had seen that young teacher's natural bond with the children, and she knew that ease eluded her.

She decided to walk to the village to pick up the new batch of ration books, hoping the excursion would steady her. She walked fast down the drive, stepping carefully over the cattle grids as she tried to unpick her thoughts.

Thomas was always busy teaching now, and enjoying it: she could see that in his eyes. He had so swiftly adapted to their new life. But she, meanwhile, had delegated all the pastoral duties, leaving herself only administrative tasks. She could feel her own confidence slipping.

No matter how many customs and rituals there were in the new school, she found herself unable to settle into any routine. She felt perpetually restless, without a rhythm in her life. Every Sunday, as Thomas prepared for the week ahead, a particular dejection would seep through her—a woe, a panic about the days to come—what should she do with the hours?

She was smoking too much. In the evenings, she would draw too swiftly on each cigarette, as if racing to light up the next one—with another drink to accompany the rasp of tobacco. While Thomas read, tactfully ignoring her disquiet.

Reaching the village post office, she admitted to herself that, as ever, what she needed, what she wanted, was her own child. She had hoped that all the many children at Ashton might cure that longing, but they had not, or not yet.

Returning to the house, she walked back by the park lake and watched the slow sway of weeds under the water's surface. Beyond, the rose garden was barren and empty, showing only the bare cropped heads of rosebushes past their season.

Without sunshine the gardens sometimes looked too bleak, she thought, but the weather never seemed to deter the evacuees. When the break bell rang, she watched a band of children run outside and circle the fountain. They often ran around the fountain, she noticed. They always wanted to dip their hands in the water.

Sometimes she wanted to reach out and touch one of them, as if that might ease her aching heart.

"What did you do this morning?" Thomas asked her at lunch.

"I went for a walk in the park, and it was looking lovely," she replied, knowing he liked appreciative remarks. But she did not mention the children.

Afterwards, as he went off to a lesson, she sat at her desk, answering letters and checking bills. *Is this it,* she wondered suddenly, *or is this just an interim stage, a preparation for something else to happen?*

Ten years with Thomas, and she no longer knew what she felt about him or their life together.

It was in the summer of 1927 that she had first been introduced to Thomas, at a London cocktail party.

"I don't believe we've met," he said to her with a courteous smile, as their stout hostess brought them together.

"No, I don't believe we have," she replied politely. But she already knew who he was. They had both attended the same parties that season, where she had regularly watched him weaving from group to group—always, it seemed, unattached. Smiling, but giving nothing of himself away.

Elizabeth had first become aware of Thomas across a crowded room. So compelling was his presence that even as he stood with his back to the party, admiring a Venetian painting with a friend, he drew people's glances. Elizabeth maneuvered her way round one side of the silk-walled room, curious to glimpse his face. He laughed for a moment, jutting his head back, and for the first time she saw a flash of him. *So that is Thomas Ashton,* she thought. *He looks like God's Englishman.* She was at once afraid of him—but also wanted to meet him.

She watched him make his way round the room. He was arrestingly attractive, with a wide, spontaneous smile which could instantly dispel any unease. She noted his steady blue eyes framed by dark brows, and his soft, thick hair swept back from his forehead in a dashing curve. And yet he did not seem to be vain: he appeared naturally modest, and quite oblivious to his own physical grace.

Elizabeth was twenty-one then, tall and slender, with a dark-eyed quickness and auburn hair which fell in waves to her shoulders. She had been feeling unsettled and fragile that summer. Three years before, she had arrived in London to "come out" as a debutante, attending all the dances of the season, with rows of eligible men always in attendance. Most of the young men were aspirant guards officers, and she often found it tricky to think of something—anything—to talk to them about. There was an unwritten rule that girls should be both pretty and chatty: hostesses were quick to abandon those girls who could not make conversation.

Her own "coming out" dance was held in her aunt's Eaton Terrace house, with the ample drawing room cleared for a ballroom and festooned with carnations and roses. But there was no particular guards officer or banker or lawyer who touched her heart. She danced with many men—tall, thin, stocky, American, clever, dull, rich. The season ended, and an autumn of foxhunting began. She drifted through London parties for the next two years, and worked intermittently at a charitable school in Chelsea, to stave off the ennui of her search for a husband.

"Are you being too particular?" her mother had asked her. The smart parties had rolled on, with the same plates of salmon mousse and tongue, and the same gilded chairs arranged around the dance floors for the debutantes' chaperones. But the older women who watched the dances could see that not every girl would be lucky in the musical chairs for a husband. They knew by now that there were four million too many women in the wake of the Great War, that four million young women up and down the country were fated to find themselves romantically thwarted. Mrs. Fairfax feared for her own daughter, though she was confident that Elizabeth was beautiful and accomplished.

"But she is *choosy*," she would say to her husband, a decorated soldier who was privately relieved to defer the wedding
bills. It was as if nothing could ever quite match the Platonic
pictures fixed in Elizabeth's mind, where the palette was always
brighter, the light sharper, the shapes fuller. She had arrived
in London so brimful of inarticulate longing, of ambition, of
spirit. But without a university education, what could she do
but wait to marry, she wondered.

She began to grow jaded, cynical and bored. She toyed with
the idea of opening a hat shop. She dreamt of voyaging to Africa. She tried hatching plans to do something, anything, with
her life.

But her sightings of Thomas Ashton fired her with a new
hope. Before she realized it, he had become her challenge. He
was a bright young diplomat on leave from the Berlin embassy
for the month of June, and she went to as many parties as she
could in the hope of meeting him.

Soon she found herself thinking of Thomas all the time. At
first it was perhaps a question of vanity: Thomas was the most
handsome, the most romantic, the most desirable man she saw
at any party, and a stubborn part of her would not consider anyone else. But a humility born of desire soon followed, because
he showed absolutely no interest in her. Every time they met
fleetingly, both of them would appear pleasantly surprised to
see each other again. But while her surprise was assumed, his
was genuine.

By now, she was entirely smitten. She saw his intelligence,
his kindness, his courtesy, but also his unusual detachment,
which hinted at private melancholy. There was something taut
and recessed about him, and she knew that when he did love, it
would be something special.

At any gathering, she was more at ease if she saw him first
from afar, for then she could compose herself. Surprise meetings were an agony because, unprepared, she shook in his

presence. She had to wind herself up to be vital, or witty and interesting. She tried, subtly, to engage his eyes. His level blue gaze fell on her, and she trembled, but could see that he felt ... nothing. There was just his smile, and polite conversation.

The season ran on—parties, dinners, cocktails. She acquired a taste for wine and went dancing at the Embassy Club with other young men, but they were coarse and dull-spirited beside Thomas. Worse, he returned to Berlin, and Elizabeth knew it would be months before she would see him again. Perhaps he had found love in Germany. She ached over his absence, but this only heightened her desire.

She sought time alone to think of Thomas. She would break away from friends and walk to the window to close her eyes and see his face. Once, she found herself stopping dead on the staircase at home, leaning against the wall and catching her breath at the thought of him. Sometimes her sense of him was so powerful that she cried out his name.

She saw herself touching his hand. She ached to reach out her fingertips to his face, and look into his eyes. She craved the darkness of her room at night, when she could luxuriate in conjuring up his image. If she screwed her eyes close enough, she sometimes fancied she grasped, for a blinding moment, some elusive sense of the intimacy she wished for—but then the moment would be gone.

She wrote *Thomas* on bits of paper. She wrote letters which she never sent. She sought scraps of information about him, just to hear his name spoken. Coming from a Yorkshire family, she knew a certain amount about the Ashtons—their house, their hunting, the deaths of his brothers in the war and his sister in the influenza epidemic. She remembered meeting Claudia Ashton as a child, and the news of her unexpected death had made a deep impression on her, but now that she loved Thomas, the Ashton family griefs swept right through her with a new force. She found herself crying over deaths which had happened a decade before. Thomas was now a figure of great and noble pathos to her.

Soon, she guessed, he would return from Berlin, and she might at least fathom if there was a woman there who held his heart. Meanwhile it was so hard to contain herself. She desperately craved intimacy with this man, and yet he appeared so entirely oblivious to her.

When Thomas did visit London in the summer of 1928, he might never have noticed Elizabeth had it not been for his Foreign Office friend Clifford Norton. Bookish, reticent and slightly austere, Norton generally avoided parties, but happened to see Thomas at an art gallery reception to which his wife Peter had dragged him. The pair of diplomats huddled together in one corner, catching up on office news, while Norton's wife strode around the paintings. Elizabeth was also there, and she saw the two men alone together. Boldly, she walked over to greet Thomas—just for a moment.

Their conversation was cursory, yet Norton divined her interest in Thomas. Through subsequent years, she gathered that Norton never much liked her, such was his habitual protectiveness about his friend. But nevertheless, when Thomas was hurriedly seeking a last-minute partner for a concert, Norton remembered Elizabeth and suggested her.

Two days later, she was sitting beside Thomas at the Wigmore Hall. Four sleek string players bowed and arranged themselves on the small stage, until their leader nodded and Debussy's plaintive string quartet flowed between them.

It was familiar chamber music of pleasurable melancholy, yet rarely had Thomas found himself so moved; he wondered whether his mysterious elation wasn't somehow aroused by Elizabeth at his side. He turned to her occasionally, and she returned his glance. Her face was rapt, or so it seemed to him; it moved him not only to hear the music, but also to feel the presence of this intense young woman beside him.

He could not know that she was shaking at his own presence, that her heart was brimming with the bittersweet joy of a long-nurtured infatuation. Whenever he turned his eyes to her, she felt her heart swooping with hope. *This is the man I love,* the music told her, her quaking body told her. She tried to steady the trembling of her hands.

From the corner of his eye Thomas could glimpse her long neck, the distinct rise of her breasts, her elegant ankles. He observed the way her fine fingers seemed almost to quiver at the music. *My mother would appreciate this girl,* he thought—then realized that he, too, appreciated her. He was touched by her feminine grace, faint fragrance, and by the lovely responsiveness of her face. He felt proud to be escorting her. More, he felt suddenly at home, as if he were understood and known. Extraordinary, he thought, considering they had barely met properly before.

When they talked in the interval, her conversation resonated with him. Perhaps because she spoke with such tact of his dead sister, Claudia, breaking through his usual reserve and allowing them to converse frankly together. He did not guess that Elizabeth had already dreamt her way into his life, that every gesture, every word she uttered was freighted with all those days and nights of private longing. For Thomas, it simply felt as if they had known each other for a long time.

A curiously intense encounter, and oddly tender, he thought, as they listened to the gentle lament of Ravel's string quartet in the second half of the concert.

Later, when he saw her home, Elizabeth ran straight up to her room and closed the door, caught between elation and fear. She knew she wouldn't be able to let this love go now, because at last she had some hope. She would have to see it through, and suffer for it, if need be.

All that had been eleven years ago. Now, walking through Ashton's corridors, Elizabeth felt almost protective about her younger self—and the way she had followed her feelings so unconditionally, never stopping to consider where they might lead her.

She paused for a moment in the stone hall, caught by its coppery light. The late afternoon sun was shafting through the hall windows, and she found herself looking upwards, trying to recall the first time she had gazed up into that azure dome as a young woman—with all the excitement and trepidation of her first visit to Ashton. Arriving in her own car, she had driven cautiously up the long white drive, but when the house finally reared up before her, she faltered. Even then, she had wondered if this vast house could ever be her home.

On that first trip, she had arrived in time for a rather confused tea, with many houseguests she did not know, and a brief meeting with Thomas's father, who looked at her with disconcerting directness, while his mother was vague and distracted.

A maid laid out her clothes while she took a bath—that was something new to her. She could remember noticing how the old-fashioned tub was stained with brown streaks from the peaty water. Alone in her room, she dressed with care: she wanted to be elegant but demure. When she pinned up her hair, her hands were clumsy with nerves, and she could not even bear to appraise her own appearance in the mirror. So she just drew her breath and walked carefully down the great mahogany staircase for drinks.

Through the drawing-room doorway, she could just see Thomas beyond, groomed to chilly perfection in his dinner jacket. She felt herself hesitating, but was relieved when he watched her entrance into the room with obvious pleasure; suddenly, she felt more at ease in her long close dress.

But dinner was more of a trial.

"Whitby was founded by the *Benedictines*," Thomas's father told her emphatically over pheasant, "but all the other large abbeys round here—Rievaulx, Jervaulx, Byland, Fountains—were all Cistercian, of course."

Of course. She knew nothing about Yorkshire monasteries, and soon ached from smiling and nodding at her host, yet still could not spark a single opinion. Perhaps as a consequence of her inadequacy at dinner she barely slept that night. Burying her head in a musty pillow, she wished she could go home.

The next day was even more testing, when Thomas walked her round the house and gardens. She was alone with the man she loved, yet she could hardly muster a thought, a view, a word to say.

"The weather this summer has been so disappointing. Too much rain."

"In Berlin we have been luckier."

"I should like to see Berlin."

"It's not a beautiful city, but it's invigorating—they have some inventive new architects working there."

No invitation to visit him at his embassy. Perhaps he had changed his mind, now he knew that she had nothing to say.

The corridors were long, and rang with the sound of their heels. The Marble Hall echoed with the closing and opening of doors. The paintings looked down at her, and through her, she feared. Thomas, all the while, was charming and considerate, strolling beside her yet holding himself just far enough apart not to graze hands. She enjoyed the easy grace of his walk.

But at lunch, his parents were still remote.

"Cumberland sauce is so refreshing with lamb, don't you think?" observed Miriam Ashton. "Do you admire Ramsay MacDonald? We are rather fond of him at Ashton, because we feel he understands the *land*," she went on, talking past Elizabeth's shoulder, without apparently expecting a reply.

Afterwards, a drizzle kept Thomas and Elizabeth indoors. They toyed with a jigsaw of a Turner painting in the drawing room until, at last, a wash of pale sunlight spilled through the somber sky and eased away the rain. Thomas suggested a walk, and led her out along the grass terraces, where the gentle breathing of the trees filled the uneasy gaps in their conversation.

At last Elizabeth began to feel a little closer to her very formal host. By the gracious Ionic temple, with the river cascading below, she felt Thomas edging towards her.

"What a wonderful view," she said with plausible conviction, sensing a sudden increase in intensity from Thomas. Short, stiff banalities were all she could offer. Thomas stood very still, and gazed down at the river below.

"It's my favorite view," he said with grave passion.

In sudden panic, Elizabeth looked down at the land spread out before them. She understood that he wanted to see if she could love this place too—if it could move her as it did him. The scene meant little to her: it was a blankly beautiful landscape which she could barely register. But as she held her gaze on the view, she sensed Thomas turn his face towards her. She could hear her own heartbeat as she waited, feeling his eyes upon her. Until she turned to look at him.

What she saw made her heart turn over. His eyes were ablaze with anxious hope in the most loving face she had ever seen. He leant forwards, fingers stretching out to hold her shoulders. His taut face came towards her, his eyes piercing her, his mouth opening her lips. They kissed, bodies pressed together. She rested her head against his shoulder and felt herself flow into his embrace. Inside, she was surging like a rip current, a delicious expectation of love flooding through her.

When she dared to meet his eyes once more, he touched her chin with one hand and they held each other's gaze: they had found each other.

They walked and walked, laughing, kissing, embracing, past the tennis court and the palm court pavilion, past the lake, the sunshine penetrating the gloomy sky in great shafts of gold.

When they returned to the house for tea, a glow of sheer joy glanced off their faces. They tingled with mutual happiness. All those in the drawing room could observe it—Thomas's father was quietly approving.

Sunday was unhurried. After a service in the chapel, Thomas rowed Elizabeth on the lake. Their fingertips grazed against each other, and they kissed many times. Elizabeth followed Thomas's distinctly decorous overtures; although she longed to touch him further, she held back.

At last, Thomas invited her to visit him in Berlin. With the promise of a future meeting secured, Elizabeth felt ready to depart. After tea, as she set off on the long drive south, she was relieved to feel all her tension seeping away. There had been enough love for one weekend. She did not want to lose him with too much too soon.

She took with her the memory of Thomas standing on the steps of Ashton Park, his arms raised in a gesture of farewell. He stood there with his shoulders thrown back in an attitude of effortless self-possession. *This is my home and hope,* his body seemed to say as he waved her off.

Even then, in the moment of her greatest euphoria, Elizabeth had felt a little uneasy. Because she knew that she had reached Thomas by stealth. Without his realizing it, she had orchestrated his emotions. He thought he had wooed her, but she knew better: that she had tricked him into love.

But now, all these years later, she felt a different guilt: that she had pursued Thomas so cannily only to let her love for him leak away.

Sometimes, across the dining room, she would suddenly glimpse Thomas talking to someone, and her heart would turn over at the sight of his smile. And a memory would come back to her of the longing she had known for him before their marriage. But she knew that now it was only a memory of a feeling, not the feeling itself.

13

⸻

A NNA WAS FINISHING her weekly letter home as fast as she could, because she wanted to get to the swing. There was only one swing in the gardens, hanging from a knotty tree by the main lawn. The children were always queuing up for turns, but Anna could see through the library window that it was free right now.

She raced outside and clambered onto the swing seat. There were only ten more minutes before afternoon lessons, so she swung her legs as hard as she could, to get into a rhythm. Higher and higher she went, pushing herself through the sky until she was really soaring.

Speed bonny boat like a bird on the wing . . .

She liked to sing her own private songs on the swing, songs her mother could play on the piano at home. But after a while, she just let the swing's momentum take her—watching the sky race towards her until she was dizzy, then leaning back to feel the breeze rushing through her hair.

It was only as she slowed down that she noticed an unexpected sound. A subtle shaking, a rustling whisper, but musical too, like wind chimes. She jumped off the swing and followed the sound, skirting the woods to the grass terrace beyond—until she arrived at the source of the rustling. A cluster of slender trees with light bark. And small tremulous leaves—some still silvery-green, others turning autumn-yellow.

They must be the aspen trees, thought Anna. Quivering trees

94

which could play their own music. She tucked a few aspen leaves into her tunic pocket and ran back to her lessons.

Only yesterday, Miss Weir had taken them outside to collect autumn leaves for their nature diaries. Oaks, elms, sycamores, silver birches. Mr. Ashton had greeted them in the Marble Hall as they returned to their classroom.

"Did you find anything interesting?"

Anna paused to show him her pressed leaves.

"Ah, but have you found the aspens yet?" he asked her lightly.

"No, sir, what are they?"

"The most unusual trees in the park, slender and silver-green. When the wind blows through their leaves, they make their own special music. They sing."

"Where can I find them?"

"Listen for them. Wait for a windy day, and you'll hear them."

"Come along, Anna . . . ," Miss Weir called after her, and Anna joined her class, wondering if he was making it up.

But now she had the leaves to show him. She waited until the end of her Latin lesson, a quiet moment when everyone was scattering for tea.

"Here they are, sir. Aspen leaves."

He was delighted with her find; she could see that, so she gave him some leaves.

"How did you find them so quickly, Anna?"

"I listened, just like you said."

"That aspen grove was a favorite place of mine, when I was your age. But not many people ever notice it, so you should keep it to yourself," he said with a smile, wheeling himself off.

Anna went back to her desk, and proudly stowed away the one leaf she had kept. If she ever wanted to get away from the other children, she had her own place to go now.

14

THAT EVENING, SITTING with Elizabeth in the drawing room, Thomas felt something in his pocket. The aspen leaves; he put them on a side table.

"Collecting leaves?" asked his wife.

"Just a gift from one of the children."

"You are popular these days," came Elizabeth's tart reply, as she rose to fetch an ashtray. Instantly, she regretted her tone; sometimes, she disliked her husband just for the acid he drew from her.

Thomas let the barb pass, and returned his eyes to his book, a Henry James novel. But it required concentration, and Thomas's mind was wandering, following his wife as she walked about the room.

The ongoing erosion of their marriage was subtly cumulative, he felt, but turned on a series of failed moments which might perhaps have been different. For which he was to blame as much as her. There had been so many times when he might have reached out to Elizabeth and stroked her cheek, or caught her eye and touched her heart. But too often he would neither look at her, nor hear her silent calls; instead, he resisted her romantic gestures because he felt too foolish, in his condition, to be a lover.

Thomas knew that he had too often shut his own door on her.

Just as he was doing now, sitting in the drawing room while Elizabeth talked to her mother on the telephone. He watched her and saw that she was lovely. His wife. She put down the telephone.

"Elizabeth?"

She looked over to him, open for a moment. Too long he paused.

"Is your mother well?"

"Yes, quite well."

"I'm glad."

He hesitated. She waited for more words, but none came. He wheeled himself away to the bookcase, feigning interest in a set of French classics.

Why could he not tell her she was beautiful? Had his disability crippled his tongue too?

He leafed through a book which meant nothing to him. She walked past him, and out of the room. Ashton was a house where you could avoid each other's silences by simply going to another room, another floor.

She went to sit on her own in their bedroom, with a drink.

Thomas picked up his novel again. Most of the time now, he had his own strategies for contentment: music, reading, listening to the wireless. But sometimes he allowed himself to recognize the acute compromises of his marriage. Two damaged people together, barely speaking.

He had hoped that this school initiative might rekindle their warmth, but perhaps it was just another false dawn. Any spontaneous intimacy seemed to elude them both at the moment. There was always that distance in her eyes. In his eyes, too.

He knew his disability had shortchanged her, but he sensed other patterns at play too. As long as he could remember, he had always been straining to know how to love. He couldn't say whether it was his stiff upbringing or his siblings' deaths which had cauterized his feelings, but he knew there remained something remote about his heart.

He could recall Norton reassuring him that he was a natural diplomat when he first joined the Foreign Office, "because you can see all sides, while taking none," he had said, as if fence-sitting was a virtue. Yet Thomas was wary of his own detachment.

He thought back to his younger self, arriving at Oxford and meeting girls for the first time. He could remember music drifting through the college quads on Saturday nights, and summer parties in damp sunlit gardens. He had worn the new clothes, baggy trousers, patterned jerseys. Modern girls had arrived, smoking cigarettes and asking to dance. But his heart had remained untouched by anyone at that time: all the girls had seemed like strangers to him.

He had avoided intimacy, retreating instead into the excusable solitude of the Bodleian Library, and seeking out neglected books from the stacks. In his days as a classics student, the ancient poets had offered him unexpected consolations; their stoic forbearance eased something in him, as if all his recent family losses were but a passing shadow beside their epic grief.

Iam seges est ubi Troia fuit.

Now there are fields of corn where Troy once stood. Ovid could conjure the vanished traces of a human glory greater than anything the present could show. As he edged towards a line's meaning, he had often felt himself almost touching the allusive grace of lost times.

By now, Thomas had abandoned his evening's reading, and poured himself a whisky instead. Rapidly, the drink relaxed him. Reminding him that he hadn't always just been solitary and bookish, that there were other versions of his past too. He thought back to his years as a junior diplomat in Weimar Berlin, where the embassy had been so formal and yet the city so free. Where he had seen all his polite assumptions so swiftly dismantled.

It had been a lucky posting for him. Inside the goldfish bowls of Oxford and London, he had always been so guarded—

but amongst foreigners, in the overcranked atmosphere of the Weimar Republic, he had at last felt liberated to experiment.

He had visited every kind of theater. At the Wintergarten and the Metropol he watched extravagant displays of bare-legged dancing girls—but then a raffish young German diplomat, Max, took him downtown to the bawdier cabaret clubs, the Weisse Maus and its rival, the Schwarzer Kater.

Tentatively, Thomas allowed his eyes to meet the predatory glances of women in unsuitable bars, and began to find himself stirred by meetings with strangers. He even took Max's lead and followed a prostitute with a swaying walk into a tenement block. Away from the mysterious shadows of the streetlamps she looked suddenly old, and the skin about her neck was loose. But Thomas's gallantry would not let him back away from the poor woman's unwilling pretense that she had any allure at all. So he had his first sexual encounter on an aging woman's narrow bed in a room which smelt of cabbage and herring. They did not kiss, nor even look at each other, and it was all a mistake, an act of strange repulsion. Nevertheless, the startling intimacy of seeing a woman's unguarded nakedness did awaken something in Thomas.

Half-repelled, half-seduced by new sensations, he began to savor the cabaret scene. The women he met in bars reeked of cigarettes, and their clothes looked faintly soiled, yet he was oddly aroused by their smudged makeup and frank eroticism.

But he still kept his distance from these women. Until one evening he found himself seated beside the fifty-year-old wife of the Austrian ambassador at dinner, after a Beethoven concert. Their first conversation was deceptively stiff, banal even.

"My name is Margarete," she told him with a tilt of her face—an engaging, intelligent face, he noticed.

"Do you follow music?" he asked politely.

"But of course. I grew up in Salzburg, beside Mozart's house."

"I'm afraid we lack your great composers."

"Ah, but London has many other things to offer. You must miss it?"

"I am too busy exploring Berlin now—"

"No doubt there are a few sad hearts in London missing an attractive young man like you."

Margarete spoke with such rueful warmth that Thomas felt suddenly self-conscious, and attended to the guest on his other side. But within minutes he turned to her once again, wanting to talk further.

Margarete was confident and worldly, with an erect carriage and a sensuous grace. In accented English she asked Thomas about his life in London, and was bemused by his formal prattle. She flattered him with her expansive appreciation of men. He resisted the eye contact with which she wooed him until the final course, but by that time he was enfolded by her warmth, and the glint of desire in her eye.

He began relaxing into the realization that she had set her mind on seducing him. She had shown him in her eyes that a connection was possible, and for the first time in his life he began to think about holding a woman. He wanted to see her again. He wanted to touch her—her fullness, her overripeness.

They met intermittently, at cocktails in the Adlon, at embassy receptions. The Austrian ambassador thought the polite young Englishman was a splendid fellow. On every occasion Margarete found a way to take the flirtation forwards—with her eyes, with a little pressure from her many-ringed hand, or the sway of her walk as she came towards him or moved away.

One evening, in the gardens of the Belgian embassy, they spoke alone for the first time.

"I have been thinking about you, Thomas," she said. Her face was relaxed, amused.

"I think about you all the time," he told her, his eyes agonized with longing. She looked at him fondly and told him where to come and when.

He arrived with a bunch of flowers at the given address. A sullen landlady showed him up to a room with a grand piano, where Margarete was waiting for him. She gave him champagne and led him to the adjoining bedroom. The heavy curtains were drawn, although it was early in the afternoon. The light was dun, with a streak of sunshine where the curtains left a gap.

She looked into his face and took him in her arms. They parted from their embrace only to kiss, and then Thomas felt her desire in the slippery urgency of her tongue. He undid her dress, then her corset, and watched her full body tumble forth. She bore all the marks of middle age—heavy breasts, stretch marks—but every imperfection only inflamed him further. She drew him to the bed and enfolded him with caressing arms. He saw the look of tenderness in her face, and heard her low, consoling voice. Years of boarding school absences from his mother vanished as he slipped into her. When the time came, her cry of release was the most intimate sound he had ever known.

Afterwards he buried his face on her breast. She stroked him and muttered tender words in German. He enjoyed her gentle hands, but even as they lay together, a part of him remained still detached: this was not love, he knew, this was a release of transgressive passion.

Nevertheless, he did feel tenderness for Margarete—a new feeling, which he cherished.

Their affair continued for six months. He loved to see her perfectly composed face at parties, so elegantly made up above the strictly corseted attire, when he knew her stripped bare, with legs apart and breasts tumbling. It was an eroticism which he worried might be unhealthy—a peculiar yearning for coarseness in women.

But his anxieties were summarily cut short when her husband was posted to Rome. There were mixed feelings in their parting, because their first lust was almost satiated, and unstated reservations were creeping in on both sides. But she insisted on an extravagantly loving final evening together, which eased them both.

Thomas tried to picture Margarete once more, and their intimate afternoons together. Her unstinting delight in his young body made him shiver a little, as he realized how sad she would be to see him now, so emasculated in his chair. He hoped she had never heard what had befallen him, wanting somebody, somewhere, to retain a clear memory of him as he had been. He was grateful now for the thought of her uncritical love.

She had sent him a telegram of congratulation on his engagement, he recalled. He had wondered whether to invite her to his wedding, but decided not to, for Elizabeth's sake; he did not want to be distracted.

A sudden image came back to him from his wedding day, of Elizabeth in her ivory silk dress walking down the aisle, her face lit up. He remembered how his eyes had welled as he watched her coming towards him; she looked so happy. After all his years of emotional distance, he had felt an unfamiliar surge inside as he made his vows. *So this is love,* he had thought. *At last.*

And yet their wedding had been followed by a spell of ill fortune. A few weeks later, as they drove around the Italian lakes on their honeymoon, a telegram reached them with news of his father's fatal heart attack.

Thomas had barely buried his father and returned to Berlin with his bride when the republic's most brilliant statesman, Gustav Stresemann, collapsed with a stroke, dying soon after.

"Germany has lost the one leader who was holding the country back from its own precipice," the ambassador announced to his staff gloomily. Three weeks later came the Wall Street crash, plunging the world into depression.

The auspices for their marriage had never been favorable, Thomas reflected. But as he turned out the lights and wheeled himself to their bedroom, he refused to lose hope, and accept that they had lost each other for good. Perhaps, with their work here together now, they might find each other again—over time.

Reaching their bedroom, he was relieved to find Elizabeth already asleep. He would try to reach out to her again in the morning.

15

⸻

IN NOVEMBER THERE was a proper freeze at Ashton, and before any of the staff could forbid it, the more fearless children slid across the lake's thick ice on wicker chairs. They had one day's grace before the frozen lake was declared out of bounds.

Outside lessons, the evacuees spent hours wandering through the park, getting their shoes muddy. Anna enjoyed kicking through the leaves, but she did wonder how much longer she would be stranded in this place.

At one end of the games field stood a somber oak tree struck by lightning, whose charred branches reached out towards the sky as if in prayer. The children often played tag there, but something about the tree's stark shape always tugged at Anna, and made her quiet—until she could feel a pulse of homesickness inside.

Her next letter home was more subdued than usual.

When she read it, Roberta wondered whether she shouldn't bring her daughter back home after all, while London was still safe. Every night she scanned the sky for bombers, and waited for apocalyptic air raids, but none came. The milk arrived, she went off to work, the BBC played music, and yet—London was a city on guard.

"The bombs *will* come," warned the papers. Roberta reminded herself that her daughter's letters were not actually *unhappy;* better perhaps to leave her where she was, she decided, as she ironed her blouse for the morning.

She missed her daughter every day. But she was, too, just beginning to enjoy the surprise taste of a different life. All of them were standing at their own crossroads now, and she felt the possible arrival of something new every time she walked down the street. Roberta was Galway-Irish by birth, and sometimes wondered if those shifting west-coast skies hadn't given her a clairvoyant streak, for she could sense things—pick up other people's minds and moods. She could make rapid connections with strangers, just by divining what they were thinking, what they were feeling. She could persuade her friends to dance down the street, so vivid was she, so vital.

She had first arrived in Fulham as a child, after her widowed mother Iris found work nearby as a maid in a large Chelsea house. Iris took care to teach her daughter poise and cheerfulness, and Roberta would sometimes join her to polish the parquet floors of the Wyndham family house in the Boltons.

She loved going there. The large sash windows opened onto half an acre of lawns and roses, and the airy reception rooms had the varnished glow of old paintings and antique furniture. A taste for fine things filtered through to Roberta. She always kept her fingernails clean, and her hair neat, and her shoes polished. If she ever met guests, they looked at her in approval, she noticed. Because she had natural manners.

At twenty-two, she found work with a small family-run firm of furniture restorers in Fulham Broadway. She was good with her hands, and her experience at her mother's side in the Boltons had given her a sure appreciation of antiques. The owner soon recognized her special social skills, and Roberta was quickly groomed to deal with customers. She would go to large houses and assess the job. Where work could be done on-site, she would be dispatched to replace pieces of veneer or leather on old desks and tables, working alone in high-ceilinged rooms with fragile, priceless antiques.

From her first week at work, Roberta caught the eye of her boss's son, Lewis. He was attracted by the way she believed in her own life; she had style and zest, and a passion for dancing. He took her to as many dances as she wanted, and danced as late as she wished. She looked into his eyes and saw his determined devotion: he was romantic enough to risk her rejection.

His emotional certainty won her over. She married him, and their child—Anna—arrived soon after. Roberta hemorrhaged badly at delivery and was advised that further pregnancies would be risky. But both parents were delighted with their daughter.

They moved into a small terraced house in Fulham, and Iris gave them a much-loved old piano as a present. Anna became the focus of Roberta's hopes. She wanted to pass on to her daughter her spirit and verve. She taught her the piano, and danced down the street with her. More, she taught her joy. That was Roberta's talent.

But now, with Anna and Lewis gone, Roberta's talent for happiness had no audience. Her working life continued, but felt like a spurious activity. What was the point of restoring furniture in houses which might soon be blasted to bits by German bombs?

For the moment, there were only false alarms. No planes, no raids, nothing but sandbags and empty streets and air-raid drills. Blackout curtains and loneliness. Roberta lay on her bed and wrapped her legs around the sheets. She thought of her husband, with his neatly cut hair and his cautious gestures. She felt tenderness for him, and loyalty, and familial love. But little ardor. Her body was in full bloom now, and she couldn't help longing for somebody new to enter her life—a passionate man, more spontaneous than Lewis.

In the morning she set off to Regent's Park, to restore a table in one of the mansions there. She arrived at the colonnades of the Outer Circle, where the houses glowed with an eerie ivory sheen under an overcast sky.

She pulled the doorbell, and a housekeeper with remote

eyes showed her to the drawing room. There was the table—walnut with inlaid brass. Years of sunlight through the long windows had warped the wood a little, and the brass detailing was sticking out of its grooves. There were a few edges of veneer missing too. Roberta set to work with her box of tools, her pliers, her glue and her wood pieces in many colors and sizes.

This vast house was so empty. Without any sound but a ticking clock and the occasional passing car. Roberta looked out onto Regent's Park, the bandstand, the empty lawns, the unappreciated trees. The looking-glass lake, so still and passionless. She felt a pang of distance, as if everything was away, apart—her husband, her daughter, her own life.

I'm alone too much, she told herself. She finished her job as soon as she could, eager to leave the silent house. Emerging onto the street, she avoided the park because it looked too melancholy without children, and headed instead down Park Crescent, towards Oxford Circus.

"Roberta!"

She turned to see Martha Cox, someone she had known back in her courting years at the local dance hall.

"I work just around the corner, at the BBC—the building that looks like an ocean liner," Martha told her.

"What do you do there?"

"Sort the archives—their shelves are overflowing with recordings. But why don't you join us? Another girl just left us for the Wrens."

As she chattered on, Roberta's heart leapt at the chance of doing something different, something somehow linked—however tenuously—to the war effort. Restoring tables in empty houses seemed altogether less valuable than sorting dance records for a deprived and grateful nation.

The women walked off, arm in arm, to the reception desk, where Roberta was fixed up with an interview.

She hoped her father-in-law would understand; their firm

had fewer and fewer job requests, after all. She had her own needs too, barely admitted even to herself. A part of her was longing for new excitement, and now this opportunity had arrived. Increasingly, she tingled with formless romantic hope. She found it hard not to look into the face of any man she met, in case she found a return. She did not want to threaten her marriage or home—but nevertheless, if she caught the glance of an interesting new stranger, she could never quite resist the thought of fresh eyes, fresh love.

16

WHEN ANNA NEXT received a letter from her mother, she learnt that she had started war work now, a busy job at the BBC. *So I'm afraid I won't be able to visit you quite yet. But I was so glad to read your last letter, my darling. You are clearly so happy at Ashton Park . . .*

Anna felt deflated. She was longing to see her mother, yet now she could see nothing ahead of her but school forever.

Perhaps it was this upset which made her reckless that weekend, because she joined up with Billy and Euan, the boys who were always in trouble. They persuaded her to go stair-sliding with them. First they sneaked into the kitchen to find some tin trays, and then took them right to the top of the art-room stairs, which were lined with a tattered green carpet.

Billy was the first tray slider. Anna watched him hurtle downstairs—banging against the wall, then thrown off his tray at the bottom.

"It's fun," he cried, and raced upstairs again for another go.

"My turn . . . ," said Anna, bracing herself and closing her eyes. Her ride was fast, bumpy, scary—and she lurched at the bottom. But she landed well, and the boys clapped when she stood up.

The three of them took it in turns, sliding faster each time. Euan, who never usually said much, took to whooping on his rides, and it was his cries which drew Miss Harrison to the staircase.

"*Will* you stop that at once—" She was furious, her face clenched and her eyes even more twitchy than usual. She stormed and spluttered at them about the danger, the broken legs and necks, then she marched them off to be punished.

Anna and the boys followed her in silence, dreading what was to come. But they were lucky: it was Mr. Stewart's day off, and so they were led to Mr. Ashton's study instead.

When they entered his room, he was behind his desk. He wheeled forwards to address them, looking at them carefully while they stood there in silence. His quietness put them all on edge: Anna could not tell how angry he was.

"I understand you have been playing a game—but a very dangerous game."

"Yes, sir, we're sorry," said Billy, shouldering the blame.

Mr. Ashton paused for a moment.

"It sounds inventive, so I can't blame you for that," he said, glancing away—but then he faced them directly, each of them in turn, and fixed them with his eyes. "But I would so hate any of you to injure yourselves. You *must* learn to take better care— you could have knocked yourselves out. Now you must promise me not to do anything like this again, for your own sakes."

Anna felt herself relaxing: he wasn't angry, just worried.

"We promise, sir," she blurted out. He nodded at her.

"Is that what happened to you, sir?" Euan's question sprang out so suddenly, Anna could hardly believe what he had said. "I mean, was it . . . an accident, sir?" he went on, scrabbling for words, gesturing at the wheelchair.

"No. No, I didn't have an accident as such," said Thomas, slightly taken aback. "I fell ill on a holiday. Just bad luck. That happens too, I'm afraid," he added, with the shadow of a smile.

Silence.

"Off you go then, but please be careful from now on," said Thomas, and the children turned to go.

Closing the door behind them, Anna was relieved to be released, and yet stricken by Mr. Ashton's words. A holiday illness?

17

Thomas was shaken by the boy's question.

"One of the boys asked about my wheelchair today," he volunteered to Elizabeth at dinner.

"That was bold. Was he rude?"

"No, just curious."

"What did you tell him?"

He paused.

"I just said that I had fallen ill on holiday."

Elizabeth felt her eyes welling, and she touched Thomas's hand.

"Don't worry, my darling," he said to her, and for a moment they were gentle with each other.

It was some time since either of them had mentioned Thomas's disability. But their holiday to Brugge in the summer of 1931 still remained vividly present in their minds.

It had begun as a simple treat for Elizabeth. Thomas had been working too hard at the office, and wanted to spoil his wife with a short trip abroad.

They had arrived in Brugge in the last week of August, when the town was torrid with heat. The picturesque streets were narrow, close, cobbled, with astonishing spires stretching upwards from hidden alleys. Through tall heavy doors they had entered the famous churches, marveling at the expanse of space within buildings that appeared so compact from the outside. The high stone interiors were vaulted and bright, with white northern light falling onto the carved pillars and polished floors. All sound was muffled, and they felt solemn, heightened.

How beautiful she is, Thomas kept telling himself as he watched Elizabeth in the filtered church light. The auburn glow of her hair was enhanced, and he saw in her face the delicate ivory of medieval art.

Afterwards they walked out into the close, muggy streets, which were teeming now with summer visitors. A threat hung in the air, of storms to come, of menacing pressure.

They took a boat ride to cool themselves, but the canals were stagnant and flyblown, and brought no relief. It was as Thomas trailed his fingers through the water that he first noticed an irritation in his throat—just a scratch.

On their second day they sought refuge from the heat in art galleries. They spent hours looking into the exquisite blue vistas of Hans Memling's paintings, serene Madonnas with feudal fields glimpsed behind. The pictures were so detailed, so crystalline, that they took on a dreamlike air. The strange blue views seemed to wash over Thomas, and his mind started to detach itself, drifting into a subaqueous world of vibrant color and line and texture. He thought he could feel the silken folds of the Madonna's cloak. Walking on the cool stone floor of the gallery, his footsteps rang out like distant bells in his head.

"Is everything all right?" Elizabeth asked him.

"Just a cold coming on," he said, clearing his throat.

By the evening, his throat was sorely inflamed, and in the early hours of the morning he lay semidelirious with fever. A doctor was called to their hotel room, and his expression soon became grave.

"It is polio," he told Elizabeth. "We have an epidemic of it at the moment. You must not drink the water."

Why didn't anybody warn us? thought Elizabeth as she watched Thomas fading further into delirium.

They took him to the local hospital. For two days Thomas drifted in and out of consciousness, incontinent, fed through a nose tube. He struggled for life like a fish without water, until the doctors had to puncture his throat with a tube for oxygen.

Elizabeth was frantic; she saw her beautiful husband lying there white and drained, so far wilted that he seemed sure to die. A boy two beds from him did pass away, his lungs giving in to the viral seizure.

Day and night Elizabeth hovered by Thomas's bed. In her limited French, she spoke to the doctors again and again, urgently, passionately. This is not just another Englishman, she tried to explain, this is Thomas Ashton, a diplomat, and heir to a great estate. *Ce n'est pas possible de faire quelque chose?*

After a week there was still no improvement. Better care was available in Brussels, but the beds were all full. Elizabeth was desperate to move him home to England, and the Belgians did not try to stop her.

Thomas knew nothing as he hovered in the plane between life and death, his face obscured by an oxygen mask. The throbbing of the engine shook through him as he lay there, limp, slack, sinking through his own body, close to death. Elizabeth looked down at Kent and Surrey spread out below them like a toy set, the roar in her ears forcing her inwards until Thomas was just a body beside her. She sensed her own heart closing off from him.

At St. Thomas's Hospital, the nurses immediately slid Thomas inside a sarcophagus-shaped contraption which looked like an instrument of torture.

"This machine will force the movement of his lungs," the doctor explained, "to make him breathe mechanically. He should be safe now."

For five months Thomas lay inside the iron lung, on the edge of life. Elizabeth was a familiar fixture in the polio ward, as were Thomas's mother and Norton. All of them urged Thomas to live, but privately dreaded the ravages of his disease. They could barely see him, encased as he was inside the machine. But the nurses who sponged him down watched his body wasting away, until his limbs were like sticks, with knobs for knees and elbows.

For Thomas, trapped inside the iron lung, it was like being tossed about in an interminable storm. Sometimes his body was lost to him, as if he were falling from himself into a never-ending pit. Yet any touch on his skin was like a scream of pain, as if his whole body was a raw burn. His soul hung on while the virus swept through him like a fire, ravaging his nerves and muscles.

Just to be able to catch his own breath and push out his lungs by himself was a terrifying ordeal. Every time they took him out of the iron lung to clean him or feed him, panic seized him as he gasped for air.

The rhythmic noise of the pump drove him inwards. His surroundings existed only as a faint echo, glimpsed as through a distant window. He slipped into his own world of dreams and visions. It seemed to him that his sister was very often by his side, and together they looked up at sunlight flickering through trees in Ashton Park. There was a scent of wild garlic. Sometimes, he was with his brothers in the trenches, wading through mud and corpses, before Claudia took him back to the woods at Ashton. At other times, when he opened his eyes, he saw his mother's aging face looking down at him with unblinking eyes, while his father stood behind. Then he did not know if he was living or dead.

Often, there was no refuge from the throb of his own pulse. Blood was beating through him—he was frantic, sweating, running over vast cracked plains. Sand slowed him down until there was no push against his legs—until he was falling through quicksand. Mother and father, brothers, sister, all falling with him.

On better days, he slipped towards a tranquil oblivion, as if he'd been released into an eternal present. There was a special quality to that light—it sang—and his soul seemed to float like a sphere. Those moments outside his body were blissful, euphoric. Seeing like a sphere. It was light somehow connected with love, with loved faces, with the morning light of his childhood bedroom, and summer holidays, and the gray-gold sunlight of Oxford. Simultaneous memories, all known at once, bringing relief.

After six months, he began to surface from his storm. He was weaned from the iron lung, and started to breathe for himself again. The nurses moved him into a convalescents' ward, where he wallowed in a bed with pillows. His head began to clear, and they sat him up. He made an effort to be wry and talkative, though his body was still emaciated and his strength shattered.

Now that he had won back the simple power of breathing, Thomas felt that anything would be possible. He assumed that as he recovered his strength would return, and he would stand again.

The convalescent ward was painted *eau de nil*. Sometimes he would wake up to glinting sunshine, which bleached the room white. Other times, the walls were pooled in shadow and appeared a rich turquoise, like a dappled pool. The pale curtains flapped in the wind with little insistent sounds, while noises from beyond—tugboat horns, distant cars, the clatter of trains over Charing Cross bridge—seeped through like a dream. Through the window he felt the presence of the river Thames, with its slow tidal exhalations.

In some ways this was a peaceful time. The doctors had long since warned Elizabeth that Thomas was unlikely to walk again, but nobody had broken this to him yet. It was only when his expectations began to return that the pain and grief of his new condition began to take hold. Some of his muscles had shriveled away to nothing. He could barely move his legs, nor could he feel any spark of strength returning to his limbs.

Finally, he confronted his doctor.

"Do you think I will make a full recovery?"

His doctor paused.

"Do you mean will you walk again? We will have to wait and see."

"Am I to be permanently crippled? I need to know—"

"I'm afraid we're not sure yet." The doctor averted his eyes. "Clusters of your nerves have been damaged by the polio virus. Only gradually will we know which of your muscles might recover, and which ones will be lost to you."

Months of rehabilitation began. Daily a physiotherapist would pull and stretch his deadened limbs, trying to unravel their tightened knots. Every part of his body ached: his bones, his muscles, his nerves. It became clear to Thomas that he would recover the use of his arms and hands. But the muscles he needed for standing upright, let alone for walking or running, were ravaged beyond repair.

He would never be able to walk again.

It all felt quite unemotional in the hospital, where there were dozens of others in the same position. But whenever he had a visitor from outside, then he felt a pang of shame and humiliation for his physical change. Never had his familiar smile seemed so forced, nor so helplessly ironic.

An outside nurse arrived to take a plaster-cast mold of his back, and she returned some weeks later with a leather back brace for him. She fitted it onto him and he sat up in his wheelchair. The brace gave him support and an unnaturally erect posture. When Norton came to visit and saw Thomas looking out of the window, his heart crumpled. There was his friend, sitting so straight in his wheelchair, his hair freshly cut and brushed away from his face, his legs wasted and useless. Thomas looked so dignified and brave, and so utterly emasculated.

Thomas hoped he might walk with calipers, and he tried many times to stagger along the hospital's parallel bars, against the advice of his doctors, but he lacked the strength to carry himself, even with crutches. Eventually he surrendered to his wheelchair.

At first, in hospital, he had felt euphoric still to be alive. *One breath of life is better than none at all,* he told himself. He balanced his ill luck with all the many misfortunes of this world, and fought his way back to hope. But little by little, a horror at his condition began to overtake him. A cripple confined to a wheelchair. When the nurse changed his sheets and he looked down the bed, the sight of his big knee joints and emaciated thighs and calves disgusted him.

He carried, too, a dull, barely articulated conviction that he was paying the price for surviving the war which had taken his brothers. An atonement.

Ten months after the fateful holiday to Brugge, he was ready to leave the hospital and all the patient nurses, who had respected his natural reticence. But he was apprehensive about his return to daily marital intimacy.

The evening before he came home, Elizabeth checked over their house in Regent's Park. She had ordered an abundance of flowers to greet his return, cheerful bowls of tulips and yellow roses. She had also removed from the drawing room a photograph of Thomas with his Oxford running team.

Thomas's months in hospital had been terrible for her too, and she had felt her heart detaching itself from him. She had at times been sunk with fear that he might die—but now, instead, he was coming home a different man. She had spent many evenings crying for him. But she had cried for herself too, and for the death of her own happiness, even though she was ashamed of such selfishness. For she had hitched her life to Thomas, and from now on all their mutual hopes would be compromised. Even in the most glorious moment, there would always be the wheelchair.

Thomas left hospital on a glittering day in June. He was waiting for his wife in the hospital hall, dressed in new flannels which flapped around his legs. Elizabeth arrived in their most spacious car, and Thomas was lifted into the backseat by

Carter, a sturdy young chauffeur who had been designated as his manservant.

The car drew up outside the house in Sussex Place, and his mother came out to greet him, along with the butler, Ropner. Even the servants were apprehensive about seeing Thomas for the first time in his altered state.

"Hello, Ropner—very good to see you again."

"It's so good to have you home, sir."

Thomas felt wretched and ashamed, but smiled politely and dredged up all his natural courtesies to make them feel at ease. Carter helped to move him out of the car and into his chair, then up the steps.

Once they were inside, Thomas wheeled himself around the ground floor, stopping to admire the new lift which Elizabeth had installed. It took them up to the drawing room, where Thomas cordially thanked the housekeeper, Mrs. Bruton, for the lavish display of tulips on the rosewood table.

"It was Mrs. Ashton's suggestion, sir."

"Well, thank you, Elizabeth. And that has always been my favorite table," he said, searching for commonplaces.

Through the windows he saw again the familiar view onto the lake and bandstand of Regent's Park. Some late blossoms still graced the trees, and swans eased through the water.

"Has it been a good year for park blossoms?"

"I haven't noticed an unusual flowering—"

"I see the black swans are still there."

"Yes, two of them this year."

He smiled and talked amiably to Elizabeth and his mother, yet felt entirely remote from both of them. He retreated to read the paper while his small case of belongings was unpacked.

Later, getting downstairs for lunch was such a business. Then what would there be to do afterwards, he wondered.

He asked to go out, and Elizabeth wheeled him off to enjoy the summertime glory of the park. But Thomas could still recall how his first outing as a man in a wheelchair quickly turned into a trial. As his wife wheeled him past the lawns and along the lake, he felt the curious gaze of the strangers they passed—sensed their snatched glances of pity for him. He sat up straight, and chatted pleasantly to Elizabeth, but felt sliced to the marrow by humiliation.

He could remember feeling compelled to keep up a banter of good cheer, not just slump into forlorn silence. But it was so hard even to sit in a comfortable position in his chair, because he had to twist his shoulders round to talk to Elizabeth, or else look ahead and talk with an unnaturally loud voice, like an idiot. More, he could feel that the chair was heavy for her to push, and this offended his natural gallantry.

Later, after dinner, there was the terror of the bedroom. A fierce modesty overcame Thomas—he could not bear his wife to see his back brace, nor his wasted legs. He had help with bathing from Carter, which was humiliating, but better than the emasculating attentions of a wife. Then he heaved himself from his chair into bed. Elizabeth joined him soon after from her dressing room.

Theirs was a marriage which had been founded on mutual beauty, yet now Thomas dreaded any physical intimacy. And Elizabeth—she was haunted by a fear of his altered limbs. He had always been covered or clothed during her hospital visits, but now she was afraid of seeing his naked body, and not knowing how to respond. She assured herself that she still loved Thomas, but now she quailed at their changed life together. And she had given up any hope of children.

But Thomas knew he was not impotent. On their third night together, under the cover of darkness, he rolled over to his wife and caressed her until their mutual timidity dissolved. Then she gripped his shoulders hard, and cried out as he penetrated her. Afterwards, they lay close together, both of them relieved to have broken through their awkwardness.

The next morning he let her dress him. When she saw his legs properly for the first time, her fear was over. They were the same legs, just thinner and slacker. Nothing particularly disgusting or odd, nothing to be afraid of. They laughed about them, and she stroked his thighs affectionately.

Thereafter, Thomas tried to begin his life again. All through the summer of 1932, he worked to build his strength, through whatever exercise he could manage. A physiotherapist came three times a week to stretch and massage his muscles. Alone in his study, he repeatedly gripped a rubber ball to strengthen his hands.

Then at last he undertook what he had put off for too long: the train journey to Ashton Park, where a suite of rooms had been prepared for him and Elizabeth on the ground floor.

Carter chauffeured them up the long drive to Ashton Park, then Thomas was lifted in his chair up the steps into the Marble Hall. His wheels squeaked on the polished floor, and all the rooms looked unusually high from his new sitting position. He would have liked to go upstairs, as he usually did, to see the view from his old bedroom, but did not want to cause any bother.

He realized how far he was cut off now from his own past.

He spent many weeks recuperating at Ashton, endeavoring once more to turn his mind to his tenant farmers, and all the other obligations of his estate.

To exercise his hands and arms, he often spent the mornings playing the piano in the saloon. Music also gave him an excuse to be on his own. He craved solitude, but was fearful of it, too. There were many empty hours when he was alone in his head, trying to brace himself for a life in a wheelchair.

Sometimes he would reach the end of the day with a degree of acceptance about his condition. But then the next morning he would wake up again at the bottom of the ladder, in despair, and then he would have to overcome his revulsion at his new bodily state all over again, right through the day.

He found himself retreating into a private interior. Despite the steadfast appearance given by his manners, he was closing himself off. He tried to remain open to Elizabeth, but there was increasingly an element of role play in their warmth to each other.

Had they ever achieved that easy, continuous, unspoken communication between spouses which works beyond words? Certainly, it was not there then. Each blocked the other, despite their smiles and little squeezes of the hand as they passed each other.

Thomas was most at peace when left alone in his study. There he could find his own level—pain and grief could be dulled by mental exercises. He could remember opening again his classics books, and reading Marcus Aurelius's *Meditations*.

Man's life goes in a flash, his flesh is fleeting, his understanding is dark, his body a prey of worms, his soul a whirling wind, his fate unknown, his reputation undecided . . . What then can be man's guide? One thing and one only—philosophy. To be a philosopher is to keep man's inmost divine spirit clear of reproach and injury, beyond pleasure and pain . . .

The divine spirit. Thomas had always secretly prided himself on his solitary epiphanies of sheer joy, moments when everything seemed to be connected. From the delicate veins of a forget-me-not to the constellations above, he had felt he could intuit a pattern, a soul—a fleeting sense, almost, of infinity. But now he only felt estranged from any such soaring intimations. All those elusive apprehensions of nature now seemed no more than the illusions of youth and health.

He could sit alone for hours, oblivious and unmoving, as his study grew dark around him. The servants did not dare to disturb him. Eventually Elizabeth would go in and switch on the lights, and try to rouse him with the trivia of the day.

He tried to stabilize himself by reaching after order and ritual, with prayers to the God of his school chapels. But when he listened for God's voice, all he could hear were the solipsistic repetitions of his own mind, driving him further inside himself.

Wanting to feel less, he drank more, though this made his nights restless. The lights stayed on in his head, jolting him awake with flashes of brightness. For a time only the translation of Greek or Latin kept him sane. The conscious pairing of words to a meaning reconnected him with his mind. But even as he held a pen to write, he could feel the dislocation between his body and soul. Sometimes his still-shocked nerves were overstrung with expectancy, his body ringing with too much awareness and his fingertips jangling with sensation. Even to look at the sky sometimes felt dangerous, as if it might break, or fall, or be sucked inside his mind.

All the while, he knew he was resisting Elizabeth, subtly closing himself to her overtures of affection and care. When they made love under cover of darkness, it was perfunctory, with each avoiding the other's eyes. His own self-disgust was poisoning any tenderness between them, he knew, but he could not help himself. He could no longer look at her properly, even in daylight.

In the end, there had been nothing left for him to do but to trust that his dark time would pass. To wait for hope. Day after day, Thomas played the piano, schooling himself with the orderly preludes and fugues of Bach. Little by little he began to breathe more deeply, and to get out more into the fresh air— until at last the threatened lunacy of despair receded to leave only a dull ache of accepted loss.

In November 1932 came the news that America had elected Roosevelt as president—a man who had been severely stricken with polio a decade before. His example gave Elizabeth hope that Thomas too would recover his energy and spark. As the depressive aftermath of his illness lifted, they began to talk of his return to work.

They moved back down to Sussex Place, and Thomas visited his Whitehall colleagues, determined to prove his fitness. Within weeks, he returned formally to the Foreign Office in his wheelchair. On his first day back, Norton took the trouble to wheel him to his office in the Central Department.

Thomas found it strange to sit at a desk without needing a chair anymore. European affairs had shifted radically since he had disappeared into his iron lung: Adolf Hitler, once a small-time agitator of street politics, was now about to become chancellor of Germany.

"It is a mercy we are no longer in Berlin," he said to Elizabeth at dinner.

"We left at just the right time," she agreed, both of them trying to seize on reasons to feel fortunate.

They had always been careful with each other since then. The death of their desire was never mentioned.

18

ROBERTA'S HUSBAND WAS now stationed in North Africa, near Cairo, and she wrote to tell him about her new job. She did not mention she would be playing band music—that sounded too feckless. Instead, she hinted that she was working for something less frivolous, like the talks programs.

Lewis replied to her with wry descriptions of his inaction under the fierce Egyptian sun. *We listen to the BBC much of the time,* he wrote, *so now I'll be able to imagine you at the other end of the broadcasts—right through the wireless, across the sea, back in London. Send me a thought wave sometimes, my darling.*

She comforted herself with the thought that he was safe for the moment, and this absolved her of any guilt about her new life. She had begun as an assistant on the BBC Home Service, doing everything from filing to timing recordings with a stopwatch. But her training was somewhat haphazard, as all the other assistants were already busy.

She soon acclimatized to the daily atmosphere of controlled panic in Broadcasting House, everyone running blinkered down corridors and vanishing through double doorways—all frantic to keep the show going.

"Continuity is the thing," explained Roberta's new boss, a bespectacled man with a bow tie. "We are all wedded to keeping the programs going without interruption—it's our first duty to the public at this time."

The program she worked on was known as *Music While You Work,* which was designed to rally the legions of factory workers to their tasks. She soon gathered that there were certain rules about the music played. "Unsuitable" numbers were those with lethargic rhythms or insufficient melody, and waltzes were deemed too soporific. Many of the numbers were played by the BBC Dance Orchestra, conducted by Geraldo, and before long Roberta was the new stopwatch assistant in the recording hall downstairs.

She was intoxicated by all this new pleasure. Here was Geraldo's band sitting right before her in shirtsleeves—and when the conductor rapped on the music stand to signal a new change to the score, dozens of men apparently dozing in their chairs would suddenly sit straight and produce heart-stopping syncopations.

Within a week, Broadcasting House felt like her natural home. She loved the contained atmosphere of the place. The floors were how she imagined the decks of a liner, with windows like portholes to the outside world. Every sound was oddly muffled, and there was always a smell of cooking drifting upwards from the lower depths.

Solemn-looking men and women appeared and disappeared down the lino corridors but she, Roberta, danced through the doorways with a bright electric step of happiness. She ran up and down the stairwells, rejoicing simply because she had never before belonged to an institution with great communal stairways like these. Even the banister rails enchanted her. She ran her hands down their smooth shafts as she moved from floor to floor.

The music was everywhere, sweeping over her in waves. The jaunty trumpets and crooning saxophones made her long to dance again, and she sensed the possibility of a new partner hovering somewhere on the edge of her life. There was a cornet player in Geraldo's band who watched her studiedly when she walked across the room. Perhaps he would be the one. Perhaps another. Suddenly, there were all these new men around her.

After work, free of family ties, Roberta took to following her

BBC colleagues off to the nearby bars of Fitzrovia. There, she drank beer and told people the story of her life exactly as she liked, perhaps hinting at minor discontent with her husband, with occasional suggestions that he had held her back. Whatever the untruths, she was enjoying this chance to reinvent herself.

Fitzrovia pubs closed in sequence, and she quickly learnt the order. After the last round at the Wheatsheaf, everyone would decamp down the road to the Duke of York. Roberta preferred the French—run, as the name suggested, by a Frenchman famous for his magnificent mustache. The same faces came and went in each bar. By the time you had seen each other three times, you were friends.

Drink and cigarettes, and a shifting company of new faces, made Roberta lighthearted. She exchanged glances with many men, soldiers on leave, BBC staff, artists, band players. As yet, no particular man had quite captured her attention, but she had not forgotten the cornet player in Geraldo's band, who watched her every time she came to a rehearsal. He had taken to sitting up properly when she was in the room, she noticed.

She worked hard all day, then laughed with strangers in pubs, and teetered home with the band music still ringing in her ears. But not forgetting her husband in Egypt, nor her daughter sleeping at Ashton Park. Visits to evacuees, she knew, were discouraged as "unsettling," but she was sure she could ask for some leave soon, then take the train to Yorkshire and see her daughter.

She wondered if Anna still threw her arms back on her pillow as she slept.

19

ALL TOO OFTEN, Anna felt lonely. What did it mean, making friends? She was never sure. Sometimes, she could only see the faces of other children stacked up opposite her: Katy, Susan, Beth. They smiled, they laughed. She might run down a hill holding hands with Beth. But then Beth might turn and walk away, and Anna would watch her go and never know if Beth wanted to play with her anymore or not. Why was it Beth, not her, who held this choice? Every day she tiptoed across the unknown terrain of other children's affections, clumsy with self-doubt. She could not work out why she feared other children more than they feared her. It was easier to walk away into the woods, and be on your own. Read a book.

She met Suzy West on the way to lunch one Saturday. Suzy was in Katy Todd's gang, a shy, tentative girl, shuffling from one foot to the other.

"What are we doing this afternoon?" asked Anna cheerily.

"That depends," mumbled Suzy.

"On what?"

"Well—I don't know."

"Know what?"

"Whether we're all going."

"What do you mean?"

"Don't you know?"

"No."

"Well, maybe I'm not meant to say," said Suzy, fidgeting with her fingers now.

"Please tell me," begged Anna, dropping her voice.

"I can't."

"*Please*—"

"Well, promise you won't tell I told you—"

"I promise."

"We're going to the water tower, to collect snails—there's lots of them there."

"Who's going?"

"Just the gang—some of the gang. Billy, Mary, me. Katy, of course."

"Why—" Anna paused.

"Yes?"

"Why can't I come?"

"Well, I think you can, but you don't always come to everything, so I don't know if you're coming to this or not."

"Should I ask Katy?"

"No! Because then they'll know I told you."

"Then what do I do?" cried Anna, holding back the tears now.

"Hang around the back-garden door after lunch. Then Katy'll ask you along if she means to." Little Suzy was scared by now, and wanted to get away. Anna let her go.

But through lunch she could scarcely talk to those beside her; she was twisting herself into knots of misery and rejection.

Perhaps she'd only missed the gang's plan because she hadn't seen Katy and the others this morning? All she had to do was bump into them, and they would say, in a cheery voice, *Coming*?

Then all would be well. Or would it? A part of Anna felt weary of hanging out with children she did not really want to be with, who did not like the same things as her, or think the way she did. Who were meaner than she wanted to be.

She decided she would not hover by the garden door, waiting not to be asked on the snail-catching trip. So after lunch she walked off on her own instead, as she often did, hoping nobody would notice her.

THE VERY THOUGHT OF YOU 129

What do I care? Anna told herself, taking herself off to her den in the luggage room. But finding an old tennis ball in the rack there, she decided it was probably safe now to play ball outside, unnoticed by Katy's gang.

She clattered downstairs, and found herself a spot in the herb garden to perfect her bounce and throw against the house wall.

From his study upstairs, Thomas heard a thudding sound. He looked outside, and saw Anna Sands throwing a tennis ball against the wall, one catch after another, her eyes fixed on the ball. He hoped she was on her own by choice.

Thomas himself was alone that weekend, with Elizabeth on a visit to London. "To do some catching up," as she put it. With what or whom she did not say, and he did not ask. He, meanwhile, had slipped into his own solitude, returning to a translation of Virgil which he had promised to an Oxford journal.

After all his years in the engine room of the Foreign Office, Thomas found it strange to be applying himself now to Latin sentences, while so many others were gathering on the front line. Eighteen months earlier, once it was clear that Chamberlain was determined to appease Hitler, Thomas had resigned from the Central Department—in sympathy with his chief Vansittart, who had been quietly ousted as head of the Foreign Office because of his opposition to Chamberlain's strategies. The atmosphere in Whitehall had grown intolerably toxic for any antiappeasers, and Thomas had felt compelled to withdraw. At the time, he told his colleagues that he was embarking on a new translation of *The Aeneid*. What had begun as a private consolation had turned into a passion, and whenever he was not teaching now, he went back to his Virgil.

But he knew that sometimes he retreated into his study to avoid his marriage, too. Lately, an unspoken truce had settled between Elizabeth and him, in which they lived together and yet separately. He had learnt not to ask Elizabeth what she did on her visits to London.

Thomas did not doubt that she had tried to love him. Over the years she had emerged as a social orchid—everything about her was always perfectly presented to the world: her hair, her nails, her clothes. But Thomas sensed that it was romantic life she craved, to be swept onto a dance floor, to walk on the arm of a desirable man, needs he could never now meet.

Perhaps Thomas divined this better than she did herself. He did not blame her for it, or despise her, or even hold it against her. He, too, prized her perfection and poise—had that not been her attraction for him as well? And yet, whenever he saw her remote eyes, he felt threatened by that look of dissatisfaction in her face.

At least he had always been able to take refuge in his work, whether the legitimate crises of the Foreign Office or, now, his teaching and his translations. But he knew she had enough empty hours to feel the holes in her life. The war had offered her this chance to reinvent herself, yet even their school had not satisfied her restlessness. Her discontent was too pervasive, and he had watched her drink too much—first wine, then spirits.

There were still times when Thomas regretted not being in love with his wife—not feeling that tenderness which might exalt daily life. As he raked over their marriage, he was haunted by one particular milestone in their mutually diminishing expectations: their holiday in Venice in the spring of 1935.

It was Elizabeth who had planned the trip.

"Venice will be easy for the chair," she had announced with brio. "No hills. We can stroll through piazzas and visit galleries."

Neither of them had ever been to Venice before. They took the train, setting off with the light spirit of travelers, both delighted by the opulence of the Orient Express. Thomas was charming and attentive to Elizabeth—who was trying so hard to fire their ailing intimacy. They passed the rolling fields of France and the mountain passes of the Swiss Alps, until at last they arrived in Venice, glittering in the late-August sunshine.

They tried to hide from each other their disappointment with the hotel. Their room had a dark, damp air, and although the window faced out onto a canal, it was too high for Thomas to have any view. But still, they changed their clothes, and set off through the pretty streets to find a restaurant for dinner.

That first evening they saw Venice at its best. The colors of the buildings glowed and blended under the mature sunshine: ocher, rose, cream, coral. The pleasure of this new place made them both light-headed. They found their way to a trattoria overlooking the lagoon, and ate seafood while watching the sunset fade to darkness over the sea. Later that night, they made love.

But the next day, for no perceptible reason, Elizabeth's habitual melancholy began to seep through, and she retreated inwards. Thomas found her distant and unresponsive at breakfast. Perhaps it was the dining room, with its inadequate light fixtures, or perhaps it was the weather, for the sun was closed out by dull clouds now. Thomas did what he could to engage her, smiling at her brightly, his old familiar smile.

They set out with their guidebooks to explore the famous city, Elizabeth pushing Thomas through the maze of piazzas and hidden streets. But they had not reckoned on the uneven paving stones, which soon began to jar Thomas's spine. Elizabeth, meanwhile, was quickly exhausted by pushing the wheelchair through the rutted streets.

Elizabeth grew irritable and Thomas dejected. Venice was beautiful, no doubt, but they found themselves too soon estranged from its beauty. In the Basilica of San Marco, the mosaics were dun and lifeless, because no shaft of sunlight kindled their glitter. So it was with all the sights. They visited the Accademia gallery, and Thomas viewed Bellini's paintings

with a cold, dead eye: his heart had closed up against so much
perfection.

When they came out of the gallery, it started to rain heavily.
The water fell down in sheets, sluicing down broken walls and
running in dirty streams along the gutters. Thomas sat helplessly in his chair as Elizabeth wheeled him back to their room,
his knees soaking, her back strained.

The next morning, Thomas woke up with a streaming cold
and felt breathless. With his lungs weakened by polio, he was
wary of catching pneumonia and stayed indoors. He lay in the
dark, airless hotel room and listened to the rain falling on the
canal outside.

Elizabeth went for a walk on her own. She sipped coffee
in Piazza San Marco, and watched romantic couples. Pigeons
flocked and flew away in waves. By the time she returned to the
hotel, self-pity had infected her every nerve, and she did not
even try to be cheerful.

Her disappointed face at least spurred Thomas to attempt a
recovery, and he roused himself to go out the following morning. The colors of the buildings, which had been so charming
in sunlight, now looked moldy and dreary in an overcast sky.
There was a stench from the canals, and the thickening air stuck
in their throats. They ate their lunch in silence, and a wave of
gloom came over them both as Elizabeth wheeled Thomas
back to their hotel.

More rainstorms were forecast, so after one final desultory
day they left for home, three days early.

Their marriage had reached an impasse. Thereafter they
hoped without hope, and their hidden crack of estrangement
began to widen. When Thomas heard the sound of Elizabeth's
step, his heart did not rise. When she saw his handsome face,
she was unmoved. There were occasional false dawns of intimacy, moments when they almost reached each other, usually
after an evening of wine, feeling each other in the darkness of

their bedroom. But each was imagining somebody else, some other life.

Divorce, however, was still not discussed. How could Elizabeth leave her crippled husband, the Ashton heir? Thomas hinted that she was welcome to her freedom by mentioning the liaisons of other London women with as much approbation as was decent. But they both still hoped for a child who might redeem their unhappiness.

Outside, the sound of the bouncing ball stopped abruptly, and Thomas realized that the girl had run off. The sudden silence prompted his return to the words before him, and he tried to switch his mind back to Aeneas's wanderings.

> *Blown far off course, we wander in the dark,*
> *Where day and night converge, till even*
> *Our pilot Palinurus must confess*
> *Our way is lost in all this wilderness of water . . .*

20

WHEN ELIZABETH RETURNED on Tuesday, Thomas was careful not to trespass on her privacy.

"How was London?"

"Dark, and empty. But no sign of an air raid yet. Just everyone waiting indoors for the worst to happen."

"And the house?"

"As ever. Well, not quite. The park is being dug up, and the railings have been removed. In fact the entire city looks oddly dismantled—"

"I think I'd rather not see it."

"I went to the gallery too. Not much life there at the moment."

She slipped in this last remark casually, as if to forestall any questioning. Peter Norton's modern art gallery was where she had worked and made her friends before the war.

"It's very nice to have you back here, darling," he said, and he meant it.

"Yes," she said with feeling, and touched the back of his hand. She seemed remarkably cheerful, and refreshed.

The next morning she rose early, and watched all the evacuees having breakfast in the dining room. As they filed past her into their assembly, she felt an unexpected calm settling on her. There was a brightness in their faces, as if this place suited them, and she was suddenly proud to have brought them all here, to have given them a home. At last she had been able to do something right.

She met the head gardener that morning, and found him

buoyant: for too many years he had watched in quiet despair while his vegetables rotted away uneaten.

"Eighty-six children is good. I can feed more," he told her.

There was plenty to be glad about, she decided, as she went through the staff rotas.

Such as her trips to London.

Her double life had begun three years ago, when she had been too much alone in their Regent's Park house, unoccupied and childless. Something in her had snapped.

Her transgression had begun in her mind only, as she sat in their London drawing room one day, wondering what to do with herself. Their housekeeper had placed a cyclamen on the rosewood table, and Elizabeth felt herself mesmerized by its tranquil poise.

Cars hummed by on the street outside. Sunshine exposed the dust in the air as she sat on her sofa, barely moving, her gaze held by the cyclamen's intense stillness. Even the serenity of a plant could rebuke her now, she realized, with a start.

She pushed herself to her feet and walked round the room, suddenly impatient, past mirrors, a telephone, papers on her desk. Perhaps she should just pack her bags and leave Thomas—sail off and nurse the poor in India, or find some other heroic new life.

She wondered whether the telephone would ring. Whether a young man would call her, out of the blue—somebody who desired her but had been too afraid to tell her so.

What was it that she was hiding from herself—what was it that she wanted? Was it a person, or a hope, or—a rapture?

She sat down again on the sofa and reached up to feel the curve of her breasts.

There must be someone, somewhere, who would want to touch her. She wanted to stand in an embrace with a man, and lay her head on his shoulder. She wanted to be held close, with arms wrapped around her.

Thomas could never be enough for her anymore. He had rejected her, and so she was repelled by him. By his perfect face, by his coldness, by his distance. Resentment was silting her heart. She could walk naked through their bedroom and still he would not look up. His inadequacy had frozen him.

Barely spoken then, even in her mind, was the whisper of her empty womb. She was so stricken with a fear of barrenness that she could scarcely bear to acknowledge it. Every month, she kept up a faith that perhaps a child would come to relieve the years ahead. But always she felt the sharp ache, the pang, the subtle inward wrench which preceded her menstrual flow. Then the blood oozed forth, washing away her hope.

A few days later, Thomas found her crying in their bedroom, after the arrival of her latest period. He sought out her face, her eyes.

"We could find our own child to love," he said softly, "we could adopt a child."

Her whole body ached for a baby; how could he understand that? She could not look at him.

"I couldn't love a child that has not grown in me."

"You might come to love the child, especially if it was with you from birth—"

"I could not love somebody else's child."

"You don't know that," he spoke as tenderly as he could. She was crumpling, her face staring downwards.

"I need to feel my own child kicking inside—"

He reached out very tentatively and, for once, she let him hold her. In his mind he said to her, *Find another man, have another man's child.* For her, for him, for both of them, he just wanted her to have a child. *Please, have your child.*

That night, she allowed the blood to flow over the sheets, and in the morning their bed was accusingly smeared with stiff red stains. The sheets were thrown away, but their mattress still carried the buried signs of her empty womb.

Yet Elizabeth had sensed Thomas's unspoken plea that night. Thereafter, every time she met a man she felt free to check his eyes—looking for the blue gaze of the Ashtons.

Not long afterwards, she fell under the unexpected spell of a revolutionary new art show in London. The International Surrealist Exhibition at the New Burlington Galleries was a surprise sensation in the spring of 1936. Salvador Dalí appeared in publicity photographs wearing a diving bell, and it was this iconoclastic image which intrigued the public.

Clifford Norton's wife Peter had loaned some of the paintings, and she insisted on guiding Elizabeth around the works of Dalí, Miró, Max Ernst and Paul Nash. Dream landscapes by twilight, human bodies in strange metamorphoses, subconscious images of desire and memory. The pictures were provocatively frank in their nakedness.

Elizabeth had come to the show reluctantly, and was surprised by the way it affected her. She walked around the exhibition again by herself, and these surrealist images spoke to her at once, with their erotic secrets and carnal glimpses. The paintings broke her open in some primal way.

So much of the work was by men, and she saw in their paintings the direct gaze of male desire. Their fascination with the female body, and the irrational joys offered by female flesh. She emerged from the show stirred by illicit impulses.

In her longing to reach out, she turned to Norton's indefatigable wife, Peter, who had always been an emancipated woman with a career. She dared to talk to her about the eroticism of the surrealists.

"Why not come and join me at my new gallery?" suggested Peter, encouraged by Elizabeth's appreciation. So many of Peter's artist friends had fled from Hitler's Germany, and she was determined to show their work in London, where very little modern art was exhibited. So she had opened the London Gallery in Cork Street—"the first avant-garde gallery in Britain," as she proudly described it. The art critic Roland Penrose had just joined her as a director. She asked Elizabeth to help her run the exhibitions.

Every morning for two years, Elizabeth walked down from Regent's Park to Peter's Mayfair gallery, her clothes crisp and chic. She spent her days attending to visitors and buyers, and felt herself in delicious counterpoint to the shambolic artists who arrived with new pictures, or came to gaze at the exhibitions there. There was a brittle immaculacy about her, with her cigarettes in a long ivory holder and her tailored suits—and yet, improbably unconventional painters flirted with her. She went with Peter to pubs where they mixed with surrealist poets and French modernists. Peter, in the innocence of her enthusiasm, rode through all her encounters with a guileless brio. But in Elizabeth there were more forbidden cravings.

It amused her to think of Thomas in his decorous office guarding the empire with pen and paper while she smoked in pubs with unknown young men who cared only for their own risqué self-expression.

She began to enjoy her own incongruity. Mrs. Ashton in Mayfair, groomed and genteel, but slumming now in these pubs. She swayed as she walked, knowing that her skin was glowing and her hair abundant.

What did she want? To be desired and pursued. To challenge her fate.

Something must happen.

In the evenings, after the gallery had closed, she began to haunt the pubs of Soho. Furtively at first, keeping herself apart, but gradually daring to engage with men who wanted to experiment with women.

In the French pub, a man brought her a whisky which she did not like but sipped anyway.

"My name is Luc," he said, and the crowd pushed them close together. It was hard to see the whole of him: he came to her in glimpses—face, forearm, flexed knee.

He was a painter, young, dark, badly shaven. His fingers were stained with nicotine, his shoes worn and tatty. He fixed his large bold eyes on Elizabeth as he told her, in broken English, about his escape from Belgium into the refreshing amorality of London. The pub was throbbing with smokers and drinkers, all gesticulating wildly in the cramped, noisy space. Luc was absurdly youthful—but attractive, too.

"Here I can paint what I see in my head, because it is clear to me. In Brussels all I had was boredom—and anger—and my mother's black dresses. And lace. There is too much lace in Belgium."

Elizabeth drew on her ivory cigarette holder and laughed, and felt the thrill of being with someone so young and cocky, who had no knowledge that she was Elizabeth Ashton, of Ashton Park. She locked eyes with him. His eyes were blue, could pass for Ashton eyes.

Later, she found herself in a Soho backstreet, mounting the stairs behind Luc's stocky thighs. In his narrow room stood an iron bedstead with gray sheets. By the light of a bare bulb they took off their clothes, Elizabeth's nipples erect, her womb crying out for a child. She let him grapple her like an animal, his legs robust and his thick erection protruding from crinkly black hair. In a rapture of procreation she rolled on Luc's unmade bed and cried out as she felt his hot rush inside her. Then she lay back to halt the ooze down her thighs, and luxuriated in the thought of her child forming within.

But still no child came. At the end of the month her womb washed itself out with blood, as usual.

In the months that followed, there was Roberto, and Julius, and Stefan, and Billy, and even a discreet guards officer, Henry, who had always pursued her when she was a debutante. But generally she preferred encounters with strangers in unknown rooms, where afterwards she could look out and see an unfamiliar piece of London sky. Sometimes at night, sometimes during an extended lunch break. Peter Norton never asked where she had been when she reappeared, immaculate as ever, in the late afternoon.

Yet in her bedroom at home, the misery of infertility still persisted. Thomas continued to fear that the fault lay with him, that his polio had made him sterile. But Elizabeth began to realize now that it was probably she who was truly barren.

Was it a punishment, she wondered, for her faithlessness, for her secret abandonment of her disabled husband? Was she cursed? She lived month by month. Her hope was erratic. Her happiness depended on the time of the month.

Thomas had learnt not to watch her moods too closely, but was relieved when she returned from London in such high spirits. He could not know that her buoyancy was founded on the hope, however slight, that her latest tryst in Soho might yet prove successful.

21

ANNA NOTICED A new arrival at Ashton. A Pole, or so Mrs. Robson told them. A dark-haired, heavy-browed man called Pawel, who sometimes sat at the Ashtons' lunch table. He did not say very much. Anna heard from Miss Weir that he had fought the Nazis before escaping from Poland, "but he'll be up and about and teaching you soon, once the Yorkshire air revives him."

The children whispered about him with awe. A man who had fought the Nazis! In England there was only the Phoney War, and nothing dramatic ever seemed to happen.

The Ashtons did not meet Pawel Bielinski properly until he joined them for dinner on his first weekend at the house. Chance had brought him to Ashton Park. In the aftermath of Poland's disastrous defeat, he had been rescued by Peter Norton from one of the Polish refugee camps in Romania. And on their return to London, Peter had sent him to Ashton to recuperate.

"He's an artist," she told Elizabeth on the telephone, "so he can teach art."

The young man whom Thomas saw across his dinner table was thin, distant and numbed. He was clearly exhausted too, for he had hardly emerged from his room since his arrival. His hollow-eyed absence reminded Thomas of those wounded veterans he had watched with his sister, when their house was a hospital in the Great War.

He wondered if Pawel had taken life on the front, but it was too early to ask him what had happened out there. He steered their conversation towards more neutral territory.

"Don't be too daunted by these wet days," he said to Pawel, "it always rains here in November, but December is often surprisingly dry."

"Oh, darling, it rained all Christmas last year . . . ," countered Elizabeth.

"*Usually* it's dry for Christmas here."

"In Warsaw, the snow is thick by now," Pawel contributed.

He spoke reasonable English, but appeared happier when silent.

Elizabeth did not yet make much effort to engage with their new guest, but she did watch him discreetly. Noting his erect posture and broad, careful hands. And his dark eyes. He reminded her of those supple, unshaven artists who had thronged the London Gallery before the war. But she feigned indifference.

Neither Thomas nor Elizabeth made much impression on Pawel that first night. For the moment, he was relieved if he could simply answer the questions of this grand English couple who had so unexpectedly given him a new home.

When the coffee arrived, Thomas asked him gently about his friendship with the Nortons.

"Peter has spoken of you with such warmth. How did you meet her?"

"She came to my exhibition in Warsaw last year, and bought some of my paintings. How lucky I was that she came," he said with his first smile, and then tentatively began to volunteer pieces of his past to them. How he had grown up in a small town, Sulejów, but had always dreamt of moving to Warsaw, a proper city throbbing with artists and musicians.

"And did you always paint?" asked Elizabeth, intrigued by anyone with a vocation.

"I was lucky enough to get into the art school in Warsaw," he said with a shrug.

As he gave this bald account of himself, he could barely recognize the person he was describing, shorn of emotional detail. He did not bother to tell them that his widowed mother had longed for him to be a doctor instead, nor that it had been no easy feat for a Jew to be accepted into a good art school.

"By 1938, I had painted enough canvases to put on a small exhibition. Lady Norton came to the gallery—she had recently arrived at the British embassy."

She was distinctive, so he had noticed her at once—her quicksilver face, her faintly disheveled short hair and awkward long limbs. She had praised the quick light of his paintings, which was just what he wanted to hear. His metaphoric scenes reminded her of Paul Nash, she said. All those defiant land-scapes and mountains of the mind.

"She bought three pictures, on the spot," Pawel said, smiling faintly. "Sometimes I dined with the Nortons at the embassy, and afterwards I was lucky enough to see her art collection: paintings by Paul Klee, Léger, Kandinsky. That was an educa-tion. She is a free spirit—"

"And always an enthusiast," added Thomas.

"Yes," said Pawel emphatically.

"How did she help you escape?" Elizabeth asked.

"I was with a troop in eastern Poland when the news came through that the Russians had invaded. Soviet soldiers arrived to round us up, but it was chaotic and many of us slipped away, crossing the river into Romania, where we were put into refu-gee camps. It was there that Lady Norton found me."

He had heard that there was to be a shipment of aid arriving from Britain, razor blades, soap, cigarettes, medical supplies, food. He went to wait for the lorries. He could hardly believe it when the door of the Ford lorry opened and down stepped a familiar figure—angular, bracing.

"*Lady Norton!*" he called out.

He saw that it took her a moment to recognize him, then joy flashed across her face.

"We must get you out of here," she said, embracing him. "Come and help me unload, and you can return home with me."

After her own escape from Poland, she had raised funds in London for the Polish refugee camps, and then volunteered to drive out the provisions herself.

They visited three more camps, with Pawel acting as her assistant. Then he accompanied her in the lorry back to Italy, where, after much string-pulling and waving of arms on her part, a British consul stamped a visa for him.

They drove back through a subdued France, closing down for war. Pawel slept much of the way, and Peter did not pester him with too many questions about recent events. As soon as they reached London, she brought him home to Chelsea to recover, hatching a plan for him to join the evacuees' school at Ashton.

"You'll need plenty of time here to recuperate, so please— take your time before you start to teach," said Elizabeth, turning to him.

"Thank you—thank you for everything," said Pawel, rising from his chair. Bidding good night to his hosts, he was struck in passing by a wary, searching quality in Mrs. Ashton's face.

He returned to his room, relieved to be released from company. He had not touched alcohol for several months, and the wine from dinner was still slipping through his veins as he undressed. He turned off the bedside lamp and lay down in the darkness, hoping for a dreamless sleep as he closed his eyes.

22

———•———

I T WAS A week before Pawel surfaced for long enough to explore Ashton Park. Until then, it had appeared to him as a series of distanced impressions, as if through thickened glass.

He began to watch the children playing in the grounds. Pretty children, with smiling faces and crooked teeth, thin and fair, different in looks to the children in Poland. He met the other teachers and matrons too, though it was some time before any of them entered his thoughts.

But he did feel some curiosity about the Ashtons' marriage. And soon, this curiosity had crystallized into pity for the wife. Thomas Ashton was a handsome man, it was true, but he seemed a desiccated character—formal, correct and closed. Elizabeth Ashton, on the other hand, was sensuous: she swayed a little as she walked, and her every gesture suggested a caged need. Had she married him as a cripple, or as an able-bodied man?

The other teachers seemed either not to know or not to want to talk about the Ashtons. In the end it was Joan, a housemaid who had been at the house for years, who recounted the story of Thomas's illness. Pawel was moved by their ill luck and could not help but wonder about their life together.

Could Thomas still make love to his wife?

Elizabeth, meanwhile, had felt Pawel's heat from his first day. The young Pole was oblivious to niceties of class and she felt that he had looked at her right from the start as a woman, without deference. She divined immediately that he was a man who was drawn to women. Might it be her he came to?

She delayed her attentions to him out of pride, but soon

she could not resist being charming to him. Since he was a protégé of the Nortons, and a foreigner, she was able to forgo that English reserve which kept her at a remove from the other teachers. And Pawel was their guest. He was soon established as Elizabeth's particular favorite, the teacher she talked to at lunch.

Thomas's instincts were more wary. From the start, he sensed that Pawel was a man without ties, made reckless by his unformed future. He had passed through war and emerged disconnected, and might pursue any sensation right to its conclusion, just to feel alive. Thomas found himself wondering how to avert any emotional collisions. He was reluctant ever to block his wife's needs. But he knew she was a woman in a delicate balance, and he did not want to see her hurt.

He was surprised to feel a prickle of jealousy, too. He noted that they did not yet look at each other's eyes—in his presence, at least. But he could feel the desire running from Elizabeth like an electrical current.

Above all, Thomas was determined to remain calm and give off no hint of his intuitions. He continued to engage the young man in conversation, using the German he had learnt during his years in Berlin. Pawel was more comfortable in that language. It gave the two men a bond which was denied to Elizabeth.

"How long would you like to stay with us, do you think?"

"Until the Polish forces have regrouped here—but that will take some months. I am grateful for the place you have given me here."

"The children will enjoy having a proper artist to teach them. Do you have all the things you need?"

"Mrs. Ashton has been very kind about finding everything."

Indeed she had. She had taken Pawel off to York herself, to a shop which had a dwindling stock of paper, paints and brushes. There, she had impressed Pawel with an extravagant purchase of art materials before taking him out to lunch.

She had chosen a restaurant where she could sit opposite

him, to be sure that they had to look at each other. As they talked, she studied his face, a decisive face, with dark eyes and brows. He was unflinching in his gaze, challenging almost.

"Will you be able to settle in England?"

"If any place in Europe is to remain free, it will be England."

"That hardly answers my question."

"I have not met many people yet, but I like the landscape. Gray-green."

Their conversation lurked far below the words they spoke. Pawel kept his distance, still unsure of his hold on this new life. But he was intrigued by Elizabeth: their flirtation was something definite upon which to hang his thoughts.

He liked the crisp containment of her body inside her clothes. There was a promise of hidden fullness beneath her blouse; he was curious to unbutton it, and see her face as he did so. He sensed that she would drop her cool stare and look grateful and vulnerable.

Their tentative intimacy moved cautiously. Both were bound by a thread of unspoken assurance that they might be lovers soon. But it was a matter of how to let their attraction thrive within the boundaries of Elizabeth's life—because Pawel found himself unexpectedly respectful of Thomas. He began to be unnerved by the older man's gentle courtesy, and his sympathy for Pawel's recent ordeals. After dinner one night, they drank Madeira together in the library.

"Is it a success for you, the evacuee school here?"

"Very much so. The house is so much more alive now, and I have never seen my wife so happy."

"Was it her idea, to make a home for these children?"

"Yes, all hers. Elizabeth has a great deal of . . . vitality."

Thomas wheeled himself over to close a gap in the curtains, then offered the young man more Madeira.

"Are you . . . alone, or do you have family to worry about in Poland?"

The question lit a flare in Pawel's mind; he saw the fire at Sulejów, which he had reached too late. The memory was indelible—that lurid scarlet glow flooding the night sky, and his sickening certainty that Sulejów was in flames as he walked over the fields to find his mother. He ran to her house, but the entire street was gutted, a series of craters and shells. Had even his mother's soul survived?

"No. No family. They are gone."

"I'm sorry," said Thomas in a low voice, not wanting to press him.

Unexpectedly, Pawel turned to him.

"I was in a troop on the border with Czechoslovakia. Our division was splintered by the invasion, and we had to make our own way eastwards. We passed through my hometown, but there had been a massacre. Sulejów was packed with Jews, and Nazi Stukas had dive-bombed the town. The wooden houses lit up like matches. When people tried to run to the woods, the planes swooped low and razed them. My family amongst them."

Thomas hesitated.

"There's nothing I can say which will help, but I'm so sorry."

"Thank you."

For a moment, the two men looked at each other.

"You will have to be careful not to close yourself off, Pawel. It is easy to do. But you shouldn't rush into any new attachments either. You must take care of yourself."

Pawel was shaken by Thomas's words, knowing that they were spoken unselfishly.

He took up his advice and resisted Elizabeth's next summons into town on some spurious mission. He watched her carefully, but held himself back because, just as Thomas had warned, he was wary of breaking himself open to any new feeling yet. And he could see her haste, her wish to throw herself towards him, every time she met his glance.

Instead he spent many hours watching the evacuees in the

gardens; he had forgotten how contentedly children could play together. Boys threw balls against the outside walls for hours on end, while in the Marble Hall there was always the *toc-toc-toc* of badminton shuttlecocks.

He began to work out his own teaching style, starting with sketches of trees in all seasons. He showed the children how to draw branches sprouting out of a tree trunk. Then they colored them in with an autumn cascade of falling leaves, or the blossoms of spring, or the full green glory of the summer. Even the bare branches of winter had their grace. Practically every child produced pictures of a sort, and Pawel mounted an art-room exhibition called Ashton Park Trees.

Ashton was thriving with life now, as Elizabeth organized the school with surprising efficiency. The Nortons came up for a weekend, and both were startled to see the house so transformed by children. They were relieved to find Elizabeth apparently sober and content, and delighted by Thomas's new role as a teacher.

The Nortons were there too briefly to pick up any nuance of Pawel's role in Elizabeth's rejuvenation. But Peter did rekindle her protégé's self-belief with her lavish compliments about his talent, which had all but leaked away through so many disruptions. He began to paint for himself once again, which somehow made him feel more able to meet with Elizabeth on equal terms.

Hope had begun to take root in him once more. He was growing fond of the children, and his natural happiness was welling up again. In a few months, he would rejoin the war effort—but for now, he would enjoy his work here with these evacuees.

Yet he also wanted to find someone to love.

There was a tree in the woods with a great swinging branch, and one crisp February afternoon Pawel was bouncing the branch up and down for a pair of robust boys. Elizabeth was out walking and joined them. Pawel felt her pleasure in seeing him entertain the boys, who soon ran off chasing each other.

"Can I give you a ride?" offered Pawel with mock gallantry as she stepped towards the tree. Playfully, she sat down and he eased the branch to and fro, but then he surprised her by rocking it much harder, with a pirate's glint of menace.

"Enough," she said, laughing, and he stopped.

There was a pause. Neither knew what to say.

"You enjoy the children, don't you, Pawel?"

"Of course."

"They like you, I can see that."

"A place like this needs children," he said automatically.

The pain on her face sliced through him.

"I mean—with this war on, there could hardly be a better place for them to be."

"Yes," she said. "I'm glad that we have the evacuees here," she went on, recovering her composure, "because Thomas and I can't have children of our own."

Pawel did not know how to answer this remark, so he took it as lightly as he could, and continued to swing the branch, very gently now.

"What good fortune that children have found their way here anyway."

"Yes," she replied, stepping away from the branch.

As they walked back to the house, no more was said. She averted her eyes as they parted on the stone steps.

Pawel felt shaken as he left her: the intimacy of her revelation had touched him to the quick. He went away surmising that Thomas must be impotent. He continued to walk round the lawns, thinking of Elizabeth and her wounded eyes, wondering if the discomfort between them could ever be cured by an embrace.

Elizabeth walked indoors, back to her bedroom, to be alone. Her conversation with Pawel had rattled her, and she had to un-pick exactly what had thrown her so much. She worried that the mention of her childlessness had been too intimate. But more, there was a further anxiety that she had cheated. *Thomas and I can't have children of our own,* she had said, knowing what Pawel would assume. While she knew by now from her failed Soho trysts that the problem lay with her.

It was something she tried to keep private, but she was still locked inside her own personal ordeal: her inconsolable long-ing for a child. Whenever she went for a walk, she could feel the shape of her womb inside her—its readiness and emptiness. She could even sense her ovaries ripening—and yet she was blighted with infertility. This desert inside was something she could not yet accept.

She longed for that flicker of life within, that inward spark which could reconnect her to the world outside. Just a light kick inside, and all could be well. She felt her barrenness acutely, as if it was severing her from anything that was alive and flourish-ing. Flowers and fruit, or any metaphors of female beauty, blos-soming, blooming, budding to ripeness—all these were lost to her. All she could see were withering roses and leafless trees. A stone-dead world.

She picked up a batch of letters from her desk and decided to post them in the village. She put on her coat against the win-ter chill, and set off alone, past the sodden leaves still festering in piles on the drive. Everything reminded her of her wasted womb. Leaves in a puddle. Or old conker shells crushed on the road by passing cars. Even just bad weather.

By the time she returned home through the park lawns, there was a band of evacuees playing there. In the last of the afternoon light, they appeared to her like angels from another world, entirely outside her reach. It seemed to her that there was no such thing as an ugly child: they were all blessed with clear faces and clear spirits. She stood there as if trapped inside her own prison, cut off, watching three small girls play chase through the box hedges of the herb garden. Their bright faces. Their fresh limbs and pure skin. Their guileless smiles, and the sure way they reached out their hands to each other.

More than anything, she longed to hold a child's hand in hers. But her own child, who would look up into her face and say, *I love you, Mummy.*

She sensed by now that this was unlikely to happen; yet the longing for it still would not let her go.

None of this could she, would she, let anyone know, least of all Pawel, and so she had implied to him that her childlessness was Thomas's fault; more, that she had made a willing sacrifice by staying in a barren marriage.

She did not feel comfortable with her falsehood. But she wanted to present herself to Pawel as a woman without problems.

23

A T ASHTON PARK, Pawel read the newspapers assiduously every day, to improve his English. Week by week, he followed the war's dismal progress as the Germans blasted their way through Europe, forcing thousands of British troops to flee from Dunkirk. Soon after, Hitler was photographed in gleeful pose by the Arc de Triomphe.

But Ashton remained serenely detached from the war. Pawel continued to teach his art classes in this placid English country house. For the younger children, he drew farmyards with pigs and chickens and a black cat sitting by a weather vane. It was a peaceful place, this crayon farmyard, a small quiet world untouched by war or hate. He liked rescuing the children into these pictures.

One morning Elizabeth visited one of his lessons. She watched Pawel's concentration, and the way he held his torso straight even as he drew his pencil over the paper for the children. He looked up.

"I came to see your class," she said, as casually as she could. Pawel smiled. He was glad she had come.

"Will you look at our pictures?"

He showed her round the tables, praising the children's work. One girl had colored every brick of her farm in a different shade. Together they admired the harmony of the colors.

Elizabeth's face glowed with pleasure, as it always did in Pawel's presence. All her previous lovers had been strangers, and that was the way she had wanted it, but this attraction was something new and different. Pawel had lived in her home for some time now, she worked with him and ate with him. He even had the respect of her husband.

She felt that they had been circling each other for weeks. The first tentative glances between them, his first touch of her arm in passing—all these moments had reached right through to her. She craved some recognition of their private bond.

"Is there anything else you need?" she asked.

"We don't have any yellow paint," said Anna Sands, looking up.

"No yellow paint," concurred Pawel, with a smile.

"Then we must get you some," said Elizabeth.

So a fresh trip to York was fixed, with another visit to the art shop. And afterwards, they once again sat face-to-face at a secluded restaurant table. Her eyes were so engaged, and her concern so transparent, that this time Pawel found himself confiding in her and discharging at last the burden of his recent past.

He told her about the horror of finding his mother's charred house at Sulejów. But more, he conjured for her the chaos of the Nazi invasion—when the panzers had broken through their defenses so swiftly that thousands of Polish soldiers had been left scattered along the border front, cut off from the retreating army.

"Transport was so scarce that hundreds of soldiers had to walk eastwards through Poland, just to find the regrouping army," he told her. "I was lucky to get a horse and cart at Sulejów, but when I reached the main road from Warsaw to Lublin, it was like a biblical exodus. The road was crammed with soldiers and refugees—all you could see was a stream of cars, lorries, horses, carts, prams, bicycles, donkeys. The sun was glaring and there was dust all around us. The German planes were so frequent that we all felt as though we were being watched from above— like ants under a raised boot.

"I helped a woman and her three children onto my cart. Her

name was Monika; she had round eyes and clung to her baby. Whenever Stukas buzzed over, we all ran for the side of the road. The bombs were a terror, but the machine-gun fire was more deadly—a chilling sound, I can still hear it.

"As we were reaching Lublin, three more planes appeared. Monika's older children moved quickly, but they were struck down with gunfire. The boy went down silently, at once. The girl wailed, a hopeless cry—"

Elizabeth watched him pinch his nose with his thumb and forefinger, closing his eyes.

"I had never seen anything like that woman's anguish; she howled over their bodies. I felt ashamed to be alive. I can still see the purple veins straining on her forehead." He paused again, glancing at Elizabeth.

"I did what I could. I helped the mother to bury her children, then she begged me to move on. So I did as she asked, leaving her with her baby and the cart."

Elizabeth tried to meet his eyes.

"Did you ever find a new troop to join?" she asked him.

"At Lublin," he said, nodding. "I heard that there were soldiers at the station, so I went there, and found at last some reservists, heading south to join General Sosnowski's army. When our train set off there was no room to sit, so we all stood pressed up against each other.

"We were attacked several times on the way to Lvov. Whenever a plane buzzed in the distance, the train stopped and we dived out of the carriages to find cover.

"I've never known such raw fear as I felt then—running over open ground, with planes above, waiting for bullets to rip through me. Each time, a few soldiers did not come back to the train—it was random, which of us escaped."

He looked away as he spoke.

"The rest you know. By the time we reached Lvov, the town was surrounded and we had to surrender to the Russians. I escaped over the border to Romania, and ended up in a refugee camp outside Bucharest. And there I remained until Peter Norton arrived in her lorry."

He was still evading Elizabeth's eyes.

"Pawel," she said, reaching out her hand. "It is a blessing that you survived . . . ," she added in a low voice, and for the first time they looked at each other frankly.

24

ELIZABETH AND PAWEL soon made another visit to York. But this time they spent the afternoon alone together in the Royal Station Hotel. Elizabeth gave Pawel money to pay for the room in advance, and then slipped upstairs by herself, careful not to be seen.

She had been brooding over Pawel's shape for weeks, wondering how the hair grew on his chest, his legs, his arms. When he removed his clothes she was amazed by the fact of his body.

They did not hide beneath cold starched sheets but looked at each other. The frankness of her desire moved Pawel; there was nothing stilted or shy in her response to him. Never before had he known such unguarded intimacy.

Afterwards, he held her in his arms, and was touched by her vulnerability. They drifted into sleep together—waking only just in time to return to Ashton for dinner.

"Would you care to try our mint sauce, Pawel? Mint, vinegar and sugar, an English speciality . . ."

Thomas's manners that night were, as always, gentle and unforced as he carved the roast lamb from the estate—a rare treat. *Can I do this?* thought Pawel. *Is this man encouraging me into the arms of his wife for some private game, or is he ignorant of our glances?*

In the months which followed, a strange triangle of complicity came into play between Pawel and the Ashtons—and all within a house dominated by the complicated timetable of schoolchildren. There was never a time without bells ringing for lessons, comings and goings in corridors, and crocodiles of children filing into the dining room. Pawel relished this constant traffic of people passing through their lives, between them, past them, obscuring their affair.

Unexpectedly, Elizabeth's relationship with her husband began to flourish. Now that she was content with another man, she liked to stroke Thomas's arm as she passed him, and show him affection in public. Such signs of marital intimacy only fired Pawel further.

Their joyous, reckless communion continued for many weeks, and Pawel's urgency was like a drug to Elizabeth. Every day, she just wanted to be with him, to lay her head on his chest and stroke his face. To adore him and care for him. To start again—she was only thirty-four. She even dared to dream that if she threw off the shackles of Ashton Park, she might conceive Pawel's child.

Yet as she grew more confident with her lover, something began to leak away. Subtly, unacknowledged at first, a canker crept in, an inequality of desire on the part of Pawel.

It happened gradually, this crack of disconnection. Was it the wild devotion in Elizabeth's face which first distanced him? He began to see her again from the outside, and there was a glint of extremity in her eyes which troubled him.

One night, Thomas was playing the piano inside, his beloved Schubert, and the music flowed through the open French windows to the colonnade. It was after dinner, and Elizabeth was a little drunk.

"Dance with me," she said to Pawel, but he was reluctant. She walked over to Thomas.

"The man won't dance with me if you play that music. Please play something else—for us."

Thomas looked up with steady eyes and even as he watched them his fingers changed the tune from Schubert to Jerome Kern.

Elizabeth laughed. Thomas and Pawel looked at each other

for a moment. Then Elizabeth swept towards the young man and they danced together on the terrace.

> Oh, but you're lovely, with your smile so warm
> And your cheek so soft,
> There is nothing for me but to love you
> Just the way you look tonight . . .

At the end of the song Pawel walked away into the gardens. Elizabeth went after him.

"Don't go," she cried out too loud. "He'll play some more, it's fine."

"I don't want to dance," said Pawel.

"Please—"

"I said, I do not want to dance."

"Is it him? Is it him you're worried about? He doesn't mind."

Pawel turned to her with quiet ferocity.

"Please—leave me alone."

He backed away. She did not follow, but stood in the half-light of the garden, peering after him.

Thomas closed the piano lid, and discreetly wheeled himself to bed.

The next morning Elizabeth felt mortified by her behavior to both men. She was contrite towards Thomas, and sought out Pawel to ask his forgiveness. But it was too late.

Pawel now wanted to leave. He did not want to witness a disintegrating marriage. He had always meant to move on after recuperating, he reminded himself. Without telling Elizabeth, he made enquiries into joining a Polish air squadron stationed in Derby, to train as a pilot.

His departure followed within days. He said good-bye to the children and packed a kit bag with the few clothes which had been bought for him by the Nortons. He bid a courteous farewell to Thomas, who, if he was surprised at his decision, did not show it. Then he went to find Elizabeth, drawing her aside from a meeting with the kitchen staff.

"I have come to say good-bye, Elizabeth . . ."

The color drained from her face.

He was brisk and robust. He left her sitting on a chair in the corridor with a childlike look of puzzled grief on her face, the tears about to pour forth, but he did not wait for that. He was off, walking to the village and taking the first coach south.

It was cruel to be so abrupt, he knew, but he could not bear to listen to her pleas. He felt a stifled pang of guilt, nonetheless. For raising up her hope, then sluicing it away.

Elizabeth hid in her room, stunned. She experienced the parting as something physical, a brutal severance which seemed to slice at the very roots of her heart. She began to shake all over. Thomas found her tightly curled up on her bed, uttering low cries of pain.

She shook so much that she was overtaken by fever and had to lie in bed for three days, her sheets soaked with sweat. Thomas stayed with her and sponged her with water.

For some weeks Elizabeth floundered in a depression in which silence alternated with tantrums, rage and bitterness. Thomas was the only one allowed into the privacy of her grief, and he did what he could to comfort her. She talked about her lover as if Thomas had already guessed everything. Seeing that she was unwell, he never made any recriminations.

He did not know what he felt in the aftermath of his wife's infidelity.

25

ONE DAY, WHEN Elizabeth was still bedridden, Thomas noticed Ruth Weir walking through the gardens on her own. As he watched her from his study window, he was struck by her abstracted air—she often appeared to be inside her head. It occurred to him that he knew very little about this young teacher; he hoped she was not too isolated at Ashton. She was always polite in staff meetings, yet reserved, too; not easy to talk to.

He had gathered from Mr. Stewart that Ruth was a vicar's daughter recently graduated from Oxford, who had come to Ashton from his school in Pimlico. She was reticent but bright-eyed, with a pale face and sandy hair—not somebody you noticed immediately, Thomas reflected. It had surprised him to look at her at lunch one day, and see that she was pretty, with very fair skin and a touching smile.

Watching her now as she walked past the fountain, he found himself curious about her; she was tentative and guarded, yet paradoxically, there was something transparent about her, too.

Later that week, as Ruth wheeled him along the west-wing corridor after a lesson, he tried to engage her in polite chat.

"Have you found enough to occupy you here?"

"Well—I love walking."

"You must make sure to visit Rievaulx Abbey in this clear weather."

"I walked along the valley to it last weekend."

"It's a fine place, isn't it?"

"Yes," she said at once, "I don't think I've ever seen . . . such beauty."

She expressed this last sentiment with such intensity that Thomas at first wanted to laugh. But instead, for a moment, he opened himself to the sincerity of her response. She still had a fresh eye on the world.

They began to talk about the park—the contours of the valley, the sweep of the lawns—and he pointed out particular trees as they passed each window. By the time they reached his study, he felt a new affinity with Ruth.

Brief, insignificant conversations followed, in the staff room, or over lunch. Polite enquiries about the places of her childhood, questions about novels she was reading. The delicacy of their mutual formality made him smile.

He began to look forward to any occasion when she might wheel him from one classroom to another. He was even storing up things to say to her, knowing it was ridiculous.

"If you go to the lower woods next week, you'll see the bluebells coming out."

"They're already coming through," she told him, "the children showed me."

"I think you'll be amazed by their abundance this weekend."

"I've never seen a bluebell wood like that before, the colors are so vivid . . ."

There seemed to be little they could say to each other beyond these mutual moments of enthusiasm, but the nothing they said was measured out with unexpected feeling.

As spring opened up their days, he found himself moved by Ruth's way of seeing; subtly, she was reawakening a part of him, his unspoken delight in nature. He sensed her eye for the elusive grace of ordinary things, the wind through the trees, the light off the lake, the roll of the moors. He had forgotten, even, that this sensibility had ever mattered to him too. Perhaps it was simply her youth, but somehow she touched the springs of his old responses, true responses, which had been blocked off for too long.

He wanted to show her that his eyes were still keen, too. It became absurdly important, suddenly, to talk about the bark of a silver birch, or the shape of a horse chestnut tree in full bloom. He wanted her to share his pleasure in the sky's slow evening closure over the park plain.

One Thursday, he was expecting her to wheel him back to the house as usual, but she wasn't there.

"She's off sick," said Mrs. Robson, as she took him back to the house in Ruth's stead. For the first time Thomas had to admit to himself that not only was he shaken by Ruth's absence, but he felt extraordinarily fretful about her. It was only mild flu, and she was up and about again within three days.

"I'm so glad you're back with us," he said to her, when she reappeared in the staff room.

"It was only a feverish cold," she said, embarrassed by any fuss. But the look of concern in his eyes touched her.

Ruth went off to her morning lessons, glad to be teaching again. It was one of her younger classes; she resumed her reading of *Through the Looking Glass*—then took the children to the window, and pointed out the statues of the lion and the unicorn on either side of the gateposts.

"They escaped from the story and settled here at Ashton Park, but why?" she asked them, before setting their first writing task: *A Conversation Between the Lion and the Unicorn at Ashton Park*. The children settled down with their pencils and exercise books.

Ruth had felt nervous when she first arrived at Ashton Park, with its wartime jumble of a school. The children had come there haphazardly from different parts of London, and the classes were unevenly populated according to age. But she had organized a slightly eccentric curriculum to suit their needs. With the older children, she was reading *The Tempest* and "The

Charge of the Light Brigade." For the younger ones, she had chosen the fairy tales of Oscar Wilde.

Teaching made her happy; she was content at Ashton because she knew she was doing something worthwhile. Yet she lacked friendship. After lessons, as she walked up the many stairs to her bedroom, she wondered if this place wasn't making her too introspective, perhaps because there was nobody for her to confide in. She drew solace from her small neat bedroom on the top floor, just wide enough to hold her clothes and books and a chest of drawers—but she worried whether she was retreating there too readily.

Her arrival at this vast, unknown house had been so unexpected, the war abruptly removing her from her tentative social life in London. In some ways she was relieved not to have to brace herself for possible relationships quite yet; she felt safe here, as if she could postpone her future a little longer.

And yet something about her spartan new life was making her dig up hidden feelings. Perhaps it was because she was lonely—or perhaps this place was only making her realize that she was too solitary by inclination.

She had always doubted her ability to find love, though she could not say why. At London parties, she had observed how the men responded to self-possessed women, but she did not know how to become one of them. She would have liked to carry herself sensuously, with painted nails, and bold cosmetics, but lacked the self-confidence to attempt any sophistication. She was low-key, invisible even—a legacy, perhaps, from her emotionally withdrawn childhood.

Hers had been a stiff upbringing, the relationship with her parents formal and semidetached. There were scholarships for vicars' daughters at a local preparatory school, and so she had been sent away at eight, to receive the ambiguous privilege of a boarding-school education. There she suffered dire homesickness, compounded by a daily guilt that she was not grateful enough for the education which she knew had been given to her at some cost.

She could still remember her first trip home from school, the stilted embrace with her mother, her shyness with her father. Before, they had seemed a part of her, but suddenly she could see them only from the outside, detached from her. She had learnt to collude with her parents' distance by being polite and cheerful, but her wounds were hidden inside. At boarding school, the letters from home were erratic and there were various birthdays on which no card arrived.

Cut off from parental affection, her sense of physical proximity had grown achingly heightened. If anyone so much as held her arm, or put a hand on her shoulder, a frisson raced through her and froze her. At Oxford, she had been dazzled by the lecture halls packed with so many young men, but her shyness had held her back; much of her time she had spent alone in her room at Somerville, reading poetry, pacing up and down her study in a palpitation of excitement about a new book.

Later, when she became a teacher, she realized that it was only with children that she felt relaxed, and open, and naturally affectionate. She was a spontaneous mentor, responsive and patient. Her own understanding of loneliness had made her especially sensitive to those in her care.

But alongside her teaching, something entirely new was happening to her at Ashton. She had met Thomas. This is what she called him in her mind. For many weeks now, every meeting between them had been polite and friendly, and no more—yet for the first time in her life she felt close to someone, even though any intimacy was unacknowledged between them.

It was as if she could read his mind. And it was unlike any other feeling she had ever known before, this sense of unspoken connection. But was there really something flowing between them, as she sometimes thought, or was it all just her imagination?

26

RUTH HAD JUST finished reading *The Selfish Giant* to her class. Anna's heart was still thrumming with pleasure at the story—the boy reaching out his hand, the giant's melting heart, the frozen garden coming to life. Already, it was her favorite book.

"Please can we have another story?" she asked, raising her hand.

"Not today," said Ruth, smiling. "Another time," she promised.

Anna had been used to very basic teaching in her Fulham school: the drilling of math and grammar, and wall charts with the royal milestones of British history. But here at Ashton, the lessons were so much more interesting.

It must be the teachers, she told herself as she ran towards the dining room for tea. There was a familiar quickening of her heart as she passed by the study of Mr. Ashton, her favorite teacher. Something in his eyes always drew her in.

Whenever he taught them Latin or history, he conjured up glorious pictures of the past for them, all based on his own house. Only last week he had sent them off to visit the two Greek temples in the park, and for Anna it was as if an air of Arcadia swept through their pillars. Indoors, he took them to the Marble Hall and showed them Apollo playing his harp among the dome's painted clouds, while Cupid shot his arrows above the fireplace and fierce griffins guarded the mantelpieces.

Intrigued by so many details, Anna was feeling the strange

pull of Ashton's past. She sensed that everything had been done for someone else, the gilded cornices in the ceiling, the paneling, the great carved fireplaces. It was as if she was only eavesdropping on another time and place. The books in the library, the clocks in the saloon, the kneelers in the chapel—all, all belonged to somebody else's life. She knew she was only a chance visitor there.

But this did not stop her from secretly carving her initials on odd corners of skirting boards, under the washstand, inside her desk. She wanted to be part of this place. To join its history.

It was during her first summer at Ashton that Anna began to feel that this house was now her home. Every day the park pulled them outside. There were boating trips on the lake, and picnics by the river. Some of the children tried fishing in the cascade pool. They began by borrowing a length of muslin from the kitchens, but when Thomas heard about it, he arranged for a batch of fishing rods to be bought. Soon after, he organized cricket bats for the boys and rounders bats for the girls, and all summer long they played ball games on the great sunken lawn, under the crumbling gaze of Father Time.

13 June 1940

Dear Mummy,
It is sunny here now and we sometimes have lessons in the gardens. On Wednesdays we have my best class, when we make up our own poems . . .

Throughout the summer of 1940, Thomas and Ruth met properly at least once a week, when they gave an optional poetry class after tea. It had begun as an impromptu class of Ruth's, but one day Thomas had asked if he could attend it too: thereafter, he joined them every week.

There was a group of some twelve children who came, mostly girls, but a few boys too. It was informal, on the grass. Ruth and he would each read out a poem, then the children would put up their hands to give a response. Everyone was encouraged to write their own poems too—on animals, or home, or their parents, or food, which Ruth returned to them the following week.

To My Mother

Time won't last forever,
Neither will my life with you,
So let us be happy together
Or as close as we can.

That was Anna's first poem. Thomas was moved that this came from a child who had not seen her mother for nearly a year, just one of the many stray casualties of war. It relieved him that the children could find this outlet for their feelings—knowing all the while that it was his own needs, too, that had led him to join them.

Every Wednesday that summer, Thomas waited for Ruth to fetch him from the house. There was an unavoidable proximity between them as she wheeled him down the ramp into the garden, and along the chalk path to the Open Temple, where the children were waiting in a grassy clearing.

The journey took a little under ten minutes, but the time was freighted with unstated intimacy. He tried to talk casually, but sometimes he would turn round to face her, out of politeness, and their eyes would meet for a moment. There was that slight pressure of her hands and arms as she pushed him up a small hill, but all the while they talked of the children's progress, or the weather, or the news from the front.

"I dread the deaths of our children's parents—"

"But perhaps the air raids will touch fewer families than we think?"

"I fear that soon we will all know someone who has died in this war."

They could talk of mortality in the general way of wartime, but Thomas was still wary of attempting any more personal conversation.

Yet with time their tentative intimacy began to find its way through the conduit of teaching. Ruth took simple verses, and uncovered their secrets for the children. As a teacher, she shone. Thomas watched and listened as her appreciation of ordinary things—more, her sacred sense of life—flowed through her teaching.

> *The Sun's rim dips; the stars rush out:*
> *At one stride comes the dark . . .*

She taught them "The Rime of the Ancient Mariner," and conjured up Coleridge's great pictures of a solitary man on the sea of life, besieged by the elements. Thomas, meanwhile, introduced them to the strange word-music of Gerard Manley Hopkins, with his tongue-twisting rhythms.

> *As kingfishers catch fire, dragonflies draw flame;*
> *As tumbled over rim in roundy wells*
> *Stones ring; like each tucked string tells, each hung bell's*
> *Bow swung finds tongue to fling out broad its name . . .*

Anna was enthralled—for the first time, she saw and breathed and tasted the world in words. In the years to come, she would remember odd lines and images, and even a sense of that particular afternoon light—supple, fluent, benign on them all.

After the lesson's end, Ruth would wheel Thomas back to the house, sometimes with the children alongside. The subtle pressure of her hands against his shoulders was met, she almost fancied, with an answering pressure from him—but both of them feared it was nothing more than their own imagination.

Would Thomas ever dare to cross the line? At the end of each journey, there was the fleeting meeting of eyes, the gallant thanks from Thomas, the shy acceptance from Ruth, nothing more. *What could this girl see in me?* thought Thomas. *What could this married man, with a beautiful wife, see in me?* thought Ruth. But at night, each of them lay awake to think about the other.

27

ANNA WAS PLAYING jacks on the long sideboard by the pantry—an intense, repetitive game with a small rubber ball.

"Here, pet, can you carry this tea tray out to Mr. Ashton?" Mrs. Robson was there at her elbow with her apron slightly askew, harried by too many tasks. "You'll find him somewhere near the garden doors."

It was a warm afternoon, still and blue, and Anna willingly carried the tea outside, gingerly. There was Mr. Ashton, sitting at the edge of the rose garden with a pile of books on a table. Marking some schoolwork in the sunshine.

"I've brought you some tea, sir, from Mrs. Robson."

"Thank you, Anna."

He smiled at her—an encouraging smile. Anna set the tray down, politely waiting to help, and so he let her pour his tea— "one spoon of sugar, please"—and she passed him the cup.

"What's that, sir?" Anna asked, pointing to the stone column in the center of the garden.

"It's a sundial," he said, and saw her puzzled eyes. "Look at its face and you'll see the sun's shadows marking the time. It doesn't often work, but even in Yorkshire we sometimes have sunshine."

Anna stepped up on the stone pediment, and saw a shadow line falling from an iron blade in the center.

"Is it working?" asked Thomas.

"Yes," she said quickly, because she was hazy about actually telling the time.

"There was a water well there years ago, but it was closed up—too dangerous for children. Somebody put a sundial there instead."

"Is there water under this garden?" she asked, surprised.

"Oh yes," he said, "all this land is limestone, full of hidden springs. I sometimes think I can hear the whisper of buried streams, but perhaps that's only because I know they're there."

Anna was suddenly enchanted by this glimpse of deep wells and secret springs, hidden just beneath them. And if he could sense them, perhaps she might too.

"Look, here's a ladybird," said Mr. Ashton, studying his finger.

"Isn't that lucky?"

"You should take it . . ."

Anna came over and watched the bright-red bug creeping over his hand. He held it up and passed it to her.

Anna had never noticed a man's hand before. There were black hairs on his knuckles where the ladybird crawled. The sight enthralled her, and scared her too, those long dark hairs which matched his eyebrows.

"The ladybird tickles," she said, looking up. As she did so, the ladybird flew away.

"Fly away home," said Thomas gently. Probably that was the child's wish too, he guessed. He looked at Anna. A sweet girl, he thought, so solemn-eyed, so serious about everything.

"Thank you for the tea, my dear. You can leave the tray with me now."

He watched her running off through the garden. *Children always run everywhere,* he thought as he sat back to enjoy his tea in the sunshine. The scent of roses sweetened the air and made him feel light-headed—until he realized, quite suddenly, that he was ridiculously happy. Because every day now, he could look forward to seeing Ruth again, in the blameless routine of school life. An unexpected blessing granted to him by this war.

28

ELIZABETH WAS DRINKING too much again, and every night the cellar was searched for more wine. When Clifford Norton came up for a weekend, he dared to mention to Thomas that perhaps his wife was too drunk too often.

Thomas rebuffed him lightly: he would not and could not acknowledge the black hole of his marriage to anyone. Norton backed off but sensed a change in his friend: a private serenity which he could not quite fathom. He went away assuming that Thomas's new contentment must come from his teaching role.

By now, Ruth had begun to enter Thomas's dreams, and he often awoke with her presence almost tangible in his mind. Sometimes he saw her as she was—walking, turning, smiling at him. At other times she appeared to him more obliquely. He would dream of Ashton's brimming lake, fringed with trees, breathing with that benign last light of the day. He would send pebbles skimming across the water's sheer surface, agitating its mirror-like calm with small ripples, until the pebbles found the center and plunged deep down into the lake's untroubled depths—whose level silence and peace he knew was Ruth.

On other nights, Thomas felt himself to be a loud waterfall, crashing over rocks before plunging into a still, deep pool which lay below and contained all the haste and flux of the falling water. And just as he found himself released into this quiet pool, it welled up into his sense of Ruth.

He clung to these waking dreams, which eased his limbs with a deep boon of sensual release. Then he awoke, and faced the strange dislocation of his actual life, split between his brittle and beautiful wife—who was as chilly and distant to him as a piece of decorative porcelain—and the slightly awkward young teacher with freckles on her nose, who was unable to meet his glance, or even stand at ease in the same room as him.

One might laugh at the situation. He did, sometimes, to himself. But as his was a devotion which was unlikely ever to be declared or resolved, he continued to indulge his thoughts of Ruth. He did not think that any harm could ever come from just thinking about someone in private.

29

THERE WERE MORNINGS when Anna woke up and could no longer remember what her mother looked like. Her face had become as elusive as a ghost, leaving behind only traces of an expression: a smile, a look in her eyes, fast receding into afterimage only. So she was thrilled when her mother wrote to say that she was at last coming to visit her.

In the summer of 1940, Roberta arrived in Yorkshire with her usual swoop of joy and laughter. Anna's happiness at seeing her mother was boundless. She reached out to hug her, and the pair swung along, mother and daughter, holding hands on their river-meadow walk.

Anna was so proud to show off Ashton Park to her mother: the river; the lake; the old palm house in the woods; the gilded saloon, which her mother admired so much; and the classrooms. Finally they climbed the stairs to her dormitory, where her mother sat on her bed to test the springs.

"Plenty of bounce," she announced, before checking the view. "And you can see the park from your window—"

"Pretty, isn't it?"

"It's *perfect.*"

Her mother knew just how to see a place. Pictures were noticed, and details of statues and clocks that Anna had never given much thought to; everything took on a new grace.

Roberta was given a small bedroom at Ashton for the weekend, and their first day together was one of undimmed pleasure. But by Sunday morning the ache of parting was already threatening Anna's happiness. Her elation at her mother's presence gave way to a ticking clock, counting the moments before she would lose her once more. She felt sick at the prospect. At tea, she was unable to swallow her bread, such was her dread of her mother's return home.

When Roberta gathered up her small bag and said good-bye, Anna crumpled into her arms. Deep sobs shook her skinny frame.

"Please don't go, Mummy, please don't, please don't go."

"Train travel is restricted now, sweetheart, so I can't get here often. But I'll come back again, I promise. When they give me some more leave from work. *Soon.*"

Anna was inconsolable. For twenty minutes Roberta tried to soothe her weeping daughter, while Mr. Stewart hovered nearby.

"It unsettles them, when they see their mothers," he murmured to Roberta. In the end, it was he who led Anna away, releasing Roberta to catch her bus to York station.

There, she resolved that she would not come back again too soon: her daughter was thriving, and this visit had only upset her.

It was a relief to see her so cheerful and well, she wrote to Lewis on the train. *We're lucky she's found her way to such a glorious house! Much better for her to be safe there, far away from German bombs.*

Or was that an excuse? Roberta felt a prick of guilt. As her train rolled south to London, she thought of her daughter crying herself to sleep in her dormitory, while she was off enjoying herself at the BBC, and not a plane in sight.

But it was not long after her visit that London was finally attacked by a wave of German bombers. The long-awaited Blitz began on the night of 7 September 1940—Roberta marked it on the kitchen calendar. At first the raids were far from her home, in the East End and the docks. But in the following weeks no part of the city was left unscarred by collapsed buildings or cratered streets.

Roberta made up her bed in the cellar, though it was hard to sleep through the wailing sirens and thundering night skies. Londoners slipped into a twilight life of fitful sleep, with waking dreams seeping through them, until they all felt disembodied by exhaustion. With all its lights switched off, London was transformed into a city of darkness. People stumbled through unlit streets, and nightlife was reconvened belowground. For the hedonistic, there were subterranean clubs and dance floors, open all hours. For the anxious, there were underground platforms packed with sheltering crowds.

With the arrival of dawn, the skies would be empty once more, revealing the destruction of the night before in all its charred strangeness. Fires from broken gas pipes persisted into the morning, with flames flaring a violet haze in the daylight—like lost souls leaking away into the sky, Roberta thought.

Meanwhile, everyone in Broadcasting House seemed more determined than ever to keep the show running. Roberta worked long hours, then relaxed with her friends in the pubs of Fitzrovia, before returning home in the dark and reluctantly finding her bed in the cellar, waiting for that night's dance of death.

She was glad now that Anna was not with her. She thought with pleasure of her daughter running around in that beautiful park.

30

ON THE EVENINGS when Elizabeth was senseless with drink, Thomas felt free to think about Ruth without any anxiety that his face might betray him. That night Elizabeth had passed out on their bed by ten o'clock. She would perhaps wake in the early hours and stumble into bed after undressing; or she would lie there as she was until morning.

Elizabeth did not want him to seek help for her. It was not that she was an alcoholic, she'd say: she merely resorted to drink a few times a week, only in the evenings, usually in the bedroom. Drunkenness enveloped her swiftly after a bottle of wine. If she added spirits, she would pass out. It was a secret ritual, behind closed doors, her dependence on alcoholic oblivion.

While she slept, Thomas sat still in their room, piecing together tranquil thoughts of his love for Ruth. When was the moment he had first known? Using Stendhal's metaphor, when had his love first "crystallized"? The feeling had crept up on him, it was not something he had pursued. At first he had only opened up a crack in himself—but still the tenderness had taken root, until that single moment came when he realized he was in love.

Looking back, Thomas believed this moment had struck on a rainy March day, when the teachers had gathered in the library. He could remember every beat of that afternoon. There was a confusion of chairs as they all assembled for the staff meeting. Thomas was placed next to his wife, and there, seated at a nearby table, was Ruth—casually placed in his line of vision. She did not say much, but sat very still and straight.

He watched her and wondered, with guilt, if she could read his mind. She never looked his way, nor did he expect her to, though he felt a strange pull between them—or was he just imagining that?

Obliquely, he gazed at the quiet grace of her face; an aura of light seemed to gather at the curve of her cheek, and he found himself transfixed.

Time stalled as the voices talked on; he did not want to leave that room, he wanted the meeting to go on forever with its soft drone, just so that he could remain there watching her.

How had he ever lived without such feelings, he wondered. Her hair, tucked behind her ears, had come loose on one side. And when she moved her hand, his heart rose—the thought of a caress from those fingers.

That was the day he had recognized Ruth for what she was: the first woman he had ever wanted to love. How could he not have known this at once? It had taken him weeks, months, to understand that her face, her soul, her actions, were everything that he had ever craved in a woman.

Yet that had been just the beginning. First there had been the joy of recognition, the secret elation of love, but dejection soon followed, as he faced the folly of his feelings.

He thought of other people, everyday people on streets, who met and courted, and knew that they loved each other, and married and procreated. Perhaps that was how it had seemed with him and Elizabeth, yet all the while it had been a pretense. And now—he felt for Ruth all the things a man should feel, but he was unable to say so. How could he blight the life of this young woman, when he had nothing to offer her? And yet he could not stop himself thinking of her, and hoping for her, and longing to hold her in his arms.

Elizabeth stirred on their bed, and Thomas watched her with dispassionate eyes. He was sorry for her, and felt culpable too. But it was distant pity, long since sieved away from his own griefs. He saw her fine dark features, but these left him cold now, because she was outside him, had no place in his heart.

He might feel guilty about Elizabeth, but she could never uproot his feelings for Ruth now, however foolish they were.

31

A T BREAK TIME, Anna would race to the Marble Hall to wait for the post. Hillary Trevor, the eldest girl, collected the letters from Mr. Stewart, and all the evacuees thronged round her as she called out their names.

Maltby . . . Rothery . . . Price . . . Rimmer . . . Hill . . . Todd . . .

Small arms popped up through the crowd, letters were passed back to answering hands and children slipped away to window seats or garden benches to read their letters from home.

My dear Anna,
We have had cloudy days this week, which has been a boon because it is trickier for the German planes. Not so many air raids lately and London has come back to life again, everyone smiling on the streets, helping each other.

For the rest of her life, Anna never quite lost that childish daily hope of getting something in the post. Letters always reminded her of those wartime messages from her mother, those treasured bulletins which reassured her that another life was still waiting for her at home. There was that surge of excitement in the roll call, which might suddenly throw up her own name, *Sands!* Then a cream letter with her mother's handwriting would dance across raised arms to her, and she would carefully prize it open and savor her mother's words.

Near my office is Regent's Park, and I often stroll there at lunch. I feed the wintry ducks and think of all the times we

have done that together. I hope school is going well, and that
you are eating enough. I miss you, my darling, and I long for
us all to be together soon, as I'm sure we will be. Keep safe,
my Anna, and say a prayer for your father. He wrote to me
from Egypt, where he had three days' leave in Alexandria
and said he had bought a gift for you.

    Write to me soon, my dearest, and all my love,
Mummy.

Anna could glimpse her mother's face in the shape of her writing, and love spilled through her as she read her words. She tucked the stiff envelope into her pocket and it pressed against her leg all day, reminding her that she had been written to, that she belonged to somebody.

Some of the evacuees never got letters, but they still could not resist hovering on the outside edge of the letter crowd with forlorn eyes. Yet even for those who were remembered, there was still a dull ache of homesickness which never really eased, running like a buried river through their daily lives.

December, in particular, was a time when many of the children grew sad, and in the years to come, Anna would never forget her wartime Christmases so far from home. But she would remember, too, how generous the Ashtons were, always making sure that every evacuee had a gift under the tree. And how on Christmas Day itself they all shared a hearty lunch, with the rare treat of roast chicken and crispy potatoes, with plenty more vegetables from the grounds.

Yet none of those consolations could ever quite staunch the Christmas-night tears in the dormitories. The remembrance of home, of mothers, of fathers. The emotional wasteland of their lives without them. It would take years for many of them to dare to love again.

The New Year of 1941 brought a spell of bad weather to York-shire, and Ashton Park was cut off for several days by drifts of snow. Thomas found himself more removed than ever from his old diplomatic colleagues, with little or no sense of what was going on in London.

We are packing up our house here, Norton reported in his last letter, *and preparing for my new posting in Switzerland. We leave in a few weeks.*

It was difficult to gauge any sense of the war's progress from a wireless in snowbound Yorkshire, Thomas reflected, as he wheeled himself to his study window. But perhaps that was a blessing.

The children had all rushed outside to build snowmen and roll great snowballs down the grass banks. They were unstop-pable, despite the cold. Thomas watched them from his win-dow, though his thoughts were elsewhere. Ruth had gone home to visit her parents for Christmas, but since her return she had behaved like a stranger to him. Their relationship, always tenu-ous, had reverted to stilted formality, as if any flicker of feeling had been erased.

"Did you find your parents well?" he asked at lunch, on her first day back.

"Yes, thank you—very well."

"And what do they make of your work here?"

"They're relieved, I think, to see me out of London."

"It was our good luck that you ended up here—"

"If you'll excuse me, I must finish some marking."

"No coffee?"

"Not today, no thank you."

Thomas found himself unable to reach her. Lessons began again and school life rolled on, yet every day he grew more agi-tated by their distance. He longed to speak to her more freely, but the bad weather had long since ended their poetry classes, and there was little excuse for extended conversation.

"There's a new copy of *Horizon* in the library, if you would like to see it?"

"Thank you, but I already have so many unread books stacked beside my bed."

"There's an article about Hopkins which I thought might interest you—"

"I'll remember to look out for it. Thank you."

Had he lost her? Twice she shied away from the empty seat beside him at lunch, crushing him with a suspicion that she might be avoiding him. He began to feel his disability acutely; his legs felt wasted, his arms weak. He struggled to keep his back straight, and took to crossing his knees in staff meetings, to show that he still had feelings, nerves, life in his legs.

Self-doubt infected his every thought. How could she ever care for a man such as him? How could he have ever imagined that she might?

He watched her as she walked out of rooms, or passed by windows. The lightness of her walk. *I can't take my eyes off you,* he told her silently in the dining room, when her face was turned the other way.

He thought of her all day, every moment, and began to fear that he was losing his mind. She was in the crack of the floorboards, and the windowpane, and the lines of every book he read. He was heartsick, soul-sick, mind-sick. His eyes saw nothing but inward images of Ruth walking, turning, smiling. The first euphoria of love had passed. Now he was consumed by longings which he feared he could never declare.

And yet when he half-awoke in the morning he still dreamt that he was holding her and his heart soared with quiet bliss.

He was in despair but it was not true despair, he told himself; that came only with no hope, no meaning, nothing. He could still think about Ruth even if he could not be close to her. He tried to appreciate her from a distance, without any need to have her for himself. *How can you feel the loss of someone you have never possessed?* He wrote this in the margins of a book, trying to reason with himself, to temper his longing.

Sometimes he would indulge in safe fantasies of making love to Ruth, holding her tenderly, stroking her inner thigh, kissing her eyes, his tongue in her furrow—knowing all the while that it was only a dream. But he grew anxious, too, that he was toppling into delusion, a lunatic shadow land more vivid than the facts of his daily life without her.

Day and night he saw her face, and he shook whenever she came near, and he watched to see if she gave any flicker of response, any pity for his distress. But she always seemed distant. Was it shyness? Was it indifference? Could it even be secret love, as he sometimes hoped? He endlessly replayed their conversations in his head, sifting through everything she had ever said, straining to find any innuendo in even the most innocent of remarks.

He wanted above all to look into her eyes, and find an answering longing there. He wanted to reach out and touch her with infinite care. Perhaps it would be possible—

Until the thought came crashing back to him, as it always did, that a young woman like her could never be attracted to a married man of forty in a wheelchair. How could she ever want him? He felt pricked with jealousy by the unknown men in her life. In his darker hours, he imagined her writing loving letters to some imaginary army officer.

But for all that, his hope still refused to die away. He told himself that he must be patient. He had to wait for the spring, and longer days, when he could revive the poetry class, and she might push him there again. With the passage of time, the intimacy they had built up before could be rekindled. Sooner or later, he would know what she felt.

32

There was a night in the spring of 1941 when the bombing in London was so loud and insistent that Roberta could barely sleep. By daybreak she had given up any hope of dozing off again, so she decided to leave her cellar and walk to work early.

She made her way through Olympia and Kensington, unnaturally silent at that hour. Several buildings were turned inside out, their rooms exposed to the curious gaze of the outside world. She saw an iron bath stranded three floors up, held aloft by chaotically twisted pipes. There were staircases leading nowhere, and shreds of rose-print wallpaper flapping in the breeze. Charred joists littered the pavements, and crushed glass was scattered underfoot.

Walking briskly, she reached the empty Bayswater streets leading towards Oxford Circus, where a few burnt-out houses looked like half-finished stage sets—skeletal frames still intimately adorned with photographs and china mementoes of family life. In the trick light of dawn, it was as though she could sense the spirits of the dead flowing round her, or sitting on the broken chairs of abandoned houses—all those people whose lives had been so suddenly cut off, now silently thronging the streets as if nothing had changed. Roberta shuddered and pulled her coat tighter, quickening her pace.

She passed a derelict house where a child's cot was poised precariously on the fourth floor. For a moment she thought she could hear the phantom cries of a child, high-pitched, helpless, unanswered; her heart turned over as she thought of Anna, and her gap-toothed smile.

She arrived at last at the doors of the BBC. The gallows ca-maraderie of her colleagues was immediately infectious: every morning was a celebration for surviving another night. Roberta spent that day cataloging old discs, the sentimental melodies of a dozen different dance bands. She came upon an old Al Bowlly number, "The Very Thought of You," intimately crooned in his sweet lyric tenor. She kept the disc aside, and made a point of adding it to the playlist.

> *I see your face in every flower,*
> *Your eyes in stars above,*
> *It's just the thought of you,*
> *The very thought of you, my love . . .*

In Egypt, later that night, Lewis lay on his back in the sand and gazed up at a cloudless night sky humming with stars. A wireless was playing from somewhere in the camp, and he thought of his wife as he listened to the song, wondering when he would see her again.

33

SPRING HAD AT last reached Ashton Park. Thomas opened his study window, feeling heady with the new season. There were lambs in the field, and children running around on fresh grass. How could he have lived through so many springs without ever recognizing its simple rapture?

Light rain fell on new leaves; he could hear the soft patter as he worked at his desk. For so many years he had been wasting in his own private desert—but here was rain, sweet rain, washing into his roots and rousing his hope.

A new air filled his lungs as he looked out of the window and rejoiced in ordinary sights: the greenness of grass, the glow of buttercups, the light of the sky—it was a shining world again because of Ruth.

And yet, all this joy still hung on the hope that he might one day look into her face and find answering eyes. That thought took his breath away—the first consummation of eyes.

But what if he declared himself only to find her laughing at him, or looking puzzled, or piteous, or just detached?

The usual loop of hope and fear played through him as he sat in his study with a pile of unmarked homework. Elizabeth came in to fetch some writing paper, and noticed his reverie.

"A penny for your thoughts," she said. Thomas glanced up at the beautiful cold face he knew so well, and felt a twinge of guilt.

"I was just wondering how the Nortons are faring at their new embassy . . ."

He wheeled himself away from her gaze and started fiddling around at the bookcase. *Stay away from me, Elizabeth,* he thought.

And then he felt ashamed; he did not want to be unkind, or even think unkindly, about anyone.

After all, he had only two lessons to teach before he would have the joy of seeing Ruth at lunch. A friendship of sorts was developing between them again. And with the change of season, they would soon begin their poetry classes once more.

The longer, lighter spring days were a relief to Anna too. Instead of knocking about the house with the others, she could go out on her own, wandering down to the river, or off to the aspen grove. Without anyone even noticing she was alone.

One Saturday, Katy Todd asked her on a trip with her gang.

"We're going down to Saw Mill Bridge," she said, "to catch frogs."

"Sorry," said Anna, "I can't come."

"Why not?" asked Katy, curling her lip. Anna had no answer, she just didn't want to go.

"Because I'm meeting people at the lightning tree," she came up with.

"Who?"

"It's secret," mumbled Anna, but her face gave her away. Katy moved on in disgust.

Ashamed at her lame fib, Anna felt suddenly defeated. She watched the gang of girls heading off towards the river, and realized with a pang that it was too late to join them now. *But I didn't want to be with them anyway. What do I care?* she told herself defiantly as she swung through the woods, a birch switch in her hands thrashing through the undergrowth. It was a familiar walk which took her to an overgrown clearing in the woods, where the old tennis court and pavilion lay disused and neglected. The moldering court was infested with tall weeds which seemed to thrive in the cracked red-clay surface.

Anna walked into the palm-house pavilion. The door was slightly warped, and the frame shivered when she pulled it open. There was a stone floor, and a smell of musty old geraniums. The place was deserted. Just an iron watering can, paint-spattered, and an abandoned stepladder. There was an old wrought-iron bench too, whose decorative pattern was fretted with rust and cobwebs.

She wandered over to the other side of the pavilion, and glanced through the misted windows. The air of neglect was completed by an overgrown lawn beyond, with a small fountain at its center—a cherub on tiptoe—which was empty save for a residue of rotting leaves. To one side stood a stark monkey puzzle tree, angular and charmless in its gaze over this abandoned place.

Anna retreated to the bench inside the palm house, swinging her legs slightly. She imagined the plash of the fountain behind her, and out in front she watched a phantom game of tennis—Mr. Ashton as a young man dashing across the court, and stretching to return a ball.

But she could not imagine Mrs. Ashton there. Women who always wore high heels didn't come to the tennis court, surely? Anna no longer liked her. Mrs. Ashton was beautiful, but frightening—she could be sharp. And she was not always nice to her husband: Anna remembered suddenly the strange night when she had overheard her shouting at him in their bedroom.

She sat there for a while in the silence, and a gloom began to settle on her. It slowed her breathing, as if something was dragging on her heart. Until the shrill call of a blackbird jolted her to her feet, rousing her to walk away from the empty pavilion.

She went back to the house and took out a novel by Rider Haggard from the library, and sat with it in the garden, letting the story enthrall her. Anything to avoid Katy Todd and her gang.

It was nearing eight o'clock when she made her way back

though the French windows which led into the saloon. After the silence of the garden, the closing of the doors gave an unnatural clatter. She stepped quickly towards the library to return her book.

"Hello."

Anna's heart stopped. Mr. Ashton was sitting at one of the library tables, surrounded by books.

"Shouldn't you be upstairs in your dormitory?" he asked, but he did not appear to be angry.

"Yes, sir, I'm very sorry."

"It's all right. But where have you been?"

"Just reading. I couldn't stop—"

"Ah! A true lover of books knows no time. What are you reading?"

Anna stepped forwards with her book.

"*The World's Desire,* it's called. It's about Odysseus's last voyage, when he goes to Egypt and meets Helen of Troy, who's become a high priestess—"

"Perhaps they marry?" he teased.

"I've come to bring it back," said Anna apologetically.

"But you must keep it and finish it—I insist. I'm delighted that somebody is using this place."

"Thank you, sir."

"Come again soon. But while you're here, let me show you the secret stairway to the gallery, so you can fetch me a book—"

He gestured to a small case of dummy book spines, and pointed out the secret brass catch which his grandfather had installed. The door swung open with a click and Anna bounded up the steep stair ladder to the gallery above. From below, Mr. Ashton directed her to an atlas on a far shelf.

She was just proudly bringing the book down the stair ladder when she heard a distinctive clack-clack of footsteps and the library doors swung open. She froze behind the bookcase door.

It was Mrs. Ashton.

"Still working?" she quizzed her husband.

"Just a few pages more," he answered in a quiet voice. Anna held her breath. Mrs. Ashton would be furious if she found her, so the girl cowered behind the door, dreading the lash of her angry eyes.

Elizabeth walked over to Thomas's table, a slow swing of high heels on wood.

Thomas stopped tidying up his papers and looked up.

"I've come to tell you that I'm not happy," Elizabeth announced, in a voice both deadpan and direct. He tried to read her eyes, to see if she had been drinking.

"I said, I'm not happy."

"I heard," he said.

"Don't you want to know why?"

Thomas paused; all he could think about was the child hiding behind the gallery door. Elizabeth drew a breath and raised herself to her full height. She spoke with deliberate precision to curb any slurring in her voice.

"I'm unhappy because of you. You're my husband and you're a stranger to me."

Thomas did not know how to reply: he just shifted in his chair, painfully aware of Anna, only a few feet away. It was too late, now, to reveal her.

"Have you nothing to say to me?" Elizabeth's voice was terse, bitter, beginning to break.

"Not here, please—in the bedroom, later. *Please*."

Her face was puckering with tears.

"You—statue. You cripple. You bloody cripple."

"Please—" He reached out to her.

"Don't touch me!"

Her voice was low, stifled. She held her hands over her face, shaking with tears.

"You won't even come to sit with me in the other room. I need *intimacy*—"

"Of course I'll come with you."

"Now?"

"Of course."

"No more books?"

"No more books."

He wheeled forwards and touched his wife's elbow, eager to dispel her anger. He held out his handkerchief to her and she wiped her face. Together they left the room.

Anna stayed rooted where she was, terrified of moving. She felt mortified that Mr. Ashton knew what she had heard.

She waited until the way seemed clear, then crept through the gallery door and carefully placed the atlas on Mr. Ashton's pile of books—then ran, fast, up the stairs to her dormitory, barely catching her breath in an effort to get past the matrons unseen.

"Where have you been?" asked the other girls in her dormitory.

"We've been covering for you," said Suzy.

"Said you were stuck in the lavatory—"

Within moments Anna was in her nightdress, and when Miss Harrison appeared there was a full complement of girls in their beds. The lights were turned out.

"We caught a whole stack of frogs by the river," said Katy Todd.

"You missed such a trip!" said another.

"We put them all back again."

"You would have enjoyed it," said Katy, "but we didn't know where you went."

"Thanks," said Anna, secretly consoled, "but I got tied up with my book."

"Bookworm!"

"Quiet now!" The matron's voice rang out.

Anna was relieved to be left alone in the dark to think about the eruption of anger she had just witnessed. She knew by now that Mr. Ashton was only lame because of polio, an unlucky illness—so how could his wife be so cruel to him about that?

She fell asleep to dreams of shouting and crying, and angry people lashing out at each other for no clear reason.

The next day she saw Mr. Ashton in the Marble Hall. He waved to her, and she came over. He looked at her with an encouraging smile.

"Can you talk to me for a moment?"

She wheeled him to his study and he shut the door behind them. She was nervous, because she did not know how to be with Mr. Ashton on her own, behind a closed door. But his face was kind, tender.

"Anna, I am more sorry than I can say that you heard an adult conversation beyond your years."

"It's all right," she said, and hesitated because she could not think what else to say.

"I should have said you were there, but I didn't want to—"

"I know," said Anna. There was a silence.

"Sometimes couples argue, but then they make up," said Mr. Ashton softly.

"My parents argue too," blurted Anna, even though she had never seen them arguing. "I won't tell anyone," she added.

"You won't?"

"No, because it's—my mother would say it was private."

"Well, your mother sounds like a sensible woman."

"She likes—private things," Anna went on, stumped for something to say.

There was a longer pause.

"I'm just sorry, my dear," he said, "that's all."

With that, his face closed up with a gentle smile which ended the conversation. So off she went, closing the door behind her, determined to keep his secret.

She remembered how Mrs. Ashton had been her favorite when she first arrived there. There was the time she had cut her knee, and Mrs. Ashton had scooped her up. But now she was scared of her. Mrs. Ashton had a temper.

Unlike her husband, who was never sharp with any of them. He would tilt his face to one side and listen to whatever he was asked in class. Of course she would be true to his secret.

Anna didn't mean to take sides. But she knew that Mr. Ashton was kind and fair, and that she didn't like Mrs. Ashton anymore.

34

It had been raining all day in Ashton Park. If anyone was feeling at odds with the world, they could blame it on the weather, thought Thomas. Ruth was wheeling him to lunch after their lessons had overlapped in the west wing.

"Summer rain, I'd call it," said Ruth, "but heavy, for July."

"We have many kinds of rain at Ashton Park—slow, fast, soft, heavy. I prefer the 'soon over' variety myself."

She laughed, but could think of no rejoinder.

Their conversation had grown a little more fluent lately, but still stalled sometimes. It was like being stranded on the opposite banks of a deep river, thought Thomas. There were all these swift currents passing between them, under a polite surface, yet they still did not know how to reach each other directly.

"What will you do when you leave here, after the war?"

"I can't imagine that time."

"But it *will* end—and then what will you do?"

"I suppose I will go back to London."

"And teach? You're a natural teacher."

"Thank you but—I've enjoyed it so much here that I'm not sure if an ordinary London school could ever be the same."

"It would give you more of a life. A young woman like you needs to get out, meet people—"

"I've been happy here, I haven't craved anything else."

"But you mustn't shut the door on new people when you're still so young."

What was he telling her? Ruth was confused by their oblique conversations; something unspoken hovered between their words, each leaving the other to decipher what was really being said. Their meetings left her at once anxious and excited, she thought, as she walked out into the gardens after lunch.

From his study window, Thomas watched Ruth walk past the sundial, towards the woods; he was still shaken by their morning conversation.

He was in love with her, it was that simple. Every room without her was empty. When she was there, his heart sang.

He saw her face everywhere now. The sky was her, and the grass, and light itself. For so many years he had waited to live, biding his time for an unknown illumination, and here, now, at last, he had such hope. A desire to love so acute it strained every nerve in him. *Love.* If there was a higher word, a further word, he would have used it.

Ruth. Ruth, Ruth. He said her name over and over, sometimes out loud. He worried he might say it in front of others, or in his sleep. *Ruth.*

It did not matter that he could not walk. It did not matter if she did not love him. Nothing mattered beyond the joy of knowing that she existed, and that he might see her again. Her face, her hair, her hands. Nothing could diminish the wonder which this love, this rapture, had opened in him. He was touched to the quick—brim, overbrimming, *my cup runneth over.* What so many had felt before but never him; now at last his time had come.

But his euphoria was volatile. There were still other times, darker hours, when his happiness plummeted. Days when she did not look at him even in passing, and his hope shriveled away.

He would never touch her. He could make love to Elizabeth, even though he didn't care if he never held her again. But he could not touch Ruth. He wanted to stroke her cheek, and run his fingers through her hair. He wanted to look into her eyes—and see them open up, to let him into her soul. He felt the displaced potency of his gaze, that he could no longer meet anyone's eyes in case they might guess he was wishing for Ruth.

He knew from his pain that this was love. All those years of hoping he might feel something, driving him to act out a pretense of love. But now, at last, he had this spontaneous joy at the thought of another person.

It was everything about her. Her generosity, her hope, her spirit. Her pale, almost transparent face. Her tentative articulacy. The hesitant incline of her neck, such an uncertain gesture. Her soul in her fingertip as she spoke. Her awkward sincerity, which asked for him to hold her in his arms. Her tenderness.

35

Every evening at six o'clock, the children lined up in the Marble Hall before walking the long corridors to the chapel. Silently, they filed into the vaulted room with its wooden pews and plain leaded windows. The walls were paneled with oak, and lightly edged in blue and gold. It was a family chapel, intimate and simply furnished. But sometimes the setting sun would strike through the long windows, and the oak paneling would glow like a lamp, intimating something more than wood and stone.

> *Immortal, invisible, God only wise*
> *In light inaccessible, hid from our eyes*
> *Most blessed, most glorious, the ancient of days,*
> *Almighty, victorious, thy great name we praise.*

Anna loved the chapel, the solemnity of the prayers and the singing of hymns. She believed in God ardently, and prayed to him daily for her mother, her father and the end of the war.

There was an age-old smell of polished wood and musty leather kneelers. Anna liked to sit near the memorial to William, Mr. Ashton's older brother killed in the Great War. His helmet hung on the wall, and she could see the bullet holes. Next to it was a wooden shield for Edward Ashton, "Missing in Action." And beside that was a plaque for their sister, Claudia.

Anna always felt a little guilty looking at these memorials, as if she were spying on Mr. Ashton's sorrows. When he taught them about Roman battles, all she wanted was to hear about his own brothers in their war—but she never dared to ask.

She fidgeted on her kneeler, and watched Miss Weir, who always sat so still in the chapel, avoiding everyone's eyes. They all knew she was a vicar's daughter, perhaps that was why. But Mr. Ashton always kept his eyes to himself too, she noticed.

Perhaps all adults knew how to look inwards when they were inside a church. She tried it herself, screwing up her eyes and praying that she might go home soon, even as she chanted the Lord's Prayer.

"... *Thy kingdom come, thy will be done, on earth as it is in heaven...*"

The same familiar prayer reached through to Ruth in her pew, as she puzzled over her feelings for Thomas. *Lead us not into temptation.* She was moved by him—though it had taken many months to admit this to herself. She knew it was wrong to keep thinking about him, and yet she could not bring herself to feel guilty.

She was not yet quite sure what was happening to her. She knew that she enjoyed being in a room with Thomas, and that she was pleased if he spoke to her. He produced a slight flutter in her limbs when they talked together, and she wanted him to think well of her. But these feelings were surely just natural signs of respect for someone older and more articulate than her, whose courtesy was so particular, even to her.

Ever since her arrival, Ruth had been a little in awe of Thomas. The scale of his house had daunted her, and he himself appeared to be so guarded and self-sufficient, without any crack of need. A part of her feared him—perhaps because his disability moved her too much, and she was uncomfortable about such feelings. So she kept her distance, barely acknowledging even to herself that she looked forward to their meetings.

Perhaps it was Thomas's apparent powerlessness which had first attracted her, easing her own romantic inadequacy. Or perhaps it was simply the kindness he showed her. But somehow, at some point, she began to recognize that she was craving opportunities to talk to him. One morning, walking to a classroom, she realized that she was speaking to him in her head: he had entered her mind as her secret friend, and there she was, rehearsing what she might say to him, and qualifying her opinions in the light of what he might think.

They met daily, but there was little chance for talk of any consequence. There were lunchtimes, which he took in the main dining room, and there were staff meetings, and twice a week she had to push him back to his study from some far-flung classrooms where their lessons overlapped. On these occasions, as they returned down the long curved corridor to the house, he always found ways to dispel her shyness with his banter.

"I have been reading Elizabeth Bowen," Thomas ventured one day. "Have you read any of her novels?"

"I'm afraid not."

"She writes about gloomy houses with secrets."

"Is there a particular book I should read?"

"I'd like to lend you *The House in Paris*. There's a watchful girl who reminds me of some of our children here . . ."

Their conversations seemed to be riddled with so many gaps that she often found herself trying to finish off their sentences after they had parted.

Eventually she realized that she was talking to Thomas in her head all the time. She caught herself practicing lines to him. *"Is there a time I could pick up the Bowen novel from your study? I know I would enjoy any book you think is special." I must be lonely,* she told herself.

Sitting beside him at lunch one day, they were just discussing the Russian Front, when she glanced towards Thomas and found him watching her face very intently. For a moment their eyes met with peculiar force, startling her like an electric jolt—it was the first time she had ever caught a glimpse of somebody truly looking at her, as if thinking about her, as if she were not quite the invisible person she felt herself to be. Or was it nothing?

All through the next week, whenever she talked to anyone, she observed how and when people looked into each other's faces. The right amount of eye contact was something she found impossible to quantify. But when she had caught Thomas's look that day it had felt personal and intimate. Or had she misinterpreted him? She longed to seek out his eyes again, but did not dare.

Did she ever cross his mind, she wondered. He sometimes remembered things she had said, and repeated them back to her weeks later. That surprised her. She was growing nervous of him, of the boundaries of their conversations. There was the time he told her he was reading Thomas Hardy's elegies for his dead wife—and he casually mentioned their erotic power. *Erotic.* Nobody had ever used such a word with her before. Surely he had noticed her discomfort, the catch of her breath? A part of her felt ashamed that she had never had such conversations before. She worried whether she was too prim.

She began to think about what he might be like to embrace—as an experiment, almost, at first. She was not afraid of his wheelchair; she intuited that he was still capable of "erotic" feeling. It was his word, after all.

Yet she was reduced to a shadow by his wife. Ruth was fearful of Elizabeth, who was so poised and could be so scathing—who would certainly scorn the mere idea that a gauche vicar's daughter might form an attachment to her husband. When Ruth looked at herself in the cheap buckled mirror in her room, all she could see was a scrubbed, slightly freckled blank face. Not even a woman's face, yet. She felt—inadequate.

And yet she kept thinking about Thomas, even if it was wrong. But she could imagine how deeply she might embarrass him by any declaration of feeling, and then she would have to leave. The thought of that separation was too painful to consider, so she continued to nurture her tenderness for Thomas, but only in secret.

36

IT WAS A special night for Roberta. For the first time she was
dancing at the Savoy, in London's most elegant ballroom.
Carroll Gibbons was leading his band, the Savoy Hotel Orpheans, and the floor was overflowing with wartime lovers seizing
their chance.

She had been invited by Billy, the cornet player in Geraldo's
band who had caught her eye in so many rehearsals at the BBC.
Sometimes he played for the Savoy Orpheans too, which got
him into the Savoy on his nights off. She had arrived in her best
satin dress.

Both of them were natural dancers. Their bodies brushed
together as he laced his fingers through hers, and they stepped
fluently across the polished floor, jubilant to have found each
other.

This affair with Billy had moved so swiftly. After all those
studied glances in the rehearsal hall, they had come face-to-face
in one of the Fitzrovia pubs. "Have you two met yet?" somebody asked, and they both smiled, because they felt familiar
already.

Their first conversation was delicate, as each wanted to put
the other at ease, to commiserate with each other's life, almost.
Both of them were married, "happily" of course. He lived in
Brockley, an easy train ride from London Bridge, and was fond
of his wife although she had "lost interest" in him. (Roberta listened with complicit eyes, knowing that they were both making
excuses.) Diabetes had kept him out of the army. He was doing
his bit for Britain by playing his music.

That was enough, wasn't it, they told each other. The Nazis had banned jazz as black and degenerate. Just to play dance music was a rebellion. Just to feel the music slide through your body, panther-like, even that was a stand against Hitler, and one embraced by Roberta with alacrity. She was an alluring dancer, languid and intimate, with a sinuous abandon in her hips and arms which excited every man she danced with.

Billy was besotted, and wanted to find a place where they could stay together in London. He told his wife he must rent a room in town for the nights when he couldn't catch the last train home. Rooms were not hard to find, with so many people away. There was the thrill of pretending they were married, and giving the name Smith, "because it's so obviously a lie." A landlord took them round bedsits in Maida Vale and St. John's Wood. Abandoned houses, stacked with empty rooms. In the end, they took a place in Notting Hill, a one-bedroom flat in Linden Gardens, furnished with a large bed and tatty chairs. There was a view onto the backs of other buildings, and a woman opposite who sat on her fire escape to feed the pigeons. The bird woman, they called her.

They locked the door and made love with a mirror perched against the wall, the more to entice each other. She, at thirty-seven, was relishing her late bloom of sensuality. Enjoying the fullness of her breasts which swelled at his touch. Feeling, for the first time, the pleasing roundness of her form, and relaxing about her imperfections, the slight thickening of her thighs which only seemed to excite Billy. His waist was filling out too, and the hair on his chest was flecked with gray, which moved her.

It seemed such a waste not to be together, when they might die tomorrow anyway. That was what they said when they parted in the morning, already planning their next meeting.

37

SUMMER LESSONS FINISHED earlier at Ashton Park, allowing both children and teachers to make the most of the long days outside.

It was a clear day, and Ruth went for a long walk through the gardens. The breeze lifted her hair and her spirit, and everything before her looked flawless and new, as if freshly hatched. The forget-me-nots at her feet were like brilliant blue eyes, startled into pleasure at the scene before them. She picked one and took it back up to her bedroom, to remember that day. She laid the flower on a sheet of paper and wrote the date, with a message. To lay down her marker—that she was in love. *Think what you have meant to me.* She folded the paper with the flower at its crease, and carefully pressed it inside a book of verse.

Ruth had realized that she was happy in this house, because being with Thomas was all she wanted. She thought about him all the time now. It took longer to admit the right word to herself. *Love.* She loved this man.

At the same time, she feared she was a fool—but she could not help herself any longer. The feeling had taken hold of her before she had even guessed what was happening. He had penetrated her soul.

Even if she could never tell him, there was still the joy of seeing him. All day long she cherished the thought of him, even as she taught her lessons. "*Thomas*"—she privately called him by his first name. After so many conversations in her head, she felt a flash of guilt whenever she saw him. What if it showed on her face?

She sensed an unseen cord stretching between them, but told herself, too, that this was her delusion. And yet—she sometimes allowed herself the gift of hope. Every expression of his eyes, every gesture he made, reached right through to her. She hardly dared to look at him, but when she did, and their eyes met in passing, she shook inside. She felt his presence so acutely now that she no longer knew how to stand in the same room as him.

A wished-for moment of disclosure began to hover in her mind and in her heart. She dreamt of daring to look into Thomas's face, and finding love in his eyes; she wanted to touch his cheek, she wanted to say she loved him. It was not something she had ever said to anyone before.

After so many years alone she longed for intimacy. She imagined that if she could just lie naked in Thomas's arms, she would be at peace for the first time in her life. Breathing with someone. All secrets, all fears, laid open. Her head on his chest. But the crossing to that place could never be possible, she knew that too.

38

IT WAS ALMOST two years since Anna had first arrived at
Ashton Park, and by now the place had settled inside her—
its peace and quiet and remove.

In the evenings, she would sit at the window seat of her dormitory and gaze out at the tranquil sweep of parkland, flecked
with oaks and elms. Sometimes she watched the steady drift of
grazing sheep. Whatever the weather, it was a view of unfailing
serenity, a landscape which reached inwards—until that pale
wash of sky was distilled into the light of memory.

Anna and the others invented numerous games and routines around the park. They made dens in the woods, and a secret camp in the derelict water tower, even though it was strictly
forbidden. In gangs, they played chase through the gardens, and
block-one-two-three by the sundial.

One girl had a pair of roller skates, and on rainy days they
would spend hours skating up and down the smooth stone
corridors of the west wing. When the leather straps broke, they
tied the skates with string instead.

In the winter, they were often cold, and constantly foraging
for food. Someone found a rusty old tin of sugar in the marmalade cupboard, and the children spooned the sweet grains onto
slices of bread until the sugar ran out. Through all those chilly
months, they wore their socks and jerseys in bed, bracing themselves against the frost. Until spring arrived, with an abundance
of wildflowers blazing along the grass terraces—buttercups,
daffodils and violet-blue speedwells. Forget-me-nots too, and
untended clumps of azaleas.

Come the summer, the children left footprints in the fresh uncut grass. The woods teemed with wild garlic, which they would pick and suck for its clean, sweet taste. And on summer evenings, if the matrons could not keep them quiet at bedtime, they would be sent outside to run circuits round the south lawn, to tire them out.

It was on one of these runs in 1941 that Anna gazed out across the gardens in the long light of evening, and was lost in a moment of complete happiness.

She loved this place, that was all. The slight stir of the trees, the wide evening sky, the moist grass. The gaze of the house, its silence. Her heart swelled with a joy she could not fathom, a surge of gladness which held her right where she was, drawing in the view around her.

"*Come on, Anna,*" called Mary Heaney, prompting her to run on and catch up with the girl in front. She ached with a sense that the light would soon leak away, and the day too—and then how would she remember all this?

She stopped still, and looked back, trying to hold this moment fast in her heart, to keep it close.

39

A S SOON AS Thomas found the poem, he knew he must read it out to Ruth. Peace settled in him, because he could at last see a way to make some kind of indirect declaration. It was by E. E. Cummings, an American poet he had chanced upon in a recent anthology. He bookmarked several other short poems for cover.

Two days later, the weather was auspiciously clear as Ruth came to fetch him for their poetry class. She straightened her skirt and knocked on his study door.

"Come in!"

Just the sight of her lifted him with hope, though he hid any elation behind his habitual manners.

She pushed him up the short ramp to the garden path. Thomas was quiet and seemed preoccupied, and Ruth was careful not to disturb his thoughts.

When they reached the group of children, and everyone was settled, Thomas told them about E. E. Cummings: an American poet who looked for new ways to make his feelings immediate, such as doing away with capital letters and some of the punctuation.

"Spontaneity—that's what he's after," said Thomas. "Capturing a moment as it happens, not as some afterthought."

Having intrigued the children with the idea of a poet who broke all the rules, Thomas started to read. He began with a poem about the moon as a balloon, then one in which spring was like a hand. The book was passed around and the children looked at the eccentric layout of the lines.

"This next one is a love poem. He raises his game here . . . ," said Thomas, retrieving the book and turning the page. He began to read again, lightly and freely, as the poem suggested.

> somewhere i have never travelled,gladly beyond
> any experience,your eyes have their silence:
> in your most frail gesture are things which enclose me,
> or which i cannot touch because they are too near
>
> your slightest look easily will unclose me
> though i have closed myself as fingers,
> you open always petal by petal myself as Spring opens
> (touching skilfully,mysteriously)her first rose
>
> or if your wish be to close me,i and
> my life will shut very beautifully,suddenly,
> as when the heart of this flower imagines
> the snow carefully everywhere descending;
>
> nothing which we are to perceive in this world equals
> the power of your intense fragility:whose texture
> compels me with color of its countries,
> rendering death and forever with each breathing
>
> (i do not know what it is about you that closes
> and opens;only that something in me understands
> the voice of your eyes is deeper than all roses)
> nobody,not even the rain,has such small hands

When he had finished reading the poem there was a silence. Ruth, usually, would spark off a discussion, but she said nothing.

Thomas felt his mistake at once—it was clearly not a poem for children. He had been too blatant.

"I liked the flower in the snow." It was Anna Sands who spoke up. Thomas had never been so entirely pleased with any child before.

"Quite so. A rose in the snow. A beautiful idea, though it is hard to say why. *That* is the magic of poetry."

"But I thought it was a sad poem," said Anna.

"Why?" asked Thomas.

"Because it was about sad love," she said.

"Why do you think that?"

"It was all distant, as if they could never be together."

"Perhaps it's a poem to woo her—"

"But it sounds as if he thinks he'll never reach her."

"Better to have loved and lost than never to have loved at all," chanted a girl with pigtails, Sarah. Silence.

"Better to have loved at all," said Thomas.

He was afraid to look at Ruth. Had she understood what he was trying to tell her? She did not speak until the children engaged her.

"Will you read to us too?" asked Anna.

"I've brought you something spooky," she said, "by Walter de la Mare."

It was a ghost poem, "The Listeners." It got them all talking about the ghosts of Ashton Park—the Blue Lady, the Girl with the Lapdog—there was no end to the ghost stories conjured up by the children. In his mood of nervous levity, Thomas laughed with them all. Ruth too.

In laughter, their eyes met briefly. His heart stalled. How could she not know his feelings for her? There was an invisible thread running between them, if only she would dare to take it. He had read the poem for her—surely she had understood that? He willed her to respond, but did not dare look at her again.

The banter of the class went on for too long, it seemed to Thomas. But then at last came the moment of parting, and Ruth began to wheel him back to the house. As she pushed him,

he realized that he had lost all his regret that he was in a wheelchair, because he felt that she might love him as he was. Or was
this his delusion?

When they arrived at his study, he reached for the door
handle, trying to think of a suitable quip. But the doorknob
stuck for a moment. Her hand came upon his in an effort to free
it. He looked up at her, right into her face. Surely, that might be
love he saw there? Together they opened the door.

"Please, come in," he said. She followed. Boldly, he shut the
door behind her. For the first time, they were alone together in
a room with a closed door. She was avoiding his gaze, but he
looked straight up at her. She crumpled into retreat before he
had a chance to speak.

"I'm sorry," she said. "I'm so sorry."

"Why?" he replied, confused. "What's worrying you?"

"I've been too—familiar."

"I can't think how," he said.

She was stooped, her face down, unable to meet his eyes.

"I'm so sorry." It was all she could think to say.

He did not know how to respond.

"Please tell me what's worrying you," he asked gently.

"You were wonderful today," she said, trying to raise her
face to his. He wondered if she was just being polite. He was in
agony. What was she really thinking?

"They enjoyed themselves, didn't they?" he said as lightly
as possible, shuffling his legs. The moment of greatest tension
was passing, and he knew he must produce pleasantries now, to
stall her retreat.

"Anna might even be quite a passable poet if she sticks at it,"
he went on.

"She's not shy of her own feelings, that's for sure."

"I wonder what becomes of the Annas of this world."

"They find it hard to meet anyone who will take life as seri-
ously as they do."

"Is that so?"

"I can only guess."

What other trivia could he muster? Was she holding him off through indifference or shyness? For surely she must now know what he felt.

She started to move, to leave the room.

"Thank you." He said it too loud. She turned.

"Thank *you*," she said, daring to look into his face for a moment. He fancied he saw tenderness in her eyes, but he had lost all sense now of what she felt. Perhaps everything had been his imagination?

Then she was gone. He sat in his chair, trying to unravel the signs. Had her discomfort signaled love or embarrassment?

———

40

R UTH WAS SHAKING as she returned to her room.
When he had read out that poem, she could only assume that he was thinking of his wife—and the thought of their
long intimacy made her ache with jealousy.

And yet a part of her indulged a thought that perhaps he had
chosen the poem for her—or was she a fool to think so? She
wanted to talk to him, and be with him, and go on seeing him
forever. But another voice told her she was going mad, that she
must leave Ashton Park, that she was deluding herself, seeing
love in everything he said where there was nothing but courtesy
and kindness.

She sat down to write him a letter. She wrote it and rewrote
it, knowing that she would only change it again. Then she hid
the letter in a book, ready to revise in the morning. She might
never dare to give it to him, but writing it was a solace.

The next day he did not meet her look in the dining room. He
seemed to snub her, even—that hurt, very much. Did he worry
that he had sparked a feeling in her and must now show her that
there was nothing there? Was he telling her to keep her distance?

Through all her lessons that day, her heart was so heavy she
could barely stand. Teaching the children, she heard her voice
as if it came from outside. Yet, whatever she was doing, she had
the flashing sensation of seeing Thomas's expectant face, smiling at her, holding out his hand to her.

In one math lesson, a sudden memory of his eyes made
her gasp and lose her concentration. She *was* mad—he was
not thinking of her, not even for a moment. The children were

puzzled by her sudden silence, but she regained herself and talked on.

The succeeding days were no easier. She tried to be alone whenever she could, because her body kept crumpling beneath her. She thought: *I must leave before I unravel.* But a part of her still wanted to finish her letter to Thomas, still wanted to tell him what he meant to her. Outside lessons, she sat on the bed in her room under the dim bulb and worked on it, copying it out again and again in a fair hand.

For three days she did not change the letter. Just read it. In those days her decision came—that she must leave before her behavior became an embarrassment. She told Mrs. Ashton, and Mr. Stewart, that she would like to seek new work in St. Albans, to be closer to her parents. Of course they understood, though they regretted her departure because she was such an accomplished and dedicated teacher—as they both told her.

It was a day or two before Elizabeth remembered to mention this to Thomas at dinner. He did his utmost to feign indifference, but was poleaxed by the news. Ruth going, at the end of the week? What would he do, what could he do?

He had lost her. He had driven her away with his poem, he had harassed her, when all he wanted was to hold her and love her. How could he have been so foolish, when his daily hope lay with seeing her? He was plunged into misery and lay awake through the night, wondering how he might talk to her, express his love to her. Every nerve in his body felt raw.

He saw her at lunch the next day and lingered to catch her afterwards.

"I hear you are leaving us?" He looked up into her eyes.

"Yes."

"I'm so very sorry."

He did not flinch from looking right into her face, her clear face. She had to clasp her hands to steady them. Was that unhappiness she saw in his eyes—regret, even?

"My father is ailing a bit, and I thought it would help him if I worked closer to home."

"Will you come back to us, or are you leaving for good?"

"I think it is better that I begin again elsewhere."

"We will all miss you so much." He paused, he looked up. "*I* will miss you."

"I will miss you all too—" She felt unable to say more, though her face perhaps suggested something else. She turned to go to her next lesson. Thomas watched her walk off, then wheeled himself away to his study.

His heart was racing; he was frantic that he might not see her properly again before she left. But what could he say? He had nothing to offer her, despite his fantasies.

He sat alone in his study, tormented by his own reticence. For so many years he had been dead inside, yet now that he had finally found someone to love, he would be denied any expression of his feelings. He had always wanted to give love—that was what he wanted to do—but he had driven Ruth away now, and she was going, would soon be gone, and he would not see her again.

He did not know how to face his life without her.

41

·——·

THAT EVENING, RELEASED from her lessons, Ruth sat alone in her room. She was still troubled, but she felt something different now, too. She had a new understanding that Thomas was unhappy about her going. There was no mistaking the pain in his eyes as he spoke to her. Even if it was only a modest affection, a mentor-like fondness, she knew now that he had some tenderness for her.

So she wanted to give him her letter. He might be disturbed by it, but she trusted, too, that he understood love, and could sympathize with the depth of her feeling. She read it again twice until, exhausted, she could not look at it anymore. Then she put the pages unsigned into an envelope and sealed it.

The next day, with her bags packed, she went down for her last morning's lessons. After lunch she was to catch a bus to York, then a late afternoon train back home.

She had her letter ready now, and her resolve made her calm. But she would have to give it to him in person: it could never be put through anyone else's hands. She knew his timetable, that he had a spare hour straight after lunch, so she hoped to find him then in his study, alone.

When the time came, she knocked at his door, shaking. The letter was in her hand.

"Come in!"

His face lit up when he saw her.

"I came to say good-bye."

"Thank you," he said, "thank you so much. I would have been so sad to have missed you—"

"I have a letter for you," she said.

"A letter?"

"Well, it's just that—" Her voice dried up.

"Oh, Ruth," he said.

He looked up at her with eyes which said everything, but she could not bring herself to meet his face. She was overcome with shyness, with fear and hope together, but she handed him the envelope. He took it.

"Can I read it now?" he asked.

"Please, yes," she said. But turned and edged away.

"Thank you!" he said, but she was going, gone.

The door was still ajar as he tore open the envelope and unfolded the sheet of paper inside.

Dear Thomas,

I'm fearful as I give you this letter, because I know it's an imposition. But I did not know how to leave Ashton Park without saying good-bye to you properly.

For what it's worth, I wanted to tell you that I love you. Never before has anyone touched me so deeply—you have changed my life and I cherish everything about you. The reach of your understanding. Your generosity and kindness. The spark of your mind. Your fair-mindedness, and determined optimism, and your gentle courtesy—all are so dearly beloved to me.

I have never loved a face more than I love yours, and I see it everywhere. Everything that moves me reminds me of you.

I know my feelings are inappropriate, but I'm afraid this does not stop me from loving you. Yet I have no wish to disrupt your life beyond this letter—which is why I am leaving now, before my feelings reveal themselves in ways which might embarrass you.

My love for you is very rooted after all this time. To cut

*it out now would be to cut off my own soul, so the tenderness
is not going to go away. I may not see you in person, but you
will always remain in my thoughts.*

*Above all, before leaving, I wanted to say—I love you
with all my heart, and I always will. I want to thank you for
the profound joy I've had in the thought of you—and I wish
you every good thing.*

Within moments of opening the letter, Thomas's heart was
quelled. Here were unequivocal words to still all his longings,
set down in ink.

The letter was truer, deeper than he could ever have hoped
for. But Thomas was mystified that she could have so misread
his feelings for her. How could she have failed to read his eyes?

Now he was like an overwound clock, close to breaking—
what if she should leave before he could respond to this? He
wheeled himself out of his study, along the corridor and into
the Marble Hall. Two children were playing badminton in the
hour before afternoon lessons—Anna Sands and Mary Heaney.

"Anna!" he called softly. She came.

"Anna, I am very anxious to see Miss Weir before she leaves.
Has she passed through this way with her luggage?"

"No, sir."

"Could I ask you to fetch her for me? I have no idea where
she might be, but it is urgent that I talk to her."

Anna looked at Mr. Ashton and saw his agitation. She
dropped her racket and set off at once.

"Anna—"

"Yes, sir?" she turned, looked back.

"Please, don't stop until you have found her. I'll be in my
study—"

"Yes, sir."

He smiled, and the child's heart jumped with pride. To be
running errands for Mr. Ashton, to be doing something special

for him—that always made her so happy. She ran to the staff room, but Miss Weir was not there. She ran past the kitchens, out towards the classrooms, where children were beginning to gather for lessons.

"Where's Miss Weir?" she called out, catching her breath.

"She's finished teaching us," said one child.

"She's gone home," added another girl, sure she was right.

"Have you tried her room?" cried a boy, but Anna was already gone, tearing towards the stairs, afraid she might be too late.

She arrived panting at the top floor of the great house, where Ruth had one of the maid's bedrooms. She knocked in a hurry.

The door opened, and there was Miss Weir, still packing her last books.

"Mr. Ashton sent me, he says it's urgent, he must see you before you go—"

Ruth's head was swimming, and her heart racing, as she followed the girl back downstairs.

Anna was bird-happy now that she had done what she was meant to do. She almost wanted to deliver Miss Weir right to Mr. Ashton's door, to get his thanks, but the class bell was ringing, so she headed off to her next lesson.

Ruth was alone now, as she knocked on Thomas's study door. Some children ran past her to their classrooms, and she had to strain to hear his voice.

"Come in!"

She went in, more nervous than she had ever been before. She closed the door behind her and turned to face him.

There he was, wheeling forwards to her.

"Thank you for your letter, but you have completely misunderstood me—"

He caught his breath and looked up into her eyes.

"—I've loved you for so long, but I thought it was only me."

She could not speak but reached out for his hand, and at his touch her heart turned over. She knelt down beside him and buried her head in his shoulder, and they fell into an embrace. He held her, and stroked her hair, then looked deep into her face. Their eyes locked into each other, revealing all the tenderness and longing that had been hidden before. When at last they kissed, their faces were so close that they could see each other's eyelashes, and the texture of their skin, and every beloved detail was one more thing for each of them to marvel at.

"I love you," said Ruth. Nothing else would do, just the one phrase which she could say now for the first time.

"How could you not have known that I loved *you*?" he said, breaking into a smile. *I love you*—he could cry it to the heavens—every grief he had ever known was assuaged in this moment. He held her in his arms and breathed as deeply as he knew how.

"I thought I had lost you. Don't leave me," he said. "Please don't leave me."

42

ONE OF THE Ashton kitchen staff was a red-cheeked girl called Sarah, from Newcastle. After many months at the school, she had grown tired of being locked away from city life and marooned with dozens of children. Instead, she wanted to take up a new job in a munitions factory. So she handed in her notice.

A girl from the village was found to replace her, who could walk in every day. So Sarah's room in the west wing was left empty.

The children were always exploring the old house, and hunting for food. Anna and Beth sneaked a peep into Sarah's room after she had gone. The place was bare, except for a chair, a single stripped bed and an old wardrobe.

Anna swung open the wardrobe door with a creak and, sitting there, to their joy, was a Huntley & Palmers biscuit tin. They opened it at once. There was still a layer of biscuits, not stale yet. Anna and Beth took three each, then carefully stowed the tin back in the wardrobe and ran off into the garden to enjoy their feast.

Nobody had seen them. It was their secret. Whenever they felt peckish, they could go along to Sarah's old room and eat a few more of her biscuits.

One autumn afternoon, when most of the children were out in the garden, Anna was hungry and decided to pay a visit to the biscuit tin. She clattered along the corridor until she came to that obscure part of the west wing where the empty room lay. She closed the door behind her and fished out the tin, then she sat in the open wardrobe enjoying the last of the biscuits, wondering if she should leave a couple for Beth.

Suddenly, she heard the noise of someone coming, so she fumbled to shut the tin. The sounds came closer. She clambered inside the wardrobe and pulled the door behind her. She didn't manage to close it fully—a crack remained—but she crawled to one side.

The bedroom door was opening, and someone was coming into the room. The door was closed. Someone was locking it. Through the crack, just passing her field of vision for a moment, Anna saw Mr. Ashton's wheelchair, and Miss Weir pushing him. They moved to the other side of the bed, and she could see no more. She could only listen.

The blood was thudding so hard in Anna's ears that she thought they must hear her. She wanted to climb out and cheerily apologize for eating the biscuits, but they had locked the door. She would have to remain hidden and make sure she didn't cough. She held her breath, terrified.

It was then that she heard soft murmurs, sighs, quickened breathing, the creak of the bed—sounds she could barely understand, and yet she knew they were secret.

Anna sat shaking inside the wardrobe with her head in her hands. Never before had she felt such shame. She did not want to eavesdrop, she wanted to cry out—her overwound body was screaming with cramp. But she sat close, tight, furled in a small ball, waiting for it all to be over.

She moved her head round, and through the crack caught a glimpse of white naked shoulders against the bed. Quickly she looked away, but still heard strange sounds—soft private cries she had never heard before.

She buried herself there for some twenty minutes, feeling faint, sick, trapped. But then it was over. The lovers dressed, without speaking much. She heard the door being unlocked, and out they went.

Anna waited there in silence, still not daring to move. Until at last she unwound herself from the wardrobe and fled. She ran down the corridor and outside through the gardens, she ran along the grass terrace, and all the way to her favorite clump of aspens. The trees swayed in the breeze, and soothed her with the deeper, calmer air of life beyond people.

Mr. Ashton and Miss Weir? Could it really be so? She would not dare to tell anyone what she had heard.

For Thomas and Ruth, this was just one encounter in the passion to which they were now both bound. For each of them, every day now brought the hope of touching the other. They only ever had snatched moments together, always in daylight, in that stripped-bare room—but they still thought themselves in heaven.

For two people who have longed for each other so dearly, thought Thomas, there could never be a joy so complete as the touch of skin against skin, fingers tracing faces, the warmth of an embrace. What had been so external with Elizabeth was now, with Ruth, charged with all the passion of true longing. Eyes finding each other, every inward part of him converging with her, their bodies unfolding into souls, both of them entwined in this private rapture of mutual love.

The discovery of an empty maid's room, to which Ruth could wheel him without difficulty, was a gift. It was he who first realized that they might find a moment's privacy there, and he directed Ruth there.

When they reached the room, they found a key in the lock, ready and waiting. Thomas locked the door from the inside.

The space between them was electric. This was the first time they had been safely alone together, and the silence hummed, as if the air had been struck with a tuning fork. Ruth closed the window shutters, then turned to Thomas; their intimacy began.

Their lovemaking continued, in the same room, whenever it was possible, with a steady increase in daring for both of them. They graduated onto the creaky single bed and felt each other, diffidently at first. Until the day of consummation. Thereafter, their desire grew frank and uninhibited.

He had already told her that he could not father children, so they never worried about contraception.

43

ROBERTA WAS CAREFUL to make sure that nobody could keep track of her comings and goings with Billy in London. Her work pattern was erratic: sometimes she took day shifts, at other times she worked through the evenings. Meanwhile, she kept up polite contact with Lewis's parents, on occasional Sunday visits. She was fond of them.

"As soon as Lewis comes home, we'll celebrate," she said, and she meant it; she was looking forward to resuming family life, she missed all its rituals.

But for the moment, she drew solace from her time with Billy. As was usual on a Tuesday evening, she posted a letter to her daughter, then made her way to Notting Hill, where he was waiting in their flat. She made an omelet for both of them, with eggs saved for the occasion. Then they made love languidly, and drifted into sleep before he had even withdrawn from her.

But Roberta woke abruptly before midnight. There was the familiar sound of sirens and bombers, in a distant part of London.

"We need to go into the shelter," she said, rousing Billy.

He tumbled out of bed, and they set off for the cellar of their building. Billy was soon asleep once more on his camp bed, but Roberta was too much awake now. She had an interview with her boss first thing in the morning, and wanted to wear her best suit, which was hanging in the wardrobe at home. She would have to make an early start to retrieve it and change.

By two in the morning, she still could not sleep, and the bombing was receding. When she heard the all-clear siren, she stirred a half-conscious Billy to say that she was heading home, to have her clothes ready for the morning. Then she slipped out into the darkness.

It was a cloudy night, and there was still a distant rumble of antiaircraft guns. But no German bombers over Kensington.

She walked down Notting Hill and headed towards Holland Road. *Why* Holland *Road?* she wondered. What had it to do with Holland? She had passed this street so often, yet never before had she thought about its name.

Suddenly, a rogue plane buzzed through the clouds and, within moments, she heard a bomb exploding a few streets away. Panic seized her. She looked round for the nearest shelter, quickening her pace.

Another plane passed, and another. All heading somewhere else, but still frightening her. She could see no shelter as she hurried down the road, but she passed railings masking cellar steps. *I will have to knock on a stranger's door,* she thought.

She ran down some steps and knocked on a basement door. No answer. The planes were still flying over. *Please, please, let me in.* She ran to the next house, and the next. No answer.

It was as she reached the basement door of the fourth house that she heard an eerie whine above her head, followed by a deafening crash.

When she came to, she could not move, though her head was free and she could crane it to either side. It took her a few minutes to realize that she wasn't badly injured; just a throbbing left shoulder.

It's a miracle I'm still alive, she thought, wiggling her toes. *Alive, and in one piece. I'll just have to wait until somebody digs me out.* "Help!" she called, and again, "Help!"

But there was no answer—nor could she hear any sound. And shouting made her splutter and choke with dust. She was completely buried in the front basement-well of a terraced house.

She assumed that any minute now she would hear cheery shouts, and gallant firefighters would pull her out with offers of milky tea. But no voices came. She realized that the fire engines must be over by the river warehouses. A few rogue bombs in Kensington could hardly attract a flurry of firemen. And the house looked so deserted: perhaps the neighbors had assumed that nobody was at risk.

"*Help! Help!*" she cried, till she was hoarse, and with each yell she breathed in more dust and sucked away more air.

Claustrophobia began to suffocate her, and a terror that she might die when she could so easily be rescued. "*Help! Help me!*"

She thought of Billy, just up the road in the shelter. Lewis, in Egypt, preparing for another day in the Western Desert. And her daughter, asleep in her Yorkshire dormitory. All of them oblivious to what might be her last hours in a random London street. She was not ready to finish her life—surely she could not be cut off so haphazardly?

The minutes seeped away, and a rising panic began to take hold of her stiffening body. Her lungs were heaving, and sweat poured down her face. She felt nauseous, with head spins. Would anybody find her? Of course they would. Soon she would hear pickaxes and shovels scooping away at the rubble. She must wait, just wait.

Yet still there was no sound.

Her panic came and went in waves. Would she see Anna again? Her beloved daughter whom she had so—abandoned. They could have been dancing down the street and laughing together—but all that would be denied to Anna now.

She wondered if this was God's way of punishing her. A pang of regret made her cry out loud, but it was no use. Her own selfishness had ruined her daughter's life. Anna's eyes flashed before her. She would never have a mother to teach her female secrets, or praise her budding beauty.

How could she have let her daughter go? She should have

visited Yorkshire more often, or found work and lodgings out-side London for the pair of them. But she had given all that up, for what? For an affair which lit up her senses.

She had always thought there would be time to be with Anna, and eat ice cream with her again, in tall glasses—

The air was thickening now, and she was fading. As her life leaked away, she grew calmer. Lewis would return from the war, to look after their child, there was that hope. She thought of him with love, and prayed for his safety in Egypt. She ended her conscious life repeating all the litanies she could remember, praying rhythmically, concentrating all her strength on Anna, beseeching God to let her own love reach through the night to her sleeping daughter.

All the while, dust was clogging the air, until Roberta could breathe no more. After four hours trapped under the rubble, she was finally released from her anguish and gave up her ghost.

It was several days before she was uncovered, by which time her body was beginning to decompose. Her papers were found damp but intact in her jacket pocket. It was her neighbor, an el-derly postman, who helped the police with their inquiries when they came knocking at her door.

The following Tuesday, Billy waited for her at their flat. When she did not turn up, at first he worried, but then he fell asleep assuming that she must have changed her work shift. The next day he tried to ring her at the BBC, where he heard the dreadful news.

44

WHEN MISS WEIR found Anna in the gardens and asked if she would follow her to Mr. Ashton's study, the girl worried at once that she was in trouble. Her stomach lurched as she wondered if she had been seen, after all, in the wardrobe with her tin of biscuits. But Miss Weir did not seem cross. She put a hand on her shoulder and steered her inside the house.

Behind the heavy door of his study, Thomas was waiting for Anna with a gloomy heart. Ruth had told him that the news would come best from him in the quiet and privacy of his study. But she was such a blithe child—he wished he could prolong her ignorance.

There was a light knock on his door.

"Come in!" he said, as gently as he could. The child appeared, her face expectant, nervous. He saw that she was trembling, and remembered his own school fears, the headmaster, the canings.

"Don't worry," he said, "you've done nothing wrong, Anna."

He moved his hand, as if he were about to speak, and yet no words came. Anna thought she could hear her own heart beating louder than the clock on his desk.

"I have some difficult news to tell you, and you will have to be brave."

He could hear himself falling into phrases. *Do I spin this out gently,* he thought, *or tell her straight off?*

The child looked puzzled, distant—hardly there, really. A surge of tenderness swept through him.

"You're a very special girl, my dear, I want you to remember that. You're blessed with many gifts and you have a life waiting out there for you which will be—wonderful. You must look after yourself, and believe in yourself."

Anna was thrilled and baffled in equal measure. She felt dizzy and important. Was he planning a scholarship for her?

"I'm, I'm afraid—" He looked down for a moment.

My father is dead, Anna thought with a thump. *My father is dead in the desert.*

He looked up.

"Your mother has died in an air raid on London—"

My mother has died. My mother.

Anna was so shocked by the surprise that she felt sharply winded, as if her lungs had been punctured.

"Oh," she said. Her face opened wide. Mr. Ashton looked up at her, his eyes serious and gentle—but it was as if she was seeing him through windows of thick uneven glass.

"Oh no," she said, and began to shake, clenched hands, clenched knees, and her body rattling.

"I'm sorry," he said, "I'm so sorry."

She did not *feel* as if her mother was dead. She was immune to the meaning of his words. The news passed through her, and she simply obeyed a blank reflex not to collapse, not to let any tears spill over, just to be brave.

"How do you know?" she asked.

"What?"

"How do you know she is dead?"

He hesitated.

"They found her papers."

"Where?" She needed to know, wanted a picture, details.

"She was—buried under a building which collapsed. Probably on her way home from work one night."

"Do you think it hurt?"

"Oh no, I'm sure not—she would have died at once with no pain."

Anna stood there shivering, hardly taking in the information. Mr. Ashton, at least, was sitting down. But her whole face and body felt as exposed as a naked cliff face. She did not know what to do, or say, or where to put her hands or her eyes. She felt a smile creeping over her face, and had a terrible fear that she would laugh.

She shuddered instead. Mr. Ashton held out a handkerchief—a large white handkerchief with ironed creases—and she pressed this to her face. She sank down in a chair, cupping her face in the handkerchief to stop Mr. Ashton from seeing that she was giggling, not crying. She felt him come closer until he reached out to her shoulder. At the touch of his hand, her strange hilarity welled into tears, and she found herself sobbing rhythmically into the handkerchief.

For some minutes they stayed there together in silence. He kept his hand firmly on her shoulder until her tears subsided, but her face remained buried in his handkerchief.

What do you say to a girl who has just lost her mother? He could barely muster a word.

"Would you like to stay in here for a while? You don't have to go to lessons this afternoon . . ."

Her head was ringing with odd phrases. *No more Latin, no more French, no more sitting on the old school bench. At least I'll miss my math lesson,* she thought.

"I'm fine now," she said to Mr. Ashton, attempting to look up, hoping the laughter would not sweep back. "I'll go now."

"Are you sure?"

"Yes, thank you," she said, standing.

Her polite smile stung him: did etiquette really oblige her to thank him for reporting her mother's death?

"Just remember to ask if we can help you with anything—"

She was fidgeting to get away now. Should he keep her back, not let her go, give her a biscuit, or what? She handed back the handkerchief.

"Please—keep it," he said, and she backed off, trying to leave the room now, thanking him again for the handkerchief, which she clutched into a crumpled ball in her hand.

She was lucky not to meet anyone as she ducked out into the gardens, then escaped into the woods. Her breathing was shallow, but she ran without stopping until she reached her favorite old aspen grove. Nobody was watching. She hunkered down there on her own, and got back her breath as she folded the handkerchief into neat squares.

Then she just sat there, shaking with laughter. She did not know why.

Anna only emerged from the woods for tea. Facing the enquiring eyes of the other children, that would be daunting. She went into the dining room knowing they would have been told about her news.

"Where have you been?" asked Katy Todd.

"In the woods."

"You missed math. Fractions."

"I know. I can't do fractions."

"Shall I help you with them?" chipped in another child.

"I could help you," said another.

Help with fractions. A dead mother.

She could see it in the avid faces of the other children, their guilty fascination to know what it might feel like to lose your mother. A part of her felt strangely important: an aristocrat of grief. But she felt self-conscious and exposed too. She was lucky that Miss Weir suddenly appeared and swept her up.

"Would you like to come and pick some tomatoes with me? The cook has asked me to fetch her some."

She went with her gladly.

They set out down the drive to the Victorian glasshouse. Miss Weir walked in a calm rhythm, putting Anna at ease.

"You know, the Ashtons were amongst the first families in England to enjoy hothouse flowers and fruits."

"Why was that?"

"They had an enlightened gardener. He gave them oranges, figs and grapes. And the gentlemen in those days always had carnations for their buttonholes."

"But we're picking tomatoes?"

"Well, carnations would hardly be the thing now, Anna."

She laughed, and Anna relaxed. They reached the glasshouse, muggy with stale heat and an odd stench of overripe fruit. Anna plucked the tomatoes for Miss Weir; she placed them in her basket, then locked the rusty door behind them.

Their way back home was uphill, and neither spoke. But as they passed the last bend of the drive, Miss Weir turned and looked at Anna with her calm, gentle face.

"If you ever want to talk about your mother, Anna, please do come to me. Don't forget that we're always here to help you..."

Anna was shaken by her teacher's gaze. Gratitude welled up in her, and for a moment she was connected with her deepest feelings, making her eyes fill up. But she clenched up her face, and they walked back up to the school, with Miss Weir quietly pointing out wildflowers which Anna had never noticed before.

It was not until three nights later, once the other children had got used to her news and no longer whispered as she passed, that she cried in her bed at night, trying to remember her mother's face.

She could not remember the last words they had ever said to each other. Had she not just cried at their last parting? She thought, *There were so many things I would have liked to tell you.*

Anna would never know if her mother had got her most recent letter. Worse still, she could not remember where she had put her mother's last letter. She had read it a couple of times, but could hardly recall anything in it now. A new dance band playing at the BBC. Wondering if the spring sunshine was as fine in Yorkshire as it was in London. Was that it?

She thought, *I never said good-bye. I will never see her again. I will never send her the picture I've been drawing in art.*

She did not dare to ask the teachers about a funeral, because she guessed they would have told her if there was one to go to. What would her father think? Would they call him back from Africa?

For days she searched for her mother's final letter, but it was not in any locker or desk or anywhere she could think of. Every morning, she looked again. But it was gone.

Instead, she carried around Mr. Ashton's white handkerchief as the token of her loss.

45

As he feared, Thomas sometimes said Ruth's name in his sleep. For so long Elizabeth had been too drunk to notice such things, but one night she heard him. It puzzled her, and she began to be watchful.

It had not occurred to her that Thomas could feel anything for another woman. But now she began to observe that he was exuding private contentment, that he was warm and animated when talking to Ruth at lunch. That they studiously avoided each other's eyes.

Was there some kind of complicity between them? Ruth seemed such a prim and formal girl that Elizabeth found it hard to believe that she would dare to flirt with her husband.

But she was curious now. She started to lure Thomas once more into lovemaking at night, and found him responsive and passionate. But she saw that he closed his eyes, and she wondered if his desire was fired by thoughts of another body, another woman.

She observed the young teacher. Ruth was unfashionable and awkward, and without obvious allure—how could she appeal to Thomas? But a part of Elizabeth grew jealous, because she knew that Ruth was intelligent. She was unwilling to admit that men might be drawn to female cleverness—and yet she could see that Thomas enjoyed his solemn, bookish conversations with the young teacher.

At lunch, one day, she could not resist complimenting Ruth on the very ordinary dress that she was wearing.

237

"It looks so pretty on you," she said. Ruth blanched, and sensed the malice. Thomas did not register the insult.

After the distress caused by Pawel's departure, Elizabeth had slowly begun to revive. She had taken over the school's practical management once again, and derived a new stimulus from this work. But she was capable of caustic impatience with those who irritated her; there was a bitter self-sufficiency in her which was forbidding to kitchen staff and teachers alike. The children were generally spared her sarcasm, and sometimes she would jest with them in their break times. But they were wary of her too, knowing that her mood could suddenly darken for no obvious reason, when she would turn abruptly and walk away.

Thomas dreaded his wife's random acts of petty violence. Sometimes these flared up when she was frustrated by one of their conversations in the bedroom. Or sometimes they were dredged from the resentful vortex of her silence. Suddenly she would smash a perfume bottle on the floor, or a china dish, just wanting to break something, unable to resist her own streak of high drama. Then she would coolly walk away, to do other things, leaving the splinters of glass or porcelain scattered around.

Perhaps it was the chilly equilibrium of their marriage which provoked her, or perhaps she feared that Ashton Park wouldn't always be filled with evacuated children. By the autumn of 1942, the tide of the war appeared to be turning at last: the Allies had triumphed at El Alamein, and Hitler's army was hemorrhaging men in Russia, outnumbered by Stalin's apparently limitless forces.

But there were still frequent casualties on the home front, keeping the evacuees at Ashton. In January, the papers reported the tragedy of a school near London which was bombed as the children watched a performance of *A Midsummer Night's Dream*. The school collapsed under a direct hit, and twenty-three schoolgirls were killed, together with four teachers. Parents worked through the night with defense workers to recover the children's bodies. *"Charles Alford, a gunner on leave, came to the school to find the corpse of his four-year-old daughter Brenda carried out from the debris,"* read Thomas, stricken by such random young deaths.

Bomb blasts were never more than a distant echo at Ashton, but there were occasional domestic mishaps. Two boys were playing a vigorous game of badminton in the Marble Hall one Saturday morning, when their shuttlecock hit the chandelier wire with particular force, putting the final stress on a fixture which had been quietly disintegrating for a hundred years. There was an ominous noise. The boys paused warily, then ran to one side as the chandelier came crashing down and shattered on the marble floor. The sound of breaking glass reverberated through the entire house.

Thomas heard the noise, and hurried over to see what had happened. Stunned children lingered at the edge of the hall, staring at a sea of smashed crystal. Slivers of glass had scattered into every corner. He saw Elizabeth appear at the other side, followed by Ruth.

Elizabeth took charge and called for brooms and buckets. From the gallery above the hall, Anna and the others gazed down onto the glinting shards. The carcass of the chandelier lay inert on the floor, with colored lights shimmering through its prisms in a show of pointless magic. The glass crunched underfoot, and tinkled when brushed away.

For months afterwards, the children were always finding tiny splinters of glass in every far-flung corner of the house, carried there on the soles of their shoes.

Ruth was unnerved by the broken chandelier; she took it as a sign. How long could she and Thomas go on as lovers before the whole precarious edifice of his life came crashing down? She was afraid of Elizabeth and her cool hard glances.

Nonsense, said Thomas; it was just an old wire. But he, too, was anxious to find a way forwards. He had no wish to continue hiding Ruth as his mistress, but he wanted to be sure that she really did want to be with him. Had their consummation marked the end of an infatuation or the beginning of a deeper bond? The months went by, and it felt to him as if they were growing closer to each other all the time.

But he still worried about the difference in their ages, and about his disability. He knew she ought to have children of her own, and that he should put her off, really, not let her get stuck with him through a sense of honor. Yet he sensed that sometimes odd love, unexpected love, could create a deeper union. At least so he tried to tell himself.

From the library window, he watched her in the gardens one day. There was a spring in her step and a freedom in her shoulders as if she had thrown off a burden.

Ruth had not yet told him that she had missed her period. At first she thought nothing of being a few days late. But the days passed and her breasts felt faintly enlarged and no release came.

The next time they were together, he read her unease, and the dread rose up in him that she was trying to part from him. She sensed his fears, so she blurted it out, that she was late, might be pregnant.

She looked anxiously into his face, but saw only a spontaneous flash of joy there.

"That's the most wonderful news I could ever hope for—"

"I thought you might be worried about a scandal."

"Do you think anyone who has longed for a child cares a thing about that? It's *miraculous* news—a child, with you. It's more than I could ever have wished for," he added, jubilant.

If he could give her children, then they could be together. It was that simple. He embraced her for the first time with the feeling that he could offer her a future: she could be his, now. He could not believe his good fortune as he kissed her.

Ruth went to the hospital in York, where her pregnancy was confirmed. Thomas felt an overwhelming urgency now to be free for her, before it showed. But he dreaded the conversation which he knew he must have with Elizabeth. He rehearsed it endlessly in his mind. No time seemed right. The days ticked away until he could postpone it no longer.

One spring afternoon in 1943 he asked his wife to meet him in his study. She knew something was wrong when she stepped into the room and he asked her to close the door. He wheeled himself forwards and tried to look at her.

"There's something I need to talk to you about."

"Go on," she said, waiting.

"I've been putting off this conversation because I didn't want anyone to be unhappy. But, Elizabeth, I think the time has come to try . . . parting."

"What are you saying?"

"I'd like us to separate."

"But why?"

"Because our marriage has drifted to . . . to an end, and there is still time for both of us to—start again, find somebody else."

"What is this all about?"

"I just think the time has come to face our mutual differences."

"You're not being truthful. You mean *you* want to be free. I don't want that."

"Surely you do?"

"I don't."

"You would feel released if you weren't locked in with me."

"You're making excuses, Thomas."

She waited for an answer, but when none came she pressed on.

"There's somebody else, isn't there? Go on, say it."

He was surprised. She knew.

"And what if there is?"

"Do you think I haven't noticed you watching your little schoolmistress? She's pathetic."

He ignored the provocation, and resisted the temptation to mention Pawel. He simply wanted his freedom, with as much dignity for them both as was possible.

"Whatever the circumstances, I am asking you for a divorce."

"I don't want to give you one."

"Why not?"

"Because you're my husband and I love you." She said this with fierce sarcasm, but he knew it was true, too, in a strange way.

"Then I'm asking you for your help," he said. "We're not happy, either of us."

"Are you going to tell me you're in love? She won't have you. People will laugh at you. The crippled Thomas Ashton and his little girl."

"I would like to leave Ruth out of this."

"Ruth? Ruth is it? Have you tried kissing her yet?" She laughed.

"Please, Elizabeth—"

"She's just fooling with you. She'll want a man her own age, and children, not a middle-aged man in a wheelchair who's already saddled with a vengeful wife."

Elizabeth looked imperious. For a moment he despised her.

"She will have children," he said quietly.

Elizabeth looked at him sharply.

"She will have children?" she asked. "What do you mean by that? *She will have children?* Tell me! Is she pregnant? Is she? Is she?"

Thomas held her gaze, narrowed his eyes.

"Yes," he said, and watched shock and pain sweep across her face. Immediately, he regretted his bluntness, but it was too late; Elizabeth's posture slumped as if some fragile inner strut had snapped inside her. At a stroke, her connection with her husband, his house, their life, was completely severed. *He had an heir.*

"These things happen," said Thomas in a conciliatory tone, retreating into truisms.

"*I wanted a child.*"

He glimpsed, for a moment, the depth of her grief. It was not so much a jealousy of Ruth, nor even of him, but more a wretched unfulfilled longing for her own child.

"I'm sorry, Elizabeth. I'm so sorry."

She was crying. He waited for her tears to ease, but the minutes passed and she would not look at him.

He knew it was wrong, but he felt impatient. He did not want her to suffer and yet he did want to be released—soon. She looked up, and finally he met her eyes.

"No," she said. "No, I will not let you go." And she left the room.

Thomas stayed where he was, reminding himself that this was just the first stage. He braced himself to talk to her again when she was calmer.

He had not yet told Ruth that he would be speaking to Elizabeth that afternoon, but they were due to meet later, when he would warn her to keep her distance from his wife.

Thomas had not divined that Elizabeth was now in the grip of a hatred so intense that a malign force seemed to be driving her. She waited impatiently for Ruth to finish her last afternoon lesson, then she accosted her briskly in the staff room, and asked her to join her on a trip to the village.

"We need to pick up a shipment of new blankets," she said, not waiting for a reply. Her face was glacial; the younger woman followed her in puzzled submission.

They climbed into the car. Elizabeth's clenched rage was such that she did not even look at Ruth. *Pregnant.* This girl was carrying Thomas's child. The thought revolted her.

She reversed the car and turned to drive out through the

forecourt gates. The gravel rasped under her wheels. Ruth sensed her bitterness, and was immediately afraid. What did she know?

Elizabeth pushed her foot on the pedal, and the car gathered speed down the long white drive. She said nothing, but gripped the wheel, looking ahead to the cattle-grid gateposts midway down the road. She accelerated.

Even as she forced the pedal, Elizabeth regretted her choice, but sheer speed hurtled them forwards. Ruth saw the moment coming, yet was mute with terror. *Please slow down, please.* The trees were flying past, the sky was rushing towards her, until the car crashed straight into one of the wrought-iron gateposts. Elizabeth lurched forwards onto the steering wheel, snapping her neck and her life. Ruth was thrown through the window onto the road, her clear face ripped by breaking glass: she and her unborn child died on impact with the concrete drive.

Up at the house, Thomas heard the crash and had a sickening instinct that it was the sound of Elizabeth's violence. He wheeled himself out into the Marble Hall, and various people ran onto the drive. For what seemed endless minutes, he waited to hear the news. He desperately wished that Ruth would appear, but she was probably up in her room and had heard nothing. Soon he would send one of the girls to fetch her.

It was Mr. Stewart who hurried back, white-faced, to tell him that Elizabeth's car had crashed: that his wife was dead.

Almost as an afterthought, he added that Ruth Weir had been with her.

"Is she all right?" asked Thomas in a rush of fear.

". . . I'm afraid she's dead too."

Thomas's heart lurched and he could not breathe. He looked up, raw with shock.

"I must see them," he said. "Will you take me to them?"

And so Jock Stewart pushed Thomas down the drive, with his chair wheels grinding over the stony surface, to the midway gateposts where the two bodies had been laid out on the grass. The car was a contorted wreck of buckled metal and smashed glass. Somebody had brought out blankets to lay over the corpses. Thomas asked to see the bodies, and they uncovered his wife.

Elizabeth's jaw was bruised and her hair had come loose, but her look was closed and finished and distant. As if in sleep.

He looked on and felt his tears welling, because it was the other body he wished to see.

"Can I see Ruth too?" He said her name. He could not call her Miss Weir: he had to use her proper name.

His chair was wheeled over, and somebody uncovered the blanket. Ruth's face was torn and swollen. There was no expression, just a destroyed face: the light in her eyes snuffed out. Where was she, the spirit he cherished so dearly?

Every part of him was stretched out into an inward howl of pain. It should not have been her. How could she be gone? And the child growing inside her—their child, who might have redeemed all the sorrows he had ever known, now lost to both of them.

He sat on the drive of Ashton Park, crumpled into his chair. His love was dead and only because of him. He felt nothing for Elizabeth—no rage, no bitterness, just a blank hole. All his tenderness was consumed by grief for this poor young woman who would have lived if she had not met him.

I should never have allowed you to love me, he thought. *Then you would still be alive, and free to live your life.*

They left him there, with his head in his hands.

The afternoon became evening. Thomas asked to be left alone in his study, and ignored the usual school routines, chapel, supper. Stewart tried to bring him some food, but he was too overwrought to eat. The undertakers had taken away the bodies, and they would have to discuss funeral arrangements in the morning. Thomas put him off till then.

At about nine o'clock, once the children had gone upstairs to bed, Thomas went into the saloon to distract himself at the piano.

The night drew in and he played on, with blunt fingers, Chopin, Schubert. Much of the time he just sat there, stunned with his loss, drinking the whisky he had brought with him.

He was sitting in the dark, but a light spilled through from the Marble Hall. Sometimes he drifted into sleep, sometimes he awoke, and his fingers reached over the piano keys once more. His whisky was sliding away. He was half-drunk.

Deep into the night, the saloon door eased open, and a child appeared, backlit by the light from the hall. It was Anna Sands, shivering. She stepped further forwards tentatively.

"Hello."

"Shouldn't you be in bed?"

"I can't sleep."

"Neither can I."

She came over and crouched awkwardly at his feet. They sat there in silence—until Anna began to cry.

"I'm so sorry," she mumbled. Thomas was weary beyond everything, but he remembered that this child's own mother had also recently died, and was moved by her, despite his own sorrow.

"Now don't you worry," he said, and reached down to her in the half-light.

Before he knew it, she had grasped his hand and pulled herself forwards and curled up on his knee, burying her face in his shoulder. His arms, at first flapping indecisively, found their way to hold her in comfort. In an instant their limbs were folded together in a silent shape of mutual commiseration.

Nothing was said. The girl wept silently, for her mother and her teacher. Even for Mrs. Ashton.

The contact with another person broke something open in Thomas, and his eyes spilled over too. For a long time they shook together, clasping each other in the dark. Slightly inebriated, Thomas had an odd feeling that this girl could read his mind.

"You know, I loved her," he murmured. Anna said nothing; she was drowsy and drained after her sobbing, and sank deeper into Thomas's shoulder.

"I loved her as I have never loved before," he went on. "I don't know if I can live without her." In the darkness, in the silence, he felt the girl's breathing settle against his chest, felt her drifting into sleep. Her gentle rhythm put him out too.

It was three o'clock in the morning before Thomas awoke, feeling parched and distressed. He found the girl still nestled against his shoulder. Anxiously, he roused her. He had woken up agitated by the thought of anyone prying in Ruth's room.

"Anna, Anna, please do this for me," he asked her gently. "Go to her room, and search it for any letters, any diaries, anything personal she might have."

Am I mad? he asked himself.

"Whose room?" said a startled Anna, blinking in his arms.

"Miss Weir, your teacher."

Anna had woken up confused, but was just sharp enough to feign ignorance. She tumbled from his arms and set off almost at a run to the top floor, in the middle of the night, not quite knowing what she was looking for.

She was breathless and dazed when she arrived at Miss Weir's room. She closed the door quietly before switching on the light. The brightness pricked her awake at once. The room was so tidy.

She opened the drawers and found clothes, handkerchiefs, folded underwear. She looked at the books in the shelves, neatly ordered. But she couldn't find any letters.

Then she thought of lifting Miss Weir's mattress. And there, sticking through the wire loops of the bed frame, she saw a bundle of papers pressed inside a book. She pulled it out. The letters were all in Mr. Ashton's handwriting. She took them out, then clapped the book shut and placed it on the shelf.

Downstairs, Thomas was waiting for her in the dark, just inside the saloon door. Anna handed him the sheaf of papers, and she could just see the gleam of his eyes. The night was waning now, and they could make out each other's faces as strange pale masks.

"They were under her mattress," she said in a small voice.

"Thank you," he said, "thank you so much, Anna. Now go to bed. And let's keep this as our secret." He was whispering in an empty room. Anna nodded and smiled. She had helped. She was not some common child with no mother: she was a favorite with Mr. Ashton. They had a secret, and she would keep it forever.

Anna hauled herself to her dormitory and fell at once into a deep sleep. When she awoke at the sound of the bell, she hardly knew whether her strange night had been a dream or not. Queuing at the washbasins, she felt giddy, almost buoyant, as if she were floating with ghosts. She had lost her mother—and now Miss Weir and Mrs. Ashton were gone too.

Yet it seemed as if dead people still went on living in your head—you could talk to them. She clattered down the stone stairs to breakfast, and every sound echoed in her ears, as if emanating from her own mind.

She felt tired and dazed all morning, but something drew her back to the tidy silence of Miss Weir's room. After lunch she sneaked back up there and took down the book which she had found hidden under the mattress. It was a worn blue book of verse by "*Alfred, Lord Tennyson*," with cloth covers and thin, frail paper. She saw some writing inside—*Ruth Weir, Oxford 1938*. Anna slipped the book under her cardigan and took it to her dormitory, where she hid it amongst the wire coils of her iron bedstead, under her own mattress.

46

IN THE MONTHS that followed the funerals, Thomas estranged himself from the other adults at Ashton Park. What went on inside him, nobody knew. He could barely muster anything more than formalities, reverting to that stiff reticence which had always been his diplomatic mask.

At the same time, an unspoken bond developed between him and Anna. The death of the girl's mother had, in a way, given him almost a parental role, and he took extra care to watch over her. He would call her over at the end of a class to clarify a point. Or sometimes he encouraged her to browse through the books in his study. Neither of them ever discussed their strange night of shared grief, but a knowledge of that intimacy underscored their bond. She was always respectful, and never overfamiliar with him, nor he with her.

Thomas picked out books for her to read, and praised her insights when she reported back on them. It was a consoling relationship, paternal and tender, mentor and pupil, both drawing from each other. Unconsciously perhaps, Anna relaxed into emotional security because she had been singled out. And for Thomas, there was the privilege of having some small daily outlet for his natural kindness.

It was an alliance which both of them came to depend upon in an unacknowledged way. So it was a shock when Anna's situation suddenly changed and the time arrived for her to leave Ashton.

In the late summer of 1943, she received a letter from her father in Africa. He was quick to assure her that he was safe, but his left leg had been injured when a mine had overturned his jeep, so he was being sent home from the front line, and would be taking a staff college job in the London area.

Now that the bombings have died down, he wrote, *I want to bring you home too.*

Anna was so excited that she did not at first consider that Ashton might now be her home, and that she would miss her friends and her teachers. Above all, Mr. Ashton.

As the day of her departure drew closer, she thought of nothing but her bedroom at home, and all the treats to come with her father. She was twelve now, and had not seen him for four years. She craved family life, and the chance to talk about her mother.

But the day before her father came to fetch her, she felt an odd rush of sadness as she sat in an English class with Mr. Ashton. She answered a question, and he looked at her with such amused tenderness that for a moment she felt troubled to be leaving him. He had been like a father to her, and yet he was not her father. She felt a complicated knot inside.

The next day, her excitement was offset by a peculiar homesickness which dragged on her heart. Longing and regret tugged at her together, as she waited and waited in the Marble Hall. She looked out of the window, and there was no sign of her father. In the end, she stopped looking and sat on the floor with a book, feeling sick inside.

It was just after lunch when she heard the sound of the great doors opening, and with a rush of joy she saw her father appear. He had a slight limp, and his face looked older and thinner than she remembered. She ran over to him so that he would know it was her.

"Daddy!"

"Anna, my darling."

His arms were outstretched, familiar arms which could hold her tight. He beamed at her, shaking his head, marveling at how she had grown. He lifted her up and swung her round, a swoop of elation racing through her as the room spiraled by. She was giddy when he put her down, and shy about exactly what to do next.

"This is the Marble Hall," she said, turning solemn as she started to give him a guided tour of the house. Children came by, stopping to meet her father, and she held his hand firmly; he was hers alone.

Lewis could barely hold back his own tears.

Her suitcase was packed, the one she had arrived with in 1939. In her happy trance, Anna still knew that there was an etiquette to be followed, and people to say good-bye to. Her friends Beth and Mary—she hugged them both at once, and promised she would write. Mr. Stewart, inscrutable but avuncular, shook her hand and told her father that she was a most promising pupil. Mrs. Robson, the housekeeper, embraced her fondly.

But there was still Mr. Ashton to say good-bye to. Anna was eager to find him: she was hopeful that he might be impressed by her polite and tidy father. But as they reached his study door, she realized with a sickening lurch that this was the last time she would see her teacher, that she was almost gone from him.

The door opened, and Mr. Ashton welcomed them in. He was charming and polite to Lewis, who was at first a touch confused by this disabled gentleman's role in his daughter's life. Anna stood very still in his study, he noticed, attentive but slightly breathless. Mr. Ashton, meanwhile, was very particular in his praise of her.

"You must be so proud of your daughter, Mr. Sands."

"Of course. Thank you for having her here, I can see she's been very well looked after."

"It was our pleasure—she's been one of our best pupils. I only hope she will keep up her studies, because all things could be open to her. Any university she chooses, I should imagine."

"Really?"

"Very much so."

Lewis looked at his daughter, who was blushing with pride and gladness. Mr. Ashton turned to her, and extended his hand.

"Good-bye, my dear," he said.

Anna stepped forwards, her eyes widening in an anxiety of love. She shook his hand and looked into the warm, smiling face of this man who had entered her heart and soul without her even noticing.

"Good-bye, sir," she said, swallowing her words.

"It's been a privilege," he said, and held her face with his smile for a moment. His eyes were liquid with tenderness.

"Thank you," she said, almost looking at him. "Thank you very much for everything."

Neither of them could muster anything more substantial to say to each other, though their handshake was firm and deep and reached through both of them.

Lewis waited for Anna to turn before thanking Mr. Ashton once again, then he took his daughter off and away on the long journey home to London.

Anna did not look back as they set off down the drive, but she was quiet and thoughtful.

Thomas wheeled himself back to his desk and continued to mark the exercise books of other children. He wondered what would become of Anna Sands, and wished her well in his thoughts. *A lovely girl,* he said to himself.

Several of the evacuees had returned home now, and their replacements were dwindling. The German threat was waning, the Allies were gaining ground. But he did not want Ashton House to be left empty of children. It occurred to him that perhaps he should try to turn the house into a school permanently.

That was his chief solace now, the sound of children running around the place.

47

Back home in Fulham, Lewis and Anna did their best to settle down together. They found their house clogged up with dust and dirt, and on their first night they simply sheltered from the miserable unkemptness of the place. But the mess gave them a task to tackle together, and the next day they cleaned and dusted and scrubbed until it felt once more like their home.

Lewis buckled several times a day at the thought of his missing wife, though he did not let his daughter see that. One afternoon he went up to Anna's room and found her hunched on her bed, clutching her old teddy and weeping over her mother's photograph. He sat down beside her and held her as she cried, clenching back his own tears.

"You shouldn't have to go through this," he said. "I'm so sorry. You don't know how sorry I am."

It occurred to him then, as Anna shook in his arms, that his own grief for Roberta was nothing compared to his anguish that Anna had lost her mother. The people at Ashton Park had clearly been kind, but that could never have been enough; his child had been left alone for too long. He wished he could comfort Anna and help her, but he knew that what she really needed was her own mother. And the stolen years of her childhood.

Lewis was naturally patient, and organized too. He found the nearest school which was working and settled Anna back there. Then he took an instructor's job with flexible hours at a staff college in Wimbledon, so he was often able to join her at home for a late tea. He cleaned their clothes and looked after the house and got up early to make breakfast for both of them.

He loved his daughter. Practical care was his way of showing it.

Anna was surprised by the feelings which crept up on her at home. The pain of her mother's absence was revived by the strange silence of the house, the lack of conversation and laughter. Her father was kind, but untalkative.

But more, she had no idea that she would miss Ashton Park—yet she did. She wrote letters to her friends, anxious for news. Then found that their short replies did not satisfy her. Only gradually did she admit to herself that it was news of Mr. Ashton that she craved. Because it was him that she missed.

Of course, she knew that he had liked her, spoiled her even. But now that she was gone, she could only imagine that some other child was his favorite. The thought pierced her with jealousy.

One afternoon, Lewis returned home from work to find her sitting in the kitchen, a picture of melancholy. He asked her what was wrong, but she would not say: she could not reveal her feelings to anyone, least of all her father. So he assumed— as always—that it must be his inadequacy as a father, and his daughter's longing for her mother.

One Sunday morning, Anna decided there was no harm in writing to Mr. Ashton: if he did not want to reply, he need not. She spent three days writing and rewriting her letter, then posted it and waited, daily, for a response.

In due course, a reply arrived. It was short and polite, but also friendly and full of jokes about the antics of a new school dog called Harold. It was signed *Yours sincerely*. Anna replied with a description of her home, her new school, and many loving remarks about her father. She also signed off *Yours sincerely*, following her teacher's lead. He replied ten days later, this time with a longer letter, one addressed to the cracks he had observed in her cheery account of school life. He wanted her to be sure, above all, to believe in her abilities, and to keep up her reading. He signed it *With my love*. Anna spent the next few days reading and rereading the letter just to try to understand whether he really meant *love* or that was simply a casual sign-off for a letter.

But she did not reply to his letter, because she did not know how to—nor did she show it to her father. It was a loving letter, but it felt conclusive: there was nothing else he might say to her, nor did he indicate any wish for an answer. So she cherished the letter, but accepted that it signaled an end to her relationship with Mr. Ashton. Thereafter, she only *thought* about him, and felt a secret comfort that perhaps he cared about her, even if they did not see each other.

Her new home life was at last taking shape, and she was beginning to feel more at ease with her father. He would tell her stories of his months in the Western Desert. How it was so hot that they could fry eggs on the jeep bonnets. How he had loved the vanishing horizon of the desert, and the star-studded velvet night skies. How he would never forget driving along the coast road, and the day he ran down a scalding sandy beach into a sea so blue, so clear, so perfect that it just made him shout with joy.

He missed out the frightening bits. Driving in bumpy convoys over miles of desert scrubland, never knowing when they would hit a minefield. Finding abandoned tanks with flyblown corpses. The boyish German soldier he had seen lying dead beside a bombed jeep, still clutching a photograph of his smiling baby. The day his own jeep had toppled down a dune, leaving him howling in pain with a shattered leg.

All that seemed to belong to another world. Here they were back in London, a city of shifting shapes: so many buildings and people had disappeared without trace.

In the summer of 1944, when Hitler's lethal V1 flying bombs were launched, Lewis wondered if he would have to evacuate his daughter again, but Anna begged him to let her stay. No more family partings. So they used the cellar shelter, and stuck to their new life. Breakfast together, then school for her and staff college for him, culminating in evenings listening to the wireless.

Once a year, father and daughter visited Roberta's grave in Putney Vale, bearing flowers. They stood there solemn-faced for a few minutes, side by side in the quiet cemetery. Sometimes, Anna would cry at the sight of her mother's name on the headstone.

Well-meaning people occasionally said to Anna that although her mother had died she would still be there for her, as a star in the sky. But whenever Anna looked up at the night sky, all she could see was blank space—a vastness which killed any hope of contact, or closeness of any kind. There was just you, and the universe beyond, and the two might never connect. All those school hymns of singing constellations, or the music of the spheres, meant little to her now. There was only cold dark space stretching on forever, split by the eerie whine of Hitler's bombs.

Until these, too, faded away, replaced at last by the pealing of London church bells as Berlin fell, and the war ended, leaving Anna and millions of others to get on with the rest of their lives.

48

Iː ɴ ᴀᴘʀɪʟ 1945, Lady Norton left the British embassy in Bern and drove across Switzerland to the German border, heading towards the concentration camp known as Dachau. She was driving a lorry loaded with medical supplies which she had rounded up from various Swiss pharmaceutical firms. Near Munich, she struggled to find fresh supplies of petrol, but soon cajoled some American soldiers into filling her tank.

The year before, Jewish refugees had escaped into Switzerland with shocking reports of German camps designed for systematic genocide. They had briefed her husband at the embassy, who had sent urgent dispatches back to London proposing that Allied planes should at least bomb the train lines to the camps. But word came back that although Churchill was sympathetic to Norton's report, the air commanders had scotched the plea, arguing that they could not afford to lose any more airmen.

Peter had shared her husband's frustration at the Allies' inaction, but with the German surrender came the opportunity to bring aid to those rumored camps. After living out the war in the strange comfort of Switzerland, she braced herself for a glimpse of what had been going on across the border.

Two hours before she reached Dachau, the first American soldiers had liberated the camp with a hasty round of illegal executions, which later became notorious. The young Americans had apparently been so horrified by what they found that they raised their machine guns and mowed down more than three hundred SS guards. By the time Peter drew up in her lorry, the place was in chaos.

Despite all the rumors about these camps, nothing could have prepared her for the shock of her arrival. There was a sickening stench by the railway entrance, where a mass grave was piled high with rotting corpses whose skeletal limbs obtruded at odd angles. Then, entering the gates, she had her first harrowing sight of emaciated figures walking towards her in staccato steps, halfway between life and death.

Peter steeled herself to her task, unloading her provisions with blinkered energy and trying to be helpful, but the horror of the place soon overwhelmed her. It was a stinking rubbish dump of dead people, and those walking skeletons still clinging to life appeared almost devoid of humanity, with sunken eyes. The aid workers were reduced to a defensive stupor, dazed by the unimaginable cruelty inflicted on these prisoners.

But it was not the brutality of the guards which made the greatest impression upon Peter—rather, it was their victims' capacity for suffering. She was finally overcome by the agonized grief of a dying mother stroking her skeletal child who was long since dead.

Escaping from this woman's flailing hand, Peter retreated to her lorry cab for a moment to gather herself. But once alone, she found herself shuddering into tears. She cried that they were too late to help these people lying at their feet in meaningless, ungrieved heaps. She cried in anger that nobody had listened to her husband's reports. She cried because she had no faith which might bring shape or sense to the calamities of this camp.

All her life, she had lived through art, but all the art she had ever known could not redeem the despair of this place. Here there was pain and anguish beyond any expression, and beyond any hope of relief.

She wiped her face and breathed deeply, and returned to the back of the lorry for the next batch of medicine. Bit by bit, she did what she could to be practical on behalf of those who might recover. Something is better than nothing: that was all she could hold on to.

After three days she had exhausted her supplies, and the survivors were all being attended to—and the dead tidied away. So she drove her empty lorry back to the embassy at Bern, and returned to the carefully anesthetized existence which passed for her life there.

She tried to tell her husband about what she had seen, yet she could not quite retrieve the truth of what she had felt.

Within months, she and her husband began to pick up the pieces of their prewar routines, and she resumed her bracing enthusiasm for daily life. But every now and again, the smell of that camp would come back to her. And for a moment, she would grasp again what the place had told her—about the limitless capacity for human suffering. And the fear would seize her again that random but unspeakable pain might strike anyone at any time, and that her own blithe disposition was a mere carapace of deluded hope, no more than a defensive illusion.

Back to
the Old House

1946–2006

49

Soon after the war, when the storage vaults of the British embassy in Warsaw were reopened, someone uncovered a stack of Peter Norton's paintings which she had left behind when fleeing the Nazis in 1939. There were canvases by Kandinsky, Klee, Duchamp and Ernst, all from Peter's prewar collection at the London Gallery.

"Let the Poles keep them for their galleries—they have lost everything else," she insisted with her usual generosity.

She and her husband had recently packed up all their belongings yet again, after being posted to a new flashpoint, Greece, where civil war was devastating a country already ravaged by the Nazis. But by 1948, the steady flow of American dollars from the Marshall Plan was beginning to revive the economy, allowing the Nortons to enjoy their postwar life in Athens.

Peter continued to support the cause of modern art, although her enthusiasm for young artists did not always suit the more dignified trappings of diplomatic life. One Christmas, she hid two young painters—John Craxton and Lucian Freud—in the embassy garage, where they kept themselves scarce from Sir Clifford, until General Montgomery came to stay and rumbled them.

More acceptable to her husband was the major Athens exhibition of Henry Moore's work, which she mounted with the artist in 1951, to international praise. Norton was proud, too, of how readily the Greeks treasured his wife for her indefatigable charity work; during the civil war, she made numerous trips up into the mountains with mules, ferrying parcels of food and clothing to camps of orphans and refugees made homeless by fighting. In recognition of her tireless initiatives to relieve poverty in outlying Greek villages, she was awarded the honorary citizenship of Athens—"a rare distinction," as Norton told their visiting friends.

After the Nortons finally retired back to Chelsea, Peter continued to fund new and undiscovered talent, supporting the early careers of numerous painters, from Francis Bacon to Yves Klein, and many others whose work was later lost along the way.

She spent much of her time in Paris too, seeking out French avant-garde artists, and it was on the Left Bank, in 1955, that she bumped into Pawel Bielinski again at a party. He had lived there since the war, he explained, and was now part of a circle of Jewish artists and writers, Avigdor Arikha and Paul Celan among them.

The following morning Peter walked up the many stairs to Pawel's studio and there, propped against the walls, stood several paintings of a naked woman with long hair, reflected in a triptych of mirrors.

"I heard about Elizabeth's death," he said to her, anticipating her recognition, "but how is Thomas?"

Peter shrugged, said it was always so hard to know with Thomas—he was such a private man, always so polite. But all *appeared* to be well with him. Ashton Park was a school now, and Thomas was still teaching there.

"I think he's probably a very good teacher," she added, to be positive.

"He was a very patient man, I remember," replied Pawel. Peter did not press him any further, but she did buy one of his paintings of Elizabeth. And when she returned to her house in Chelsea, she hung it in her study.

Her husband recognized the portrait at once, and it moved him, even though he had never liked Elizabeth.

"Keep it there," he said, "to remind us of the past." They did not mention the picture to Thomas, not knowing what his reaction would be.

The Nortons did not see Thomas very much anymore—nor did any of his old friends, because he hardly ever came down to London after the war. His Regent's Park house had been half destroyed in the Blitz, so he had sold it to a developer in 1946, unable to face its renovation himself.

As Thomas grew older, he only really felt comfortable in Yorkshire, and so he settled there permanently—continuing to teach at Ashton Park, where a girls' boarding school was established soon after the war.

Every September, he would watch as a new group of eight-year-old children arrived in the Marble Hall with their freckles and pigtails and school trunks—before emerging four years later as reflective girls who would tilt their heads to one side and frown slightly before answering a question.

There were always so many children passing through his life now, each year a fresh generation to be moved by—but Thomas did still sometimes pause and wonder what had become of those first children he had known, those who had been evacuated to his house during the war. Too many of them had vanished from his mind, like footprints in the sand.

50

London, 1957

Anna Sands entered an anonymous hotel lobby in Holborn. A brash chandelier cast an unnerving flare onto muted green walls, and she was half aware of the reflected glare of a polished floor, with shimmers of light unsettling her balance.

Her partner was thirty years her senior, aging, balding, with a thickening waist and a grizzled beard. Three weeks earlier they had met at the Frankfurt Book Fair, where both of them were guests at a raucous party in a baroque hotel bar. There was a crush of publishers with cigarettes and wineglasses, and when a mutual colleague introduced them, she had to repeat her name twice in all the noise. He was the sales director of one of the bigger publishing houses—self-confident, determinedly lowbrow—while she was a junior editor at a literary imprint.

At first, she only talked to him out of politeness, and hardly listened to his questions. He was overripe, his body going to seed, a heavy man who liked to drink and smoke. She was a fresh-looking twenty-six-year-old, with a girlish face but a woman's body.

She was about to move off when he insisted on buying her a drink. As he handed her the glass, she saw a flash of tenderness in his eyes, and he called her "my dear." That was always the giveaway—their connection was made.

Ten days later he rang her office and asked her out to lunch, at an Italian restaurant near the British Museum. They sat at a corner table and played with their food while talking about Graham Greene's novels and his understanding of odd love.

He had been married for twenty-five years, she for three. She felt herself growing wet as he studied her face. When he reached out to hold her hand, she was afraid to raise her eyes to his in case they welled up.

He had already chosen the hotel, within walking distance of their lunch. It was raining and the pavements were slick—people walked with their coat collars up and their heads down. They shared his umbrella and he steered the way.

There was discomfort for her as they checked in, and the neat brunette receptionist was careful not to meet her glance. Anna wanted to say, *I am a decent educated woman with a husband at home.* But she did not want to leave either. He was more at ease with the procedure.

They reached their room and closed the door behind them.

For the first time they were alone together. It was a moment they had both hankered after, ever since she had accepted his lunch invitation.

He took off his jacket and smiled at her in a way that was ribald and wry, but tender too, and vulnerable. Their eyes locked into each other as they reached forwards to kiss. Then he held her tightly wrapped in his arms.

She undid his tie, then his shirt, and saw the grizzled hair on his chest. She rested her head against him and felt his pleasure at this yielding.

The uncovering of her breasts was a moment of excitement for him; she knew that she hid their size beneath her clothes. "*Look at you!*" he said, and she sank once more into his arms, feeling self-conscious for a moment, until he led her to the bed and their lovemaking began.

Later, when they dressed, neither of them knew if there would be a second time. As they parted, he looked into her eyes with sentimental kindness, and told her she was lovely.

She had no umbrella, and her hair was disheveled with rain by the time she reached her office. It was late, too late, and she invented a spurious meeting with an agent to satisfy a curious colleague. She could not concentrate on any of the manuscripts before her.

After work, riding home on the underground to her husband, Anna sat down on an empty seat and tried to stop herself shaking. What was this transgressive streak in her, she asked herself. She was scared, and close to the edge, and could not fathom why she felt this need for intimacy with men old enough to be her father.

She loved her husband, Jamie, who was dark haired and attractive, and successful in every way—in his spontaneity, in his friendships, in his creative life as a radio producer. His boyish vitality spilled over into every moment of his day: whether he was running for a bus or charming a receptionist, there was always a bounce, a smile, a dash about him which captivated anyone he ever met.

For two years now, they had been trying for a child without success. The doctor had told them there was nothing wrong with either of them—that they must be patient and relax, and a child would come.

But Anna feared it was all her fault. In the intimacy of their bedroom, she could feel her husband's desire and yet her own body would not respond with an answering release. She could not understand why, nor did they discuss it.

Yet that night, as her lithe young husband made love to her, she did come for him—but only by closing her eyes to think of the aging sales director with his crumpled face and grizzled body, and his sentimental eyes.

"I love you, my darling," Jamie said afterwards, as they lay together. He stroked her inner thigh, a place he loved to rest his hand.

"I love you too," she said. And the word *love* unleashed a shudder of confused guilt right through to her womb.

51

London, 1964

CHILDREN HAD ARRIVED in the end for Anna. She was a mother now, with a son and daughter. Every Friday to Monday, she would stay at home in Bayswater, playing with her children, hanging their washed nappies on a rack over the bath, and taking them for walks in Hyde Park. But midweek she would still set off to her old publishing house in the West End.

On those days, she would emerge from Oxford Circus station and make her way through Soho knowing that she was lucky and blessed—or so it would appear to anyone watching her as she swung along the streets in her skirt and boots and colored raincoat. Here she was, a young woman in her prime of life, with children at home and a husband at the BBC, setting off to work with a face which could engage anyone she passed on the pavement.

Just before nine thirty she would arrive at the Georgian building which housed her publishing firm, a literary imprint founded by a Viennese émigré. It was her job to find fresh voices which might uncover new emotions for the reading public. Every Wednesday the company held an editorial meeting in which they would discuss the latest submissions.

But in the last few weeks, something strange had been happening to Anna: she could no longer read. Her in-tray was spilling over with unread manuscripts as she struggled with her mental block. All week she had been staring at the same piles of paper, and secretly crying. She went for walks to disguise the tears, then returned to the stack of unread novels, facing once more her word-blindness.

It seemed as if the link between words and their meanings had somehow been severed, until all she could see was neat rows of black marks. Just ink—just the shape of ink. She sat at her desk, quietly stringing paper clips together, not knowing how to stop this unraveling. Soon every part of her life was infected.

"You're not listening," said her daughter, as Anna crouched on the stairs at home and stared at the wall, not hearing her questions. Instead of playing with her children, she just sat still and watched them. Their washing piled up.

When Jamie returned home, she would cook supper like an automaton. Sitting down to eat with her husband, his voice came to her as if from an ill-tuned radio.

Every day, she continued to brush her teeth, and lay out the breakfast things, and walk the children to nursery. She put money in the machine to buy her Tube ticket and heard the clunk of the coins falling down the chute. She followed safe routines which might keep her on a steady track, but secretly she was gone, off and away into a silent place with no gravity, where all you did was float and look.

She began to see things in trancelike, subaqueous colors. The world came to her as a flicker of disconnected details, raindrops on a car roof, chewing gum on the pavement, a stray white hair on a man's navy coat, her own hands chapped and red in the cold weather. Sometimes the world seemed to be breaking up before her, scattering into bits, a rainstorm of fragments which would not fit together.

There were still moments when the faces of her children broke through to her. How could she not respond to those small hands reaching out to her, that electric current of love, when she returned home from work and they ran forwards to greet her? But her helplessness when facing their expectant eyes made her buckle sometimes, so fearful was she of letting them down.

She could not sleep. She feared her nights, when darkness only intensified her claustrophobia. She was trapped inside her own mind, stuck in an endless loop of repetition, and the empty hours stretched away as she tried to lie still, to trace inward circles, any soothing pattern that might hypnotize her away from her own consciousness. But she could find no release from the kaleidoscope of her own ever-multiplying thoughts.

Thoughts of love. Of her failure to love her husband. Could she ever love anyone, or even desire them? She would lie there awake while Jamie appeared to sleep so soundly beside her. Jamie, who was her husband and used to find her attractive, even love her. How could it be possible that their marriage was failing?

In their courtship they had gone for walks in the park, and looked at each other fondly across tables at Italian restaurants. They had laughed together at the theater, and queued for tickets to the Proms, sharing all the rituals of a young couple in love, and so she had thought, *This must be it.* She took it on trust from his desire, his urgency, that this was love. He had chosen her, and so she followed his lead and hoped that her buried feelings would surface soon.

But a part of her had always been a little afraid of him. She would watch him as they walked down the street and suddenly it would strike her, *Jamie is too good for me, too handsome, too perfect.* Sometimes she tried to take their bond on trust, but other times she felt like an impostor who would soon be found out—that one day Jamie would look at her and think, *Why did I end up with this woman?*

Their marriage had at least been blessed with children. Sometimes, when she went to rouse her son and daughter for breakfast, she could not bear to wake them, but stopped to watch their sleeping faces: Joe's arms thrown behind him onto the pillow, his mouth slightly open; the stillness of Amy's eyelids, and the tendril of fair hair which fell over her ear. And then the wonder of their waking eyes—that unquestioning love in their faces, that assumption that she was their mother, and that they were depending on her.

Why am I falling apart? she asked herself. With so many blessings—her children, her husband, her work—she should have been happy. But it was as if a depth charge of buried grief was shaking all the foundations of her carefully constructed defenses, pulling her downwards into her own quicksand.

Her thoughts turned obsessively to her childhood, and her absolute, unquestioning adoration of her mother. She still cherished her memories of their last day together in London, shopping, eating ice cream in the roof-garden café. But had their wartime separation been necessity or choice on her mother's part? There were those cheery but infrequent letters, then just one visit before her death. She could not help blaming her mother for being so careless. Why had she not hidden herself away in a shelter?

If you lost your mother too young, didn't that cripple your courage to love? Had she not been cut off at the roots? These were the thoughts which tugged at Anna. Perhaps she had resisted her childhood pain for too long, hiding it away in a box. But she could not fathom why all this forgotten life was now rearing up and unsettling her. It was an odd self-pity, a retrospective grief that she had not been loved as she loved her own children. More, she felt guilty that her unhappiness was now creeping up on Joe and Amy too.

She might fall asleep at six only to be woken, exhausted, by the alarm clock at seven. Then she had to get the children ready for nursery, smiling and cheerful, and set off to work, kissing her husband good-bye.

"I'll be out late tonight," he said.

"Oh," she said, hoping it was not obvious that she knew why he would be out late.

"There's a performance of a new play by a dramatist we

might want to commission. I would've asked you too, but the children hate us both going out—"

"It's fine, you go," she said.

Later, when he returned home after making love to his BBC researcher, he found his wife slumped at the kitchen table beside an empty bottle of wine. He took her to bed and she kept saying, "I'm sorry, I'm sorry, I'm sorry."

She did not seem to mind about Jamie's lover. But why did she not mind? It did not make any sense. She began to drink every evening now, after the children had gone to bed. When Jamie wasn't watching. The wine gave her a gentle oblivion, but then she would wake up at three in the morning, and the insomnia would drain her again.

One lunch hour she drifted onto Oxford Street, and then found herself wandering up past Broadcasting House, home to her mother's wartime life. Beyond the traffic and fumes of Marylebone Road, she felt the pull of Regent's Park, with its wide open lawns and empty paths.

But the sudden quiet of the park only sharpened her overwrought senses. Even though she was hardly looking, she felt as if she could register every leaf on the tree before her, and every vein in each leaf. Like the veins in her hand and neck. The sky before her was open and infinite, and she thought she could feel the weight of the stars beyond, even in clear daylight. Everything was out there and upon her: the constellations singing and her pulse ringing and every leaf on every tree calling out for attention. *Enough, enough, enough, enough.*

She closed her eyes and covered her ears, and sank to the ground underneath a chestnut tree, where the grass was sparse and the shells of old conkers lay half-sunk in the earth. There she hunkered down and wept, until her body started heaving, her face pressed against her knees.

A retired doctor was walking his dog in the park, a wiry man slightly stiffened by arthritis.

"Can I help?" he asked, when he saw Anna.

She looked up.

"No, thank you." Her face retreated back into her knees.

He sat on a bench nearby and threw a stick for his Labrador to fetch. Anna sensed that he was still there and raised her eyes again.

"Are you sure you don't need any help?" he asked. Then he stood up and pulled out a folded white handkerchief for her.

It was at that moment that it hit Anna, a pain so deep inside that it reached back twenty years: the white handkerchief given to a child who could not cry. Mr. Ashton's handkerchief, pulled out to comfort her on the day she had lost her mother.

She looked up at the stranger and saw a creviced face, thinning gray hair, dark serious eyes.

"Thank you," she said.

"Keep it—I hope it helps," he said, dipping his head. "I have a drawer full of these at home . . ."

Then he was off after his dog, his arm raised to her in a backwards wave.

He left her folding up the handkerchief. Then she picked herself up and began walking through the park, along paths, past playgrounds.

Something in her shifted as she allowed the thought of Thomas Ashton to surface in her mind; he had always been there, hidden inside her, she realized. She hadn't seen him for over twenty years—he must be past sixty now. But she began to admit to herself that there was a part of her still pining for him, however ridiculous that might be. That nobody else could quite fill the hole in her heart because it was a shape made when she parted from him all those years ago.

She did not even know if he was still alive, or whether he would want to see her. But she at least wanted to try to visit him. And in the days that followed, she began to unscramble the patterns of her past in the light of these submerged feelings for him.

She remembered how hard she had worked to win her place at Oxford. Was it not to fulfill his hopes for her? She had arrived there with a green bicycle and a new set of clothes, all ready for love. But nobody there seemed able to reach her. By the end of her first year she had lost her virginity to a smooth lanky boy who had wooed her with chat about Albert Camus and *L'Etranger*. Yet she did not know how to feel at ease with him, and the relationship soon stalled.

She had found it so hard to form any bond with young men. Even when she met and married Jamie, her own lack of desire had confused her. He was so appealing and yet she had felt so remote from him. She longed to be held, but Jamie could not give her the embrace which she craved—he was too much her own friend, her own equal, it was like a sexless sibling relationship. So when they made love, she closed her eyes and sought out other images to ignite her feelings.

Lurking somewhere in her mind had always been the thought of Thomas Ashton. She remembered that look of care in his eyes, and a part of her wanted to imagine him as a lover. Forbidden thoughts, even in the privacy of her own mind. Yet she had divined the force of his feelings for Miss Weir, and she retained a sense that nobody else could be quite so tender, so passionate, so fixed in love as Thomas.

The great swinging sensation of her childish heart came back to her. But had he really ever had any special affection for her, or was it all her imagination?

She kept thinking about the night of Miss Weir's death, when he had asked her to perform that unexpected errand to find his letters; their secret.

It was as though their strange embrace that night had penetrated right through to her unconscious. She remembered sitting on his knee, and quietly crying as she crumpled against him. She could still feel her tears soaking into his checked flannel shirt. He had put his arms around her and held her gently, with kind words, soft words. "My dear," he called her. His chest was big enough to contain her trembling, and she melded with his adult shape, felt completely held by him. When she looked up into the white disc of his face in the darkness, she knew him as closely as she would ever know another person. His gaze had reached right inside her.

It had been a true intimacy, she felt now. Whenever they had seen each other in the months thereafter, that physical bond had been there between them, never mentioned, never acknowledged, but still there.

She began to wonder if she had ever recovered from him. In every embrace she had ever known, she now felt, she had been searching to recapture that look of tenderness in his eyes. Perhaps for him it had been no more than a look of lost hope, in which he saw only the child he did not have. But for her, it had been a look of love which had penetrated her soul and fixed her forever at Ashton Park, in the summer of 1943.

At home, she returned to the objects from that part of her life, buried at the back of her desk drawer. His white handkerchief, monogrammed with *T.A.A.* His two formal, courteous letters to her. The book of Tennyson's verse she had taken from Miss Weir's room.

Feeling rash, she called Directory Enquiries one day and discovered the telephone number of the Ashton Park estate office. A middle-aged man answered the phone and confirmed that Mr. Ashton was alive and well, but living now at a more convenient house on the estate. He told her the address, and she read it back to him, checking that she had noted down the postcode correctly.

Then she sat down, a thirty-three-year-old wife and mother, and wrote a formal letter to her childhood teacher, hoping for help of some kind.

52

Ashton Park, 1964

IT WAS A subdued spring afternoon, and Thomas Ashton was at his desk, as usual.

"Come in," he said, to the knock on his door. Every day at four o'clock his housekeeper would appear with a tray of tea and ginger biscuits. He never ate the biscuits, but she always put them there, just in case.

This housekeeper had been with him for six years now. He had called her Mrs. Smithie for the first two years, until she had boldly asked him to call her Mary instead. He was unfailingly polite and considerate to her, and she regarded him as a perfect gentleman, if hard to know.

She had studied all his old photographs, the framed one of his wedding, and later pictures of him with his wife. But she still knew only fragments of his past: that he had survived polio as a young man only to lose his wife in a wartime car crash; that he had been alone ever since, and had chosen to leave the big house, Ashton Park, after a fire there had gutted one of the wings.

She had heard tales from the villagers of the night when Ashton House nearly burned to the ground. An electric fire in one of the housemaids' rooms, it was thought. The people in the house were all safely evacuated, but it was the treasures inside which were at risk. Word went around the village, and people hurried up the long drive to help, right through the night hours. There was a chain of men passing the paintings and furniture out onto the sunken lawn, where Mr. Ashton sat in his chair, watching the flames and smoke rising from his home.

Fortunately the fire brigade arrived in time to control the fire, and the damage was contained to one burnt-out wing.

But it emerged that Ashton House had not been properly insured, so the restoration of the east wing proved impossibly expensive. Mr. Ashton had apparently lost the will to live in the big house thereafter, and so he had leased Ashton Park to a girls' preparatory school with an enterprising headmistress.

He had moved into this lodge deep inside the park. Some of the better pieces of Ashton furniture had come with him, but none of them quite fitted: his new home appeared curiously over-crammed with distinguished tables and dressers and desks which clearly belonged to the main house. When she first came for her interview, Mary Smithie was a touch unnerved by the family paintings which loomed from the walls and dwarfed any visitors. But she was also struck by Mr. Ashton's gentle, detached demeanor. *He's a philosophical man,* she said to her friends, *never critical, never demanding.*

For many years he had continued to teach Latin and English at the school in Ashton House—but he had recently retired, and spent most days in his study working on a commissioned translation of Virgil's *Georgics.* From time to time he had visitors from London, "old friends from my days in the Foreign Office," as he explained to Mrs. Smithie, such as Sir Clifford Norton and his energetic wife, Peter, "who escaped from the Nazis in Warsaw in 1939," and Lord Vansittart, who was tall and broad chested and stood before the fireplace with his legs apart—"the one Englishman who might have stopped the war, if only he had been heard."

Mrs. Smithie was glad he was not entirely alone. Solitary, yes, but not without a few old friends. If he was unhappy, or lonely, she never saw it.

The clock chimed as she put down the tea tray. He looked up to thank her, but she sensed he did not want to talk further and so she left the room.

She closed the door behind her without knowing the day's significance for Thomas, that this was the anniversary of the day on which he had lost his wife, his lover and his unborn child. *Twenty-one years without you,* he wrote in his notebook, *and I'm still thinking of you.*

The years had passed, week by week, hour by hour, and Thomas still awoke to the thought of Ruth—still talked to her in his head and wondered what she would have thought of the things he saw, the people he met.

He could not let her go. Her memory reverberated around the empty shell of his present life like a lost sea.

Thomas was sixty-four now, yet he still saw Ruth as she was on the day she had died. Sometimes he tried to imagine her as she might have become—a mother, a fuller figure, with the first signs of aging. He would have liked to see that, to trace every new line on her face. The lines of their time spent together.

Nobody had ever guessed the true nature of his loss; he had never shared his grief with anyone. Those who worked for him no doubt wondered about the misfortune of his polio, or the tragedy of his wife's death, but none of them knew of his unspent love for the young teacher who was carrying his child. Perhaps it was thought that he must miss Elizabeth, but she had vanished altogether from his heart, leaving him only with guilt that he had not freed her to another life before it was too late for all of them.

He did not believe that Elizabeth's crash had been inevitable. He was sure it had been a fit of temper, a momentary aberration of jealous rage. Another day or two and she would have found less irreparable means of wounding him. She might even have let them both go with grace. No, it had been the fault of his own pride—that he had in some way gloated over Ruth's pregnancy in the face of the woman it would hurt most, inciting her violence.

Resigned guilt was all he had left for Elizabeth. The tenderness which still welled inside him was only for Ruth—a tenderness so acute that he sometimes felt himself haunted. Working at his desk, he would suddenly feel her subtle presence behind him, creeping up on him, silently entering the rhythm of his breathing. Until he would pause and gather himself to stillness, then turn his head to see what might be there.

Nothing. Dust and air.

And yet he felt her at his shoulder, at his elbow, a tweak in his soul. The grief should have faded by now, he told himself, but sometimes, when he woke in the morning, his sense of her was so fresh that he still reached out for her.

At other times he wondered if he had gone quietly mad. Here he was, an aging cripple in a damp Yorkshire house, dreaming daily of a dead woman. Unable to move beyond her, unable to take anyone else into his life—into his confidence, even. Any conversation about Ruth would only trivialize her memory, and the elixir of her presence in his heart.

He had grown accustomed to his double life. There was the polite surface of each day, with his estate business, and then there was his hidden life with Ruth. His memories of all the things she had said, endlessly raked over in his mind to uncover lost embers of feeling. His sense of her face as they kissed, the yielding curve of her breasts, her hair falling over her cheek, the touch of her.

The grief would not go, but sometimes he cherished it. It hung about him, like a loyal ghost. The wind at the window, the sudden fall of a petal from a vase, the last flicker of twilight, all spoke to him of the strange shadow land of his heart.

Stars! Stars! And all eyes else dead coals!

He could still see her eyes—sometimes they flashed right through him, like the cry of remembrance from *The Winter's Tale.*

He had no photograph to remember her by, only the consolation of her one letter. He loved her handwriting. It flowed forwards, and curled back on itself, and embodied her intelligence and passion, but also her tentative modesty, her gentleness. It was her—all he had of her. After each of the words had passed into his mind and heart, it was the writing itself which moved him. He had opened her letter so often that it was faded now, and worn by the touch of his fingers.

The letter lay before him as he wrote in his notebook, his eyes passing over the familiar shape of her writing. But a part of him was numb, and the words would not yield up any fresh emotion: today it was just a dead letter whose life had leaked away.

There was a knock at the door, and Mary appeared to remove the tea tray. She gave him a stiff white envelope.

"This arrived in the afternoon post, sir."

It was a personal letter, in a handwriting he did not recognize. He laid it on his desk and waited until he was alone. Probably an academic correspondent. Sometimes he received letters from fellow classicists with new thoughts on a word or phrase.

Mary closed the door and he took the letter in his hand, and opened it.

Dear Mr. Ashton,

It has been many years since we met, so I would not be at all surprised if you did not remember me. My name is Anna Sands, and I arrived at your house as an evacuee in 1939. I very much enjoyed my time at Ashton Park, and am particularly grateful for the education I received there. Later, I completed a degree at Oxford and now I am a fiction editor at a publishing house. It is an enjoyable job to mix with my family life: I am married with two children.

I have recently been recalling my wartime years with much fondness. In particular, I have remembered your kindness, and also what a remarkable teacher you were. I will be coming to York in April, and wondered if I might possibly come to visit you? That would be a treat for me, but I quite understand if you are disinclined to meet ex-evacuees. You probably get a number of letters like this.

But if you would be so kind as to let me visit, I can be reached at the above address or on Fremantle 2104.

Yours sincerely,
Anna Sands

Thomas remembered her at once, the child whose mother had died in the Blitz. An image of her flickered through his mind, a girl with a gap-toothed smile putting up her hand in class. He was seized with gladness, and replied at once with uncharacteristic effusion.

My dear Anna,

Of course I remember you. It was a great pleasure to hear from you, and I would be delighted if you would visit me on your next trip to York. I am happy to hear that you have enjoyed Oxford—my old university, too—and that you have a family of your own now. I will look forward to hearing your news.

Tea is served here at four o'clock daily, so please just let me know when you would like to come.

Yours sincerely,
Thomas Ashton

There was a flurry of calls with the housekeeper. Anna, it seemed, was nervous about speaking to him directly. Tea was set for 25 April.

53

Ashton Park, 1964

O N   T H E   A P P O I N T E D day, Anna found her way to the estate lodge in which Thomas Ashton was now living. She drove up to a plain, square Georgian house, perhaps once a steward's quarters. Ample, but not the house to which she knew he had once been accustomed. The flower beds at the front were sparse and untended.

She parked her car, then checked her face and hair in the driver's mirror. When she rang the doorbell, a closed-faced housekeeper let her in.

She found herself standing stiffly in his empty hall. Clearly a bachelor's house, she noted, lacking any signs of family life, and somewhat unloved. The hall windows were streaked with the gathered grime of several seasons, and newspapers were piled carelessly by the fireplace, as if inertia had overtaken the place.

Anna stood there waiting, trying to breathe evenly and adjust herself to the obvious decline in Thomas's standard of living.

Another door opened, and suddenly there he was, wheeling forwards to greet her with his right arm outstretched, his face welcoming, smiling, expectant.

"Anna! How lovely to see you."

With a start of pleasure and relief she saw that he looked the same. Older, but the same. His ankles were slightly thickened, his shoulders shrunken a little, his belly a touch fuller. But his face—it had the same astonishing clarity. Perhaps it was even more arresting now, etched with character lines, his hair still swept back from his forehead and flecked now with silver. Just as she remembered, his soul was almost tangible through those eyes.

Anna was instantly flooded by a wave of love for him. Here was the man in her head, her heart, her soul, the one man who could reach right through to the empty spaces inside her.

He leant forwards, perhaps for a kiss, but she was awkward and fumbling, and so he converted the move into a firm handshake.

"You look so different, yet I'd recognize you at once," he said with a quizzical smile. With a familiar gesture of gallantry he tossed back his hand. "I haven't seen you since you were—what?—eleven, twelve? Anyway, you're looking wonderful."

"It's lovely to see you too," she said. "You look just the same."

"Oh come now," he said wryly. Then he swiveled his chair with a practiced swing of his hand.

"There's tea for us both, if you come through with me."

She did not know whether to push his chair, but he wheeled himself forwards with such resolute dexterity that she simply followed.

They arrived in a room of faded green—but she had only the most glancing impression of the place: all her attention was riveted on Thomas. There were a few stiff pleasantries about where to sit, then the charade of pouring tea, which Anna volunteered to do. She called him "Mr. Ashton," and he raised his hand: "Please—call me Thomas."

The teacups were rimmed with a gold line; one had a tiny chip. Anna's hand shook as she held the slight brittle saucer and poured in the tea. She feared she might drop the china with her clumsy hands.

But she delivered his cup without mishap and once they were both successfully armed with tea, she sat down and they turned to look at each other.

Thomas saw a woman of unusual youth: her face unlined and glowing, as if arrested in a kind of preadolescence—charming, if a little unnerving—with something fearful or distanced in her eyes.

"It's so good to see you," she said, stuttering at the banality of her remark.

"It's very kind of you to come," he said. He rested his eyes on hers for a moment, and her heart turned over.

She brought out photographs of her children, which were stashed in a small slip album deep in her handbag. Crouching by his side, she was closer to him now as he concentrated on the children's faces, their names, their ages, trying to find something particular to say about them. He paused at one image of her daughter.

"This one," he said, "she's like you." He looked up at her, to corroborate his claim. She put the album away and retrieved her teacup, sitting down once more.

He was silent. Anna shifted in her chair, looked down at her cup.

The nothing that you say. She thought, *Is there anything between us, some invisible thread, or is there really nothing there?*

"Does the management of the estate occupy you a great deal?"

"I am fortunate to have a marvelous manager. Mr. Reynolds. He has energy, and a passionate attachment to the park—does a tremendous job."

"And the house?"

"It's still a school. A rather successful girls' school. They have a proper gymnasium now, and a small swimming pool."

"It's a wonderful house for children—"

"Do you think so? I'm so glad you remember it that way."

He smiled at her with unguarded warmth, and she wanted to say, *I have been looking for you all my adult life—that look in your eyes.*

"Do you get the morning sun in this room?"

"Yes, indeed, and we've had plenty of winter sunshine this year."

"These Georgian windows must give you a whole theater of light."

"How well you put it."

She just wanted to reach out and touch his hand—but they sat there stiffly, talking instead of Thomas's newly purchased recordings of Schubert, and the new fiction which Anna was publishing.

Was that it? Just tea and cakes with a polite, aging man?

She longed to unlock him, to prize open some memory of their unacknowledged intimacy. Tentatively, she fished into her handbag to pull out Miss Weir's faded blue book of verse.

"Do you remember that night—when I fetched your letters?"

"Yes," he said, "of course," and he settled his face on hers for the first time, warily revealing himself at last.

"Well, I never told you, but I found your letters stashed away in a book of Tennyson's poems—and I went back afterwards to fetch the book. Just as a reminder of . . . Miss Weir. And I brought it along for you today, in case it meant anything. There's a note of sorts in there."

The shock of this news jolted him: he was almost shaking as he reached forwards to take the book from her.

He ran his fingers through the dry crackling pages, and lodged near the center was a single folded sheet of yellowing paper. Thomas opened it out and there, crumbling at the crease, was a pressed flower. A forget-me-not, its tiny blue-veined petals as sheer as a butterfly wing, alongside a note in smudged ink.

> *18 June '41*
> *A forget-me-not to remember you.*
> *Think what you have meant to me—*

It took his breath away. It was the handwriting that did it, the flow of the letters conjuring up Ruth's face, her eyes, her very spirit. Like a ghost released from the pages of a book. A message for him, from more than twenty years ago. He shifted in his chair, and his voice was faint.

"Thank you. Thank you very much indeed. This means a great deal to me."

He went on staring at the page and could not look up. The shock of emotion was visible on his face.

Anna watched on with rising unease, feeling a hot, fierce jealousy tearing through her. How could she not have known the depth of what he felt? She had sat in their poetry classes. She had carried his letters. She had heard them from the wardrobe.

How could she possibly think it would be over now—just because Miss Weir was so long dead? He was shaking with emotion over a scrap of paper she had withheld all these years—yet all she wanted was for him to reach out to her.

He finally looked up. She was brushing some imaginary dust from her skirt, keeping her hand busy. But she felt his gaze and glanced over.

In that moment, Thomas sensed that he was not the only one locked in with his own phantoms. He felt her need—that she wanted to be something more than just a conduit for fresh memories of Ruth.

"Thank you for this, my dear. Thank you so much. But is there—something else you came to talk to me about?" he asked gently, his eyes steady on her face.

"Yes," she yielded.

"Tell me, then," he said.

He waited, shifted his gaze, patient. She moved her hands, rolled them in the air as if the gesture would set her talking.

"I wanted to see you because I have thought about you over the years—"

She stopped dead, tilted her head. Then the words spilled out.

"I still have—feelings for you," she said. "I think perhaps I fell . . . in love with you as a child and I've been carrying the thought of you hidden inside me all these years. I've been reaching out to strangers and wishing it was you—because I always loved everything about you, every detail—"

Thomas found himself staring at her. Had she been nurturing these feelings for so long even though they had not even seen each other? He did not flinch, but it was unnerving.

"All that was a long time ago," he replied, hesitating. "You've grown into a lovely woman with a husband, and children."

The compliment thrilled Anna—she had never felt herself to be lovely, but even as he said it, she hoped that it really was what he saw.

Emboldened, she thought of those letters he had written to her so long ago. How she had treasured them for years. Slept with them under her pillow, until they had grown worn at the crease.

"When you wrote to me all those years ago and signed off 'with my love,' I spent so many evenings wondering if 'with my love' meant something—or if it was just what you always put on your letters."

"I'm sure I meant it—in the right way," he answered carefully, but she wanted more.

"I do remember that I wanted to help you," he went on. "You were in a sorry state after you had lost your mother. You needed . . . someone to watch over you."

"Yes," she said, almost overlapping his words.

He looked at her and saw a smooth woman's face in place of the skinny freckled child he had once known. But her eyes spoke right back to the past: that searching gaze asking, inexplicably, to be close to him.

She waited, longing for him to say more—to open up. She

wanted him to look at her, and say, *I have thought about you all these years, and waited to tell you how much I cared about you.* Of course he did not, would not. He was closing, retreating, while she slid into her quicksand.

"That night—the night when I fetched your letters—I fell asleep on your knee—and I can still remember the tenderness I saw in your face when I woke up—"

She wanted to say, *I have been searching for that look in your eyes ever since*—but she could no longer speak. She shuddered, until at last her tears spilled over.

He was embarrassed, and sat there waiting in silence. But as her tears went on, he was stirred by a distant memory of the child crying in his arms so many years before.

He thought he did remember looking down into the girl's eyes on that terrible night. Of what had he been thinking? Of the woman he had loved and lost—of the child he had lost. Yet it must have been that moment which had enslaved Anna.

He was moved, somehow, by this young woman's sorrow, seeping through the deep walls of his own private grief. He wheeled himself forwards and looked into her eyes as she raised her face towards him. Then he reached out to her with his arms and she fell against his chest. He wrapped his arms around her and held her. Until she lifted her head once more to face him.

He could see the purity of her love, and he looked at her with a tenderness he did not know he could still find in himself. He had given her nothing, and yet—the long years of her waiting had released something in him.

He wanted to set her free.

"You did mean something to me," he said. Even as he spoke he was unsure whether he was talking to Anna or to the ghost of Ruth, resurrected in this strange afternoon through a scrap of paper and the lovestruck eyes of another woman.

"You meant a great deal to me, and I was very unhappy when

you left. I have thought about you often. And I am very, very happy to see you again."

There are many kinds of consummation in this world, Anna realized later. It might be a letter, or a conversation, or even just a look. He just said the words she wanted to hear. And then he kissed her lightly on the cheek.

She returned to London knowing that a door of sorts had been closed. Theirs was a definable relationship now, with boundaries, and she had reached as far as she could with Thomas. She knew she must let him go now.

54

In the months which followed Anna's unexpected visit, Thomas sometimes wondered if he should have told her what a difference she had made to his spirits. But decided he could not; because he knew it was the chance message from Ruth which had rejuvenated him, not Anna.

Think what you have meant to me—

He could not look at Ruth's handwritten note enough. It was as if his patience had been rewarded with a sign. *A forget-me-not to remember you.*

Her memory could sustain him now. More than twenty years after her death, she had come back to him in a scrap of paper, releasing him back into the present. And by some strange alchemy, he began to see himself in a new way, as somebody connected to life by love.

He did not forget Anna. It surprised and puzzled him to think that he had unwittingly existed in anyone's heart or mind for so long, but he felt moved and honored that she had found the courage to talk to him; it was her visit which had triggered this strange and unexpected reconciliation in him.

He continued a gentle correspondence with Anna. Christmas cards, and careful readings of the novels she occasionally sent him, with considered letters. More, he took to praying for her on Sundays, in his local church. He did sometimes wonder if he should have done more for her, but knew that would have been inappropriate; there was too little he could offer her, beyond prayers from a distance. But he hoped that his warmth would somehow reach through to her.

One breath of life is better than none at all. Thomas could remember trying to rally himself with that mantra when he was recovering from polio in hospital, forty years before. That was what he had wanted to believe then. But as he grew older, he really did feel it. Every morning he was glad to see the sky. And whenever spring came around once more, he found himself surprised all over again by the cherry tree flowering outside his window, whose pale mauve blossom was always lighter and more profuse than he had ever remembered.

The passing years never diminished the force of his feeling for Ruth. Whenever the sun broke through the clouds, or wind shook the trees, her face was there, even in the rain. And every day was eased by this contemplation, right until the end.

He's always so serene, Mary Smithie used to say to her husband. The year before he died, she could remember fretting about leaving him alone on Christmas Day. She had to visit her aging mother, not far, in Harrogate, but she did worry whether he would be too lonely by himself, and kept trying to suggest people he might visit for the day.

"Please, Mary," he said gently, "you really don't have to worry about me."

"Are you sure you're not just being brave, sir?"

"More than sure."

"But Christmas is a time to celebrate, with other people—"

"I don't lack for anything here, please don't worry."

Mary could remember pausing, and looking at him doubtfully. And it was then that he had confided in her—for the first time in all their years together.

"Let me tell you my secret, Mary," he said, tilting his head. "When I was younger, I met a wonderful woman, the right woman, and she loved me. We loved each other, and we both knew that. Isn't that what everyone wants, Mary? Mutual love? The memory still sustains me, every day. So

I may seem like an old wreck to you—but inside I'm still dancing, as they say."

As he spoke, she knew he meant it. That was the secret of his eyes, then—they were filled with private joy, because he had known proper love with his wife. She felt her tears rising, and had to pinch her palm to stop herself from crying as she left him that day.

55

THOMAS CONTINUED TO hold his place in Anna's heart, but for many years his presence there was dormant. Until one morning she saw his name in the *Times* deaths notices, and felt instantly winded.

The small piece announced the death of Thomas Arthur Ashton "after a short illness" on 29 December 1979. Christmas was still in the air, and the papers were overfilled with New Year quizzes, so only two of the broadsheets carried obituaries. These were inadequately sketched with notes of his Foreign Office career, and snatches of information which excited and saddened Anna in equal measure: the little she had known of his life. Thomas Ashton was noted for his service as a young diplomat in "Sir Robert Vansittart's group of antiappeasers" in the 1930s. In *The Telegraph* he was remembered as a classicist of distinction, and the last of a certain kind of Englishman, though the obituarist did not say quite why. The school at Ashton Park was mentioned, and his wife too.

He and his beloved wife Elizabeth were childless, but at the outbreak of war they opened up Ashton Park as a home for evacuees. Tragically, Elizabeth was killed in a car crash, but her husband was determined to carry on his wife's work, and after the war Ashton became a full-time boarding school for girls. Pupils have fond memories of Ashton's genial presence as a teacher, and he was extremely proud of the school . . .

Anna read the obituaries several times over, then put them away in a drawer. Who had written these generalized fictions about him? Nothing was said which caught his spirit.

Her final exclusion from his life now struck her with deep force; there had been nothing more than Christmas cards by the end. She did not even know the date of his funeral, nor was there any mention of a memorial service. She did not know whom to write to, but assumed, with a pang, that other family members close to him would deal with his death.

What Anna could not have guessed was that there was no family. No children, no brothers or sisters, no nephews or nieces. Just polite friendships. Sir Clifford Norton was wheel-chair-bound after breaking both his hips, frail and fearful of travel, so he stayed at home in Chelsea, hoping others would turn up for Thomas's service instead. He spent the day wondering how his old friend could have vanished so thoroughly from his life. His own wife, Peter, had died several years earlier, after complications from a fall in Orly Airport. With her gone, Norton never ventured far from Carlyle Square anymore.

It was left to Thomas's housekeeper, Mary Smithie, to ensure that his passing was accorded some respect. She was the one who visited him in hospital when he came down with pneumonia. And when the doctor rang to say that he had passed away, it was she who cried for him, and worried about his funeral flowers. She tidied up the papers on his desk, and opened the letters which still arrived for him. She put away his pen and ink—but then took them home with her, as a memento of the man she had watched writing his translations for over twenty years.

Two months after the funeral, the daughter of Thomas's first cousin arrived from South Africa to view her inheritance. Mrs. De Groot had grown up in Cape Town, and her visit to Ashton Park was her first trip to Europe. Her children were unhappy about her journey, and begged her to come home soon.

"I'll be back in ten days," she promised them at the airport.

She arrived in York on a wet afternoon, and struggled to find a taxi to Ashton Park. The driver dropped her at the lodge by the park gates, so she had to walk up the apparently endless drive to the house in the rain. When at last she reached the great front doors, she was breathless and wet.

Mr. Tyler, long-term caretaker, was standing by to let her in, but was too shy to shake her hand or meet her face. Led by this awkward guide, Mrs. De Groot was given a rapid tour of the house. They began with the stone hall before venturing down linoleum-lined corridors which led to empty classrooms. When they stopped briefly in the old school lavatories, she was appalled by their primitive plumbing.

Afterwards they toured the upper floors, passing through deserted school dormitories of iron bedsteads and stained horsehair mattresses. There were washstands and old-fashioned water pans, and unlined curtains with broken hooks hanging at odd angles. The girls' boarding school had finally been closed down after years of dwindling admissions, but its aging apparatus remained.

The whole house echoed with emptiness. As the sky outside dimmed towards darkness, Mrs. De Groot was chilled by the sense of other people's past. The place reeked of ghosts and lost history, and the dusty portraits of her unknown cousins unnerved her.

Under the bare strip-lighting of the kitchens she met Mr. Tyler's wife, a stout woman with a cheery face marred by exceptionally stained teeth. Mrs. Tyler had prepared a simple meal of sausages for Mrs. De Groot to eat in the old parlor, a room with a fire stoked for the occasion. Then she was led for the night to the Ashtons' old master bedroom.

There was a stately four-poster bed, and a misted dressing table with a triptych of mirrors. The Tylers did not tell her whose room it had been, and she did not ask. But when she awoke in the morning, chilly and stiff, she resolved to return home as soon as possible, back to the swimming pools and sunshine and hygienic plumbing of Constantia.

She felt like an impostor there. It was an unviable house, she could see that at once, and she feared the strain it might place on her marriage. So when the keen-eyed curators arrived to meet her from the National Trust, she readily accepted their proposal to take over Ashton House in lieu of death duties. She extended her trip for another ten days, trying to be swift and decisive about divesting herself of this vast decaying house with its bad weather. She met with lawyers and valuation experts from Christie's, and signed as many papers as she could to strip the estate of its more valuable assets, while leaving the house and its mementoes to the heritage trust.

When finally she met the redoubtable Mrs. Smithie and went through Thomas Ashton's personal effects in the park lodge, she caught a more sentimental glimpse of the Ashtons. She picked up a photograph of Thomas, and his face moved her. Mrs. Smithie suggested—or, rather, pressed the point—that he was a distinguished man of letters whose book collection should be moved back to the library at Ashton House. Mrs. De Groot was touched by her determined devotion, and instructed the estate lawyers to be guided by Mrs. Smithie as to which books, portraits and pieces of furniture should be returned to the main house. She began to justify her hasty retreat as no less than a respectful wish to keep the Ashtons' family history intact for the National Trust.

Then Mrs. De Groot took a taxi down the long drive and did not return to the estate for several years. Not until Ashton Park had been reclaimed and restored as an Edwardian-styled stately home open to the public. An award-winning day out in Yorkshire, a triumph for the National Trust.

56

EARLY IN 2006, Anna Sands thought she saw her mother on television. She sat down one night to watch a program about the Blitz, and the documentary began with tranquil shots of prewar London, men in bowler hats streaming off to work, women wheeling their prams through the parks. But then came an abrupt shift to color footage of wartime London, and there—apparently—was Anna's mother, walking down the street in a pillbox hat and high heels.

The sighting of her was so brief that Anna wondered if she had seen a ghost. Her mother had appeared just for a few seconds, trancelike, during an elliptical sequence of burning buildings. The next day Anna rang the BBC to trace the archive footage. For weeks she followed a trail of phone calls and messages, until she found herself in an annex of the Imperial War Museum, with a slip of paper requesting a viewing. A chatty film archivist led her to a cutting room, armed with a can of sixteen-millimeter film.

"It's one of our most popular reels," he told her, "our only amateur color footage of the Blitz. Shot by a woman, on a simple windup Bolex, so it's a little overcranked in some places—it makes London looks strange, like a dream."

The film was running now, spooling through a noisy editing machine with a small screen. Anna sat back and watched random shots of wartime London, captured in the vibrantly simple colors of old film. People walked by, smiling at the camera. Workmen drank tea and ate sandwiches, all casually nonchalant against a background of destroyed buildings and cratered streets. For ten minutes or so, Anna saw nothing but strangers flickering by, until suddenly there she was—her mother striding down an empty pavement, ridiculously poised in her hat and suit as she passed the daytime debris. Anna cried out. The young man stopped the machine and rewound the footage.

The shot lasted for nine seconds. That was it. Just one extended glimpse of her mother walking down a street, before the reel cut to somewhere else altogether.

Robin was the archivist's name. He showed Anna how to replay the shot, then left her to watch her mother over and over, as he went out to make a phone call. "Not strictly allowed," he told her, "but I can see you need some time to see it properly."

Anna played the scene repeatedly and watched her mother glide off, apparently without a care in the world. She was tantalizingly recognizable, though there was no eye contact with the camera. Or was it really her?

It was more than sixty years since Anna had seen her. Here she was, an old woman watching her mother in her prime. But as she rewound the shot over and over, the spirit of her mother began to depart from the scene. As if seeing Roberta there, beyond the control of her own imagination, had set her free.

Her mother had had her own life, and that was that. She was Roberta Sands, walking away from all of them to do her own thing, until, by chance, she became one of the war's many casualties.

Anna had waited for so many years to say good-bye to her mother. As a child, there had been no funeral, only her mother hovering as an imagined observer in her life. Causing her guilt sometimes. But now she saw that her mother had been an independent soul, striding down streets to meetings which Anna knew nothing about. She could let her go now—or might let her go, once the shock of seeing her had dwindled.

It was some months before Anna recovered her equilibrium.

She had retired from publishing now, and was living alone, but with plenty of visits from her children and grandchildren.

Her marriage had ended many years before.

"I wanted to set off on a journey through life with you," Jamie had told her when they parted, "but you wouldn't join in. You were always somewhere else." It was true; in the aftermath of her visit to Thomas Ashton, Anna had allowed herself to grow too detached from her husband. She had never even tried to tell him about her odd retrospective love for her teacher; Jamie would have thought her mad.

When he had left her, it had been a relief, in some ways. She was able to enjoy their children without worrying anymore about her inadequacies as a wife. With Jamie, she had always felt an emotional fraud—and over the years, whenever she saw him, she always thought how handsome he looked, and was amazed that she had ever been with such a man. Jamie, for his part, always explained away their broken marriage by saying that Anna had been too much defined by an unhappy wartime childhood.

After the divorce, she and her children had moved to a run-down Georgian house in Clerkenwell and she had begun a long process of reclaiming it: restoring the old fixtures, cleaning out the cornices, reconstituting the fireplaces and window shutters. She had even steamed off the wallpaper to uncover several layers of earlier paper, reaching right back to a Regency original.

"It's like turning the pages of the house's history, and peeling back the past to release its ghosts," she would explain to curious visitors. Her children thought her a little eccentric, but enjoyed their trips to architectural junkyards, too.

After her own displaced childhood, Anna had drawn such comfort from motherhood that she was never much troubled by being single. She had her friends; that was enough for her.

By now, she had narrowed her life down to its essentials— books and music, and a simply furnished home. And the three slender volumes of poetry which she had written over the years, her careful distillations of a lifetime. Books which had been respectfully reviewed in their time, though none of them remained in print. But recently even the impulse to find words for feelings had left her: that was the measure of her placid self-sufficiency now. She might be a little solitary, but on good days, she knew how to value life's everyday beauty. A mind-set, she sometimes reflected, which she had first learnt from Thomas Ashton.

One Sunday lunch, just after her seventy-fifth birthday, one of her grandsons asked her if she had been rich as a child. The question puzzled her.

"What makes you ask that?"

"Because you wrote a poem about a house with long corridors, so you must have grown up in a huge house," he said. She smiled and explained how she had been evacuated to a stately home during the war.

"*That* was the house with the corridors, somebody else's house."

A memory of handstands on a sunlit lawn came back to her. Later, once she was back at home, she sought out the poem from her bookcase, and read it to herself before going to bed.

Back to the Old House

Let us go back to the old house
The house we once knew
The familiar door
The airy rooms
The light on the stairs,
Still at the back of your mind.

And if it is not quite so tall
As the house you used to know,

And less bright too, and emptier,
You need not turn away;
For a place is a time, too,
And you are older now,
And long since lost
From your own past.

Let us go back to the old house
The house we once knew, even
If it is a stranger's house,
With windows blind to you,
And long, featureless corridors
Oblivious to all the old times.

The old house—the valedictory note was catching. Even though Anna was old herself now, she was still a child running down the long corridors of Ashton House. Her memory of the house's exterior was like an architect's model: she could see its whole shape as if photographed from afar. Yet, inside, the house seemed to stretch on forever in her mind—unexpected passages and high staircases, surprise landings and tall empty rooms.

She had been to so many places in her life, but inside her it was still Ashton Park which spread its contours: the long white drive, the light off sandstone walls, the morning view onto empty parkland. Sometimes, as she sat in a room, she could still be swallowed inwards to the long shadowed corridors of Ashton and the sound of children on the grass outside. It was a healing place, she thought, as she put away the book.

She awoke early the next morning to the sound of slow rain, a soft rhythmic pulse which lured her into a waking dream. The sound seeped deep inside her, returning her to old times, lost places, rainy days long gone. Once more she was inside the landscape of her childhood, a vista of wide sky and gray-green parkland, Ashton in the late bloom of evening light. All unease was stilled in the infinite calm of the place—its remove, its serene undulations. There was an inexpressible bliss in the light of the sky.

Yet even as she felt herself walking on grass, the dream began to fade. She struggled to hold on to the line of the horizon, but it eluded her like a vanishing melody—going, gone. She surfaced to consciousness with a deep ache of regret not to be there, not to be running on the lawns, through the woods, down the hill to the river. The landscape receding, the light dying—that private rapture evaporating into silent, colorless air.

She lay in bed, fully awake now, still yielding to the impact of her dream. It was so many years since she had been back to Ashton Park, and yet the place had never left her. She was stirred by a fresh longing to return to her old childhood home—for it had been that, even if she had only ever been a visitor. She must go back.

And so she took a train, early the next day. The station at York still had its curving platform. From there, she caught a bus straight to Ashton village.

When she arrived at the park gates, she hesitated. Here it was, her place, her past. Yet it was open to the public now, and there was a lodge where visitors had to buy a ticket just to step into the park.

But curiosity and excitement were spurring her now. She paid her money—a ticket for both "house and garden"—and set off on foot up the drive. A woman of seventy-five with aching joints and heavy bones, walking slowly to catch her breath.

She passed the same trees, the same sky. Thistles alongside the drive, she recognized those too. The aroma of wild garlic. The rotting hulk of a fallen oak which she had clambered over as a child, all those years ago.

She turned the corner of the drive, and there at last stood

Ashton House, with its curved wings. She paused to observe its unflinching façade, and a wave of sadness passed through her. What was it? The regrets of age, for her own childhood? She could not say.

The lion and the unicorn still stood on the gateposts, more begrimed than she recalled. Smaller too. Their expressions fixed, closing her out from their mutual past, stones that could not remember. A mix of memory and longing was flooding through her now, though she could not tell whether she felt sad or elated. All she knew was that the place was stirring up sediments of old emotion which made her heart ache.

She turned to face the rising plain before the house, a view which had filled her with such hope as a child. She could remember her first weeks here, autumn at Ashton Park, the great oaks flaming with gold, the coppery sunshine reaching right through her fingertips to the unawakened spaces inside her.

Today's sky was white and still, muting the October colors. She sensed that in the weeks to come, the withdrawing tide of the dying year would slowly pull on her pulse, as winter set in. But today there was no hint of that. She had arrived just in time to see Ashton Park in all its sober autumn glory—so why did she feel so curiously detached from the scene before her?

> . . . But there's a tree—of many, one—
> A single field which I have looked upon,
> Both of them speak of something that is gone . . .

Perhaps life was one long story of separation, just as Wordsworth had said. From people, from places, from the past you could never quite reach even as you lived it.

But she did not want to give up yet on this place. She turned to the house and walked up the stairs to the tall mahogany doors which were still stiff to open. Then into the Marble Hall—she remembered waiting here for her father's arrival, so many years ago. And all the hours spent playing badminton on this checkered floor, with the sound of Thomas playing the piano in the saloon beyond.

Now there was a local woman selling postcards at a small table, proffering well-intended information about the house's classical details.

"That's Apollo playing his lyre in the dome, and those are griffins over the stone fireplaces . . ."

Anna turned and stood in the center of the Marble Hall. Voices came to her, ringing through the years, Hillary Trevor calling out the names of children with letters, all of them crowded about her, longing for news from home—*Maltby—Bailey—Peet—Rothery—Todd—Russell*. And there was the place where the Christmas tree stood; she remembered hanging the baubles, and all their spontaneous pleasure at the prospect of Christmas, that fresh, uncomplicated happiness of children—*Tyler—Dixon—Burnham—Peake*.

She went towards the stone stairs, past the door to Thomas's bedroom. *Is anybody there?* The place was thick with ghosts of the past, the lost, the dead. Memories of Thomas and the winter light of his eyes.

"Excuse me, madam—" A man in a tweed jacket stopped her, explaining that she could not wander around at will but must follow one of the house tours. So she joined a group and saw the dining room, and the saloon, and all her old familiar places now redecorated in high Edwardian style—everywhere looked so different to the tattered school of her day with its desks and dormitories.

But when they reached the library, she was relieved to find it unaltered; it was still the same galleried room glowing with old books.

"The late Thomas Ashton was a classical scholar, and he completed many distinguished translations," said the tour guide with as much enthusiasm as such information could merit. "We have his collection of old Greek and Latin books up there in the gallery."

Anna looked up. She saw where the guide had pointed, and recalled the day Thomas had shown her the secret door to the gallery. A flicker of rebellion crept into her, and she lingered behind as the group moved on.

She found the hidden handle, and the click of the door was just as she recalled. Here she was, an old woman sneaking up the steep library steps on her own to find—what? She could not say. But she stood in front of Thomas's books, and ran her hand along their covers.

Her fingers snagged on a slender book sticking out. Her heart jolted, because she knew it at once; it was Ruth Weir's book of Tennyson, the one which she had taken to Thomas all those years ago. She slid the book out and opened it. Here was the folded sheet with the pressed flower. But there was another letter there too—in Thomas's handwriting.

Nobody was looking, so she removed the book and tucked it into her handbag. Then she slipped down the gallery stairs and stepped out into the gardens with a fragile heart.

She paused for a moment by the sundial in the rose garden, strangely elated to have retrieved Ruth Weir's book. Seeking a quiet place to sit down, she made her way to a bench by the copper beech tree which had been planted, she knew, to mark Thomas's christening. Gingerly she sat down before opening the book. There was the new letter, in Thomas's hand. It was dated the year she had visited him. But the envelope was addressed to Ruth. An unsent letter written to a dead woman.

May 1964

My dearest,
    Of all the many people we meet in a lifetime, it is strange that so many of us find ourselves in thrall to one particular

person. Once that face is seen, an involuntary heartache sets in for which there is no cure. All the wonder of this world finds shape in that one person and thereafter there is no reprieve, because this kind of love does not end, or not until death.

For the lucky ones, this love is reciprocated. But for so many others, everywhere, anywhere, there follows an unending ache of longing without relief. Incurable love is a great leveler. Yet I believe that this bittersweet love is better by far than the despair which blights those with a dead heart.

You are the woman I loved, Ruth. I have lost you all these years, but I believe and rest in the thought that we had our time of love together; it was extraordinary and I cherish the memory of it.

Today was a glorious day. There was a glow to the evening light which fired the trees into a green so radiant that I could feel the life of each leaf. The sight stirred me to a rare joy; I sat by the window, and my spirit reached out into the fields beyond until I was blessed with this recognition: that everything was illuminated by the auxiliary light which you once gave me. You may be gone, but you gave me love, and you opened my eyes to the daily miracle of the world about me. On good days, I can still see you everywhere. An inestimable blessing, for which I thank you, my best beloved.

Anna read the words and felt her heart puncturing, all the life leaking away from her. She tried to steady herself, and rocked gently on the bench, taking deep breaths.

It was a shattering letter. An expression of absolute love, nothing less, the love which Thomas had carried for Ruth Weir through all those years. The love which she had heard as a child through the wardrobe door, but never known for herself.

What was it, this pain which sliced through her? Jealousy?

Awe? His letter revealed the one love for which she had longed, and yet it belonged to somebody else, in dead time beyond reach. And she had always been, and would remain, outside such love.

What she had witnessed all those years ago was somebody else's unconditional love. And what she could read here in Thomas's letter, so many years later, was the boundless patience of his love.

> *Love bears all things, believes all things, hopes all things, endures all things. Love never ends . . .*

The words from Corinthians surfaced in her mind, but in them she recognized her own devotion too. His was a love lost. Hers was a love never quite known. Even so long after Ruth's death, she could sense the consummation of his love in that letter: even in the leaves of a tree he could find his peace. But all such things remained outside her; she could stand in Ashton Park, and look at the lawns of her luminous childhood, and see only life beyond her reach.

How did she find herself here now, all her years gone, still in love with someone long dead? How had it happened? After all the many people she had met, all the places she had been to. Surely there should have been somebody to enter her heart, at one stroke wiping out her devotion to this man she had met as a child? Yet here she was, back at Ashton Park, still locked into her first love, still remembering his eyes.

Her body was aching now, and she felt breathless, as if a vise was tightening her heart. She began to cry, the dry eyes of old age welling up and overflowing until at last her tears were spent, and her weeping began to ease. Then she breathed more deeply and grew quieter.

She looked down again at Thomas's unsent letter. *The light of love.* Even so many years after Ruth's death, he still had moments when he could retrace the shape of his wonder. Was it not so for her too? She would have liked to tell Thomas that walking down the street and seeing buildings and trees and people—or any detail of anything, really—had been a daily wonder because of the love he had lit in her so long ago.

Her life rolled before her, flickering in glimpses: moments of tenderness, moments of reaching out—her mother dancing with her, or her daughter's first day back from school, that look of loving dependence on her face.

Perhaps it was enough that she had loved Thomas. Perhaps just to have loved was enough—just to have seen this world, and known it, through the eyes of love.

Anna was panting a little, and could feel her own heartbeats. But as she looked around now, the park seemed to flower for her once more, as if touched with grace—it would only be fleeting, she knew, but here was Ashton Park quickening again before her eyes—

Later, when Anna was found dead on the bench, nobody knew who she was, or why she was there, or what it meant that she had collapsed beside this copper beech tree.

One of the house guides, Rufus, was just finishing his tour when a visitor ran into the salon to raise the alarm.

He had never seen a dead person before, but as soon as he reached the old woman, her inert body was unmistakable. He rang the estate office to tell them.

"There's a house visitor here who found her, says he saw her earlier in the rose garden. Yes, she seemed fine then."

Rufus noticed how his supervisor's face was blanched with shock as they waited for the ambulance to arrive. But he was ashamed to find himself edgily checking his watch, because he didn't want to be late for his date that night. He did spare a quick thought for the woman's family, but only while wondering which shirt he should wear, even when the paramedics arrived. She was old, after all, he told himself.

An hour later, he replayed the unexpected scene to his girl-friend at dinner.

"An elderly day-tripper with a freak stroke," he said, putting her out of his mind.

The ambulance had long since gone when the caretaker began closing up Ashton House for the night. Shutting the windows, securing the garden doors, checking that nobody was left wandering through the corridors. The last of the evening light was still pooling unseen in the saloon's antique mirrors, but then the caretaker came in to close the wooden shutters and lock the door, and any remaining light was shut out there too.

Only darkness and silence now flowed around the empty rooms, until at last the house lay quite still, like a photograph, ready for tomorrow's visitors.

Acknowledgments

Several years ago my father gave me a batch of papers belonging to our cousin, a diplomat called Sir Clifford Norton. It was eerie to read his letters and dispatches from the Warsaw embassy, written just before and after the Nazi invasion in 1939. At around the same time, I visited a beautiful house in Cornwall which was open to the public. The visitors' tour included a very touching archive of children who had been evacuated to the house during the Second World War.

Reading my cousin's Warsaw diaries and seeing the photographs of evacuees in Cornwall sparked something in me. I was struck by the unexpected repercussions of war stretching right through to the stately homes of England, where small puzzled children were dispatched, often not seeing their parents for several years.

Clifford Norton and his wife, Peter (her confusing nickname), are the only "real" characters in this novel; they remain at the margins of this story, but act as an occasional chorus on the wider world beyond Ashton Park. As a couple, they had a knack of turning up at some of the defining moments of their century. Clifford was an Oxford classicist who survived the trenches at Gallipoli, and then joined the Foreign Office. Through the 1930s, he was private secretary to Sir Robert Vansittart, the charismatic head of the Foreign Office, whose persistent efforts to tackle Hitler's threat were repeatedly ignored and thwarted by two prime ministers, first by Baldwin, then Chamberlain. Norton was a central figure in Vansittart's group of "antiappeasers," and when he was posted to Warsaw, he did all he could to stiffen his government's support for the Poles. As ambassador in Switzerland during the war, it was Norton who sent reports of the death camps to Churchill, though his pleas to bomb the lines to the camps went unheeded. But his most effective service came after the war, during his years as ambassador in Athens: there, recognizing that the Greek civil war could open the door to rapid Soviet expansion, and that Britain was unable to provide the requisite aid, he played a dogged backroom role in wooing the Americans to intervene in Europe, with the Truman Doctrine. His obituaries painted him as an unobtrusive but tenacious diplomat who quietly played a key part in ushering Marshall Aid into Europe.

His wife, Peter, was a more flamboyant figure, a woman of infectious energy and vitality. As a young advertising agent, she fell under the spell of the Bauhaus group, and became a close friend and supporter of Gropius, Klee and Kandinsky. During the 1930s, she was drawn to the surrealists, and in 1936 she opened what was the first avant-garde art gallery in Britain (called the London Gallery), together with Roland Penrose. She was passionate about art's potential to change people's lives, and her Cork Street gallery immediately became a center for new art in London. When the Nortons were posted to Warsaw, she handed the gallery over to Penrose and E. L. T. Mesens, but continued to support emerging artists all her life, and was a founding member of the Institute of Contemporary Arts. An archive of her papers can be found at the Tate.

Peter was also known for her tireless charitable work. She was a great one for driving aid lorries across Europe, and after the Nazi invasion of Poland, she threw herself into work for Polish refugees, setting up a camp for them in Scotland. During the Greek civil war, she was decorated for her many strenuous efforts to provide aid for war victims, particularly orphaned children. Anecdotes about Peter's generosity abound.

Amongst Peter Norton's papers were several wartime testimonies collected from Polish refugees, from which I was able to draw some details for Pawel's escape from Poland.

I'm very grateful to the friends who encouraged me through this book's various stages, particularly Katy Emck and Stephen Wall, who were patient enough to read several drafts. Special thanks to Anna Webber, Elisabetta Minervini, Alessandro Gallenzi, Mike Stocks, and for this edition, I feel so fortunate and grateful to have been looked after by Grainne Fox, Sarah Branham and all the team at Atria Books. Finally, my heartfelt thanks to my family, Tim, Lucy and Daisy.

THE
VERY THOUGHT
of YOU

ROSIE ALISON

A Readers Club Guide

INTRODUCTION

In the summer of 1939, as the impending German Blitz looms on the horizon, thousands of children are evacuated from London to the secluded English countryside. Among them is Anna Sands, a quiet but determined eight-year-old girl who soon finds herself living in a vast manor house on the Ashton estate in Yorkshire.

Thomas and Elizabeth Ashton are an enigmatic, childless couple, struggling with their slowly unraveling marriage. In an attempt to salvage their life together, they open their home to these children—turning the estate into a school and attempting to keep the war from entering their isolated little world. But in doing so, they irrevocably change the course of their own relationship.

Anna, sensitive and observant, soon becomes aware of the secrets and intimacies that live behind closed doors in the house, enacted in shadow by its occupants. Growing deeply attached to the gentle, compassionate Thomas, she ultimately finds herself part witness, part accomplice to his love affair—an affair that she does not quite understand, an affair whose unforeseen and unexpected consequences changes their world forever.

QUESTIONS AND TOPICS FOR DISCUSSION

1. The title of the novel is *The Very Thought of You.* Discuss the power of thoughts as a theme in the novel. How do internal realizations, observations and perceptions shape the various characters' views of the people around them? How do these unspoken thoughts influence the paths they take? What does the title mean to you?

2. Elizabeth Ashton is a complex character. She is blighted by her inability to obtain the one thing she wants most, to the point of madness. Do you feel that—in a way—she is *more* trapped by her inability to have children than Thomas is by his disability? Why or why not? Do you feel that her deep unhappiness excuses her behavior and final betrayal? Or did you find her entirely unsympathetic? How much of the fault in their damaged relationship do you feel lies with Thomas?

3. Thomas tells his students, "Things are not always quite as they seem." The theme of appearance versus reality recurs throughout the book. Discuss some obvious (and not so obvious) examples of this theme. Do the characters use appearances as a shield? As a mask? Is there a difference? What happens to the various characters when appearances are ripped away to reveal the realities beneath?

4. After the death of Thomas's two brothers, his mother says to him: "I believe you have *luck with you.*" (p. 75) Do you think this is true? Why or why not?

5. Anna witnesses two deeply personal moments that leave a lasting impression on her, both involving Thomas. The first is when she spies the naked Elizabeth in their bedchamber,

screaming at him in her drunken despair. The second is when, stuck in the wardrobe, she hears Thomas and Ruth making love. How do you think these moments affected her, her view of Thomas and her ideas about love and relationships? What other moments during her time at Ashton might have contributed to these views?

6. Did adult Anna's similarities to Elizabeth Ashton (drinking, feeling disconnected from her husband, feeling the unquenchable pull of wanting something more, engaging in affairs) surprise you? Why or why not?

7. There are various examples of marriage, romance and sexual relationships in this novel. Based on your reading, what do you make of the attitudes about marriage during this time? What about attitudes regarding fidelity, sex or love? Do you think the impending war had any role in the way relationships were formed and carried out in this novel? Provide examples.

8. Ruth presses a forget-me-not flower between the pages of her book of Tennyson's poems, with a note that says: "Think what you have meant to me." She does this as a reminder to herself, as a marker to the knowledge that she is in love. But in the end, her note becomes a message. Discuss the importance of those words, and the idea of this message, in relation to Thomas, Ruth and Anna.

9. Using the following two quotes as a starting point, discuss the connection between light, love and the importance of memories throughout the novel.

• *"It was on one of these runs in 1941 that Anna gazed out across the gardens in the long light of evening, and was lost in a moment of complete happiness. . . . She ached with a sense that the light would soon leak away, and the day too—and then how would she remember all this? She stopped still, and looked back, trying to hold this moment fast in her heart."* (p. 209)

- *"Today was a glorious day. There was a glow to the evening light which fired the trees into a green so radiant that I could feel the life of each leaf. . . . I was blessed with this recognition: that everything was illuminated by the auxiliary light which you once gave me. You may be gone, but you gave me love."* (p. 307)

10. Did you feel Thomas was right to tell Anna that he had, in fact, thought about her all those years—that she did mean something to him? If he hadn't said this, do you think she would've been as shocked and devastated to read his final letter to Ruth?

11. At various points, Thomas, Ruth and Anna all observe that perhaps "just to have loved was enough." Do you think they truly believe this? Do you believe it?

12. In her poem "Back to the Old House," Anna writes, "For a place is a time too." Discuss the meaning of this line. Has there ever been a time in your life that felt like home?

ENHANCE YOUR BOOK CLUB

1. Poetry and the power of words are vital to the novel. Have each member read a favorite poem. As a group, discuss your interpretations of and reactions to each poem.

2. From the leaves of the aspen tree to Ruth's forget-me-not, nature plays an important role throughout the novel. Bring in a favorite leaf or flower and tell the group why it means something to you. Like Ruth, try pressing your finding in a favorite book. For a list of flowers to press and ideas for using your pressed flowers, visit http://gardening.about .com/od/craftsanddecor/a/PressedFlowers.htm.

3. Compare this novel to other historical novels depicting WWII, such as Ian McEwan's *Atonement* or Kate Morton's *The House at Riverton*. How are they similar? How are they different? If *The Very Thought of You* were made into a movie, who would you cast for Anna, Ruth, Elizabeth and Thomas?